A Turkish Folktale

WORLD FOLKTALE LIBRARY—VOL. 4

Garland Reference Library of the Humanities—VOL. 1994

THE WORLD FOLKTALE LIBRARY presents the oral art of the greatest and most representative storytellers from diverse folk traditions. Each volume, assembled by a leading expert in the field, features authentically collected and painstakingly transcribed texts designed to capture the personal styles of the oral artists. Introductory materials offer historical background on the folk community, describe the contexts for taletelling, and provide biographical information on the storytellers. Each book is annotated with comparative notes that help place the tales in relation to international oral traditions. The series is designed both to meet the highest scholarly standards and to reach all readers who take delight in the limitlessly rich art of oral storytelling.

General editor
Carl Lindahl, University of Houston

Volume 1. *Cajun and Creole Folktales: The French Oral Tradition of South Louisiana.* Collected, transcribed, translated, annotated, and introduced by Barry Jean Ancelet.

Volume 2. *Hungarian Folktales: The Art of Zsuzsanna Palkó.* Collected, transcribed, annotated, and introduced by Linda Dégh. Translated by Vera Kalm.

Volume 3. *Folktales of Newfoundland: The Resilience of the Oral Tradition.* Collected, annotated, and introduced by Herbert Halpert and J.D.A. Widdowson, with the assistance of Martin J. Lovelace and Eileen Collins. Music transcription by Julia C. Bishop.

Volume 4. *A Turkish Folktale: The Art of Behçet Mahir.* Annotated and introduced by Warren S. Walker. Collected by Ahmet E. Uysal. Translated by Necibe Ertaş.

A Turkish Folktale

The Art of Behçet Mahir

edited by
Warren S. Walker

Routledge
Taylor & Francis Group
LONDON AND NEW YORK

First published 1996 by Garland Publishing, Inc.

Published 2013 by Routledge
2 Park Square, Milton Park, Abingdon, Oxfordshire OX14 4RN
711 Third Avenue, New York, NY, 10017, USA

First issued in paperback 2016

Routledge is an imprint of the Taylor & Francis Group, an informa business

Cover photograph of coffeehouse at Izmir, May 16, 1962, by Warren S. Walker

Library of Congress Cataloging-in-Publication Data

Mahir, Behçet.
[Hamzai Sahip Kıran. English]
A Turkish folktale : the art of Behçet Mahir / edited by Warren S. Walker.
p. cm. — (World folktale library ; v. 4) (Garland reference library of the humanities ; v. 1994)
Translation of Mahir's Hamzai Sahip Kıran, a Turkish version of the Romance of Amīr Ḥamza.
Includes bibliographical references and indexes.
1. Tales—Turkey—History and criticism. 2. Epic literature, Turkish—History and criticism. 3. Mahir, Behçet. 4. Ḥamzah ibn 'Abd al-Muṭṭalib, d. 625—Legends. I. Walker, Warren S. II. Romance of Amīr Ḥamza. English. III. Title. IV. Series: World folktale library (New York, N.Y.) ; vol. 4. V. Series: Garland reference library of the humanities ; vol. 1994.
GR280.M3313 1996 96–5793
398.2'09561—dc20 CIP

ISBN 13: 978-1-138-98624-4 (pbk)
ISBN 13: 978-0-8153-2366-2 (hbk)

For
Barbara K. Walker
Masalcı

Contents

Series Editor's Preface vii
Introduction xi
The Legend of Hamzai Sahip Kıran 3
Bibliography 123
Index of Tale Types 127
Index of Motifs 129

Series Editor's Preface

A ten-hour tale, long enough to fill a night in the telling, artful enough to keep all its listeners eagerly awake: such marathon narratives constitute a recurrent theme found in folktales worldwide. Scheherazade, of course, stands as the fictional prototype of the inexhaustible artist, spinning tales all night long for nights on end.

Scheherazade's feat, however, is not pure fantasy: it possesses a handful of real-life imitators. "She can tell a tale long enough to fill a night"; "he can begin a story so engaging that his audience will return to hear him continue it night after night": praise of this nature has been extended to flesh-and-blood storytellers and passed on in some places as the highest tribute that an audience can pay a narrator. Accounts of such gifted men and women are magic tales in their own right, constituting a major motif in folklorists' folklore about the folk. In Siberia in the 1920s, Mark Azadovskii heard of a man who practiced "the sly politics of Scheherazade" (1974: 19), telling one tale in the space of two days in order to earn his room and board. In 1948, at a wake in Kakasd, Hungary, the great storyteller Zsuzsanna Palkó told a version of "I Don't Know" that lasted "from six o'clock in the evening until the bell-ringing early the next morning"—a performance that audience members would recall with awed admiration for years to come (Dégh 1989: 105-106).[1] In Ireland, where the "night-long märchen" (Dorson 1966: xxx) is fabled among both storytellers and folklorists, W.R. Rodgers speaks of a legendary Gaelic wordsmith whose rendition of "The King of Ireland's Son" filled two weeks of evenings (1962: viii).[2]

A living monument to both oral art and endurance, the person who can tell a brilliant ten-hour tale is extremely rare. Few folklorists ever have the chance to hear such a narrator, and—because of the great effort and expense required to translate such marathon artistry into written form—few such tales ever reach a reading public.

This entire book records, annotates and interprets one such rare performance, by Behçet Mahir—"undoubtedly Turkey's greatest storyteller of the twentieth century" (Walker and Uysal 1992: 3)—a man who shares

[1] Although no folklorist was present to record Zsuzsanna Palkó's legendary nightlong performance of "I Don't Know," Linda Dégh has recorded and edited a somewhat shorter version of the same tale by the same great artist. "I Don't Know" and thirty-four other tales by Zsuzsanna Palkó are found in volume two of the World Folktale Library (Dégh 1995).

[2] The best general discussion of the arts and habits of the greatest European storytellers is provided by Linda Dégh (1989).

the stature of Éamonn a Búrc, Zsuzsanna Palkó, Natalia Vinokurova and a very few other great storytellers whose art has survived their deaths and transcended their native communities to become the shared heritage of a worldwide audience of lovers of oral tales.

Behçet Mahir has reached the English-speaking world largely through the efforts of Warren S. Walker, who resembles the great narrator both in his dedication to Turkish storytelling and in his endurance in its service. The publication of the present volume marks the thirty-fifth anniversary of Professor Walker's first fieldwork expedition to collect Turkish narratives and the thirtieth anniversary of the publication of his first collection of Turkish folktales (Walker and Uysal 1966).

In the past thirty-five years, Professor Walker has worked in numerous ways to make Turkish folk culture accessible to readers of English. Many of his greatest accomplishments are the products of special partnerships. He was co-translator and editor of the monumental *Book of Dede Korkut*—a Turkish epic surviving in sixteenth-century manuscripts and preserving the distinct flavors and styles of oral narratives of earlier centuries (Sümer, Uysal, and Walker 1972). He worked with Ahmet E. Uysal to coedit *Tales Alive in Turkey* (1966) and *More Tales Alive in Turkey* (1992), two volumes "meant to provide a representative selection of the various forms of Turkish oral narrative" (Walker and Uysal 1992: 1)—a set that has earned the praise of folklore scholars and many other lovers of story.

Warren Walker has also enjoyed an impressive scholarly partnership with Barbara K. Walker, his wife. Together they manage the formidable Archive of Turkish Oral Narrative (ATON) on the campus of Texas Tech University, Lubbock. He serves as director, she as curator of ATON, one of the world's largest collections of recorded and transcribed Turkish tales—numbering more than 3000 narratives—which has been repeatedly cited as a treasure-house of Turkish folk culture (Burrill 1992; Halman 1990).[3] Although the Walkers are not native Turks and although they have established their research base thousands of miles away from Turkey, they have earned the sincere admiration and respect of Turkish educators, folklorists, and diplomats. "In recognition of the Walkers' selfless determination, perseverance, and taste, the Turkish authorities have awarded them honorary doctorates from Seljuk University in Konya and made them the only foreigners ever to be honorary members of the Atatürk Culture, Language and History Supreme Council" (Crowley 1995: 245).

It is thus with no small experience and authority that Warren Walker titles Behçet Mahir the greatest taleteller of twentieth-century Turkey. It was after thirteen years of collaborative collecting work that Walker and Uysal first met this remarkable artist in 1974. As described by Professor

[3] The holdings and classificatory system of ATON are described at some length in Walker 1991. The Walkers' Turkish colleague Ahmet E. Uysal serves as archivist of ATON.

Walker in the pages that follow, Behçet Mahir became one of the major contributors to ATON, which possesses recordings of many of his longest and most artful narratives, most of which have yet to be published.

Two of Behçet Mahir's longer tales appear in Walker's and Uysal's *More Tales Alive in Turkey*. Together they testify to the depth and variegated nature of his art. "The Ordeal of Lâtif Shah and His Family"—a tale of more than five hours' duration told on two successive nights—is an interlacing work of high complexity, a multi-stranded account of the separation, individual fortunes, and eventual reunion of seven different family members. By contrast, "Hatemi Tey"—told in one session of just under three hours—presents only one major character, yet generates its own kind of complexity by embedding the life stories of six other characters to whom the protagonist is sent on his quest for a story. Both of these tales are so labyrinthine that Warren Walker provides charts to summarize their actions for Western readers accustomed to far more simply structured folktales.

Behçet Mahir's longer tales usher the Westerner into the presence of a type of oral art far richer than many folklorists have been willing to acknowledge. Axel Olrik (1965) and Francis Lee Utley (1976) are among the many who have characterized oral art as decidedly simpler than literature: according to Olrik, folk narratives possess single-stranded plots; according to Utley, oral art states its themes far more simply than does literature. Such condescending stereotypes dissolve as soon as one encounters the elaborate and often profound performances of Behçet Mahir.

The ten-hour tale that follows is far more than an endurance test. *Hamzai Sahip Kıran* masterfully intertwines the styles of carefree märchen and semisacred narrative. As Behçet Mahir has said, "The greatest knowledge is acquired not through longevity but through travel" (Walker and Uysal 1992: 131). As the reader follows Hamzai through landscapes filled by turns with monstrous birds, holy objects, giants, mortal combats, fairies, and divine trials, the journey itself will prove far more memorable than the time it takes.[4]

Carl Lindahl,
General Editor,
World Folktale Library

[4] I thank the University of Houston for awarding me a Limited Grant in Aid to support editorial work on this series, and Sandy Jordan for her superb performance as the Series research assistant.

Works Cited

Azadovskii, Mark. 1974. *A Siberian Tale Teller*. Trans. James R. Dow. Austin: Center for Intercultural Studies in Folklore and Ethnomusicology. [Trans. of *Eine Siberische Märchenerzähler*; Helsinki: Suomalainen Tiedeakatemia, 1926. *Folklore Fellows Communications*, no. 68.]

Burrill, Kathleen R.F. 1992. "Foreword" to Walker and Uysal 1992. Pp. vii-ix.

Crowley, Daniel J. 1995. Review of Barbara K. Walker, *The Art of the Turkish Tale. Western Folklore* 54: 244-45.

Dégh, Linda. 1989. *Folktales and Society: Story-Telling in a Hungarian Peasant Community*. 2nd ed. Bloomington: Indiana University Press.

——. 1995. *Hungarian Folktales: The Art of Zsuzsanna Palkó*. World Folktale Library; vol. 2. New York: Garland Publishing, Inc. Pp. 4-34.

Delargy, James H. 1945. *The Gaelic Storyteller*. London: British Academy Rhys Memorial Lecture.

Dorson, Richard M. 1966. "Introduction" to *Folktales of Ireland*, ed. Sean O'Sullivan. Chicago: University of Chicago Press.

Halman, Talat Sait. 1990. "Foreword" to Barbara K. Walker 1990 and 1993.

Olrik, Axel. 1965. "Epic Laws of Folk Narrative." Trans. Jeanne P. Steager. In *The Study of Folklore,* ed. Alan Dundes. Englewood Cliffs, NJ: Prentice Hall. [Trans. of Olrik's "Epische Gesetze der Volksdichtung," *Zeitschrift für die Deutsches Altertum* 51 (1909): 1-12.]

Rodgers, W.R. 1962. Introduction to Peig Sayers, *An Old Woman's Reflections: The Life of a Blasket Island Storyteller*. Oxford: Oxford University Press. Pp. vii-xiv.

Sümer, Faruk, Ahmet E. Uysal and Warren S. Walker, trans. and ed. 1972. *The Book of Dede Korkut: A Turkish Epic*. Austin: University of Texas Press.

Utley, Francis Lee. 1976. "Oral Genres as a Bridge to Written Literature." In *Folklore Genres*, ed. Dan Ben-Amos. Austin: University of Texas Press. Pp. 3-14.

Walker, Barbara K., ed. 1990 and 1993. *The Art of the Turkish Tale*. 2 vols. Lubbock: Texas Tech University Press.

Walker, Warren S. 1991. "Turkish Oral Tradition in Texas: The Archive of Turkish Oral Narrative." *Oral Tradition* 7: 171-75.

Walker, Warren S., and Ahmet E. Uysal. 1966. *Tales Alive in Turkey*. Cambridge, MA: Harvard University Press; rpt. 1990. Lubbock: Texas Tech University Press.

_____. 1992. *More Tales Alive in Turkey*. Lubbock: Texas Tech University Press.

Introduction

Turkish Tales—An Overview

So broad is the range of Turkish folktales and so varied are the tellers that one must proceed guardedly in making generalizations about Turkish oral narrative. Stories differ in performance time from two-minute anecdotes through complex tales of several hours' duration to full-scale folk epics that cannot be presented in a single session. Narrative styles tend to echo tradition but not to the extent that individual creativity is cramped. And subject matter? Well, here is God's plenty!

Situated at what has been called the Crossroad of Empire, Asia Minor has for millennia provided an interchange between cultures East and West. It is not entirely surprising, therefore, to discover Turkish tales with either or both Asian and European variants. Nor is it surprising (after one has experienced it a few times!) to come upon narrative passages of ancient origin: Biblical tales that did not become part of the canon, pre-Christian and preclassical myths, and an occasional motif as old as the Gilgamesh Epic. Such living antiquities add a haunting dimension of resonance that invites one to reach for the universal, grope for the eternal.

Until around the middle of the twentieth century, the oral tradition remained very strong in Turkey, especially in rural areas. The national requirement of five years of formal education for all children—it is now eight years—greatly increased literacy, but failed to inspire a desire for or competence in literary entertainment. Theirs was still largely an oral culture informed to an appreciable extent by such genres of verbal art as the proverb, the riddle, folk poetry, folk drama, and the folktale. Folktales were then ubiquitous, and seemingly almost anyone could, with varying degrees of skill, narrate at least a few of them. Since World War II radio, television, cinema, and newspapers (now distributed even into remote districts) have diminished but not extinguished the functions of these traditional forms. A synopsis of the holdings of the Archive of Turkish Oral Narrative (ATON) may serve to demonstrate the viability of the Turkish folktale and identify some of its major categories.

Located at Texas Tech University, ATON is the most convenient and best-organized collection for this purpose. Its scope would seem to be sufficient to give it reasonable claim to being representative of Turkish oral narrative in general. It is one of the largest facilities of its kind in the world and by far the largest in the United States. It contains more than 3,000 narrative specimens in two media: original field tapes in Turkish and bound typescript volumes of translation into English. ATON is formally divided into eight sections, but because the parts are not—actually *cannot* be—always mutually exclusive, one might understandably take some exception to the taxonomy.

I. More numerous than one might expect at the end of the twentieth century are stories whose plots turn on one or more supernatural forces. (Excluded from this division are elements of organized religious belief systems; these appear in a subdivision of VIII.) The word *supernatural* here designates that which scientists would say lies outside the laws of nature, beyond the dialectic of cause and effect. Magic, enchantment, transformation, and otherworldly powers influence the action of these tales, as do such imaginary creatures as giants, witches, demons, dragons, fairies, jinns, and animals capable of human speech and endowed with human concerns. This is to a large extent the province of the märchen (*masal* in Turkish). Of ATON's holdings, 19 percent appear in this category.

II. Far fewer in number but often presented with consummate artistry are tales based upon puzzle solving, ingenious deductions, or other efforts to explain the mysterious or seemingly unknowable. Occasionally such a story may be quite brief, perhaps little more than a narrative jeu d'esprit. More often, however, they are long, convoluted, sometimes telescoped like a set of Chinese boxes. Well distributed both within Turkey and elsewhere are variants of "The Three Princes of Serendip," listed in the Aarne-Thompson type index (1961) as 655A—*The Strayed Camel and the Clever Deductions*. Of even greater intricacy is the Middle Eastern/Central Asian "The Adventures of Hatemi Tey," a series of seven tales within a tale, all of them so mutually interlocked that successful narration of the whole is a tour de force beyond the talent of many storytellers. The best rendition available in English translation is that of Behçet Mahir (Walker and Uysal 1992: 94-138), narrator of the text of the present volume. This division comprises 3 percent of ATON tales.

III. While humorous narratives are legion in Turkey, only a fraction of those in ATON are entered under Humor. The distinction here is not a matter of subject but of structure. The remainder of the comic narratives appear among several subdivisions of section VII—Anecdotes. Although some of the items in III may be short, each is a fully developed story with beginning, middle, and end. Escapades of the trickster are frequently enacted in III, for although this character type may be predatory, even viciously so at times, his successes are often grudgingly admired and acknowledged to be perversely amusing. Scatological accounts and recitals of sexual exploits are among the entries in III; perhaps there would have been more of both of these if the field collectors had been solely Turkish and the audience had been solely male. Although a few of the stories in III may be perceived by some listeners as being decidedly unfunny, they all generate laughter in Turkish coffeehouses and homes alike. Humorous tales constitute 15 percent of the collection.

IV. To the extent that they reflect (and thereby reinforce) a value system, most oral stories might be considered moralistic. But the tales in this section described as Moralistic Narratives go farther than that in being overtly didactic about right and wrong actions. The points they make are often as obvious as those that conclude many of Aesop's fables. Not intentionally Judaic, Christian, Muslim or otherwise parochial, these are parables expressing universal truths about basic human behavior. Despite their simplicity, the tales in this small section (7 percent of those in ATON) are not by any means aimed exclusively at children.

V. Romances—amatory and/or heroic—are primarily productions of Turkish minstrels. These are markedly different from other items in ATON. They are partly in verse, and the verse is usually sung to the accompaniment of a lutelike instrument known as a *saz*. They are composed by a folk poet—generally unschooled and often functionally illiterate—who rarely commits his lines to paper, recording them only in his memory. This composer/performer is called an *âşık*, which literally means *lover* but, by extension, *lover poet*. He is so designated both because the "calling" to his profession and the basic motivation for pursuing it are parts of a highly stylized, never-ending ritual of love.[1]

The partly sung, partly narrated minstrel tale (*hikâye*) tends to be longer than the *masal*, and some of these which involve both love and war reach epic proportions. Seldom (if ever) is any *hikâye* reproduced verbatim,

---

[1] Traditionally the *âşık* does not determine his own career but is tapped by fate for that role. As a young person, usually a teenager, he has a dream in which one or more aged, white-haired, and long-bearded dervishes introduce him to a girl who is to be his lifelong love. Of course she is very beautiful, often said to be "the most beautiful girl in the world." To plight their spiritual troth, each of the young lovers is required to drink a goblet of sherbet (in the Middle East a cold fruit drink, not the icy confection it may be elsewhere). That moment of mystical drama has two unmistakable implications: (1) the young man will start searching for the physical girl in the real world, and (2) he will become a lover poet and henceforth spend at least part of his time composing and singing songs in praise of her.

In folktales (as well as in literary works based upon them) the *âşık* actually finds his dream girl; in real life he usually marries an ordinary woman and lives with her while pursuing the ideal one. Occasionally the imaginary becomes the real, as it did for *âşık* Talibi Coşkun, who found and married the girl of his dreams, as he recounted (1977) in an autobiographical passage in ATON tale No. 1093.

As with minstrels in most places, in most times, the *âşık* is a wanderer whose travels are undertaken for two reasons, one explicit and the other implicit. Avowedly he is in quest of the dream girl, but en route he performs in coffeehouses, where (because he is a stranger) he can offer previously unheard songs for which audiences will give more generous gratuities than would neighbors for familiar pieces in his hometown. Seldom does either the *âşık* or his admirers acknowledge this economic incentive.

While the *âşık* never relinquishes his celebration of love, he soon introduces other themes into his *hikâye* repertoire. Patriotism, military action, religious proselytizing, charitable ventures, and efforts to relieve persecution—these are frequently the concerns that challenge the minstrel's talent (see Başgöz 1952).

even by the same *âşık*. The structure and the major episodes may remain largely unchanged, but that spontaneity which is a factor of oral composition almost inevitably reshapes minor elements and some descriptive details. The concept of orality put forth by Ong and the "formulaic theory" developed by Parry, Lord, Foley and others are as applicable to the Turkish *âşık* as they are to Homer (see Lord 1960; Foley 1988; Ong 1982).

Although minstrel tales add up to only 6 percent of the number of titles in ATON, their length fills a considerably larger proportion of the Turkish tapes and the volumes of translation into English (see Eberhard 1955).

VI. Anticlerical tales are not to be construed as being antireligious. Quite the contrary, they are usually satires on the foibles, the pretensions, and the improper conduct to which clerical personnel (like many other people) are sometimes prone. Such stories may sprout anywhere, but they seem to proliferate most readily in places where the prevailing religious organization is large and hierarchical. In the spaces that separate the many ranks of Catholic clerical office there was ample room (as Chaucer suggested in *The Canterbury Tales*) for graft, other corruption, and exploitation. It took relatively few misdemeanors to prompt folk fantasy to create numerous apocryphal accounts. So too, the many-tiered Islamic establishment between powerful Caliph and lowly dervish permitted enough ethical and moral laxity to produce a wealth of gossip that sometimes evolved into scandalous narrative.

In this area the ATON taxonomy is again admittedly ambiguous, for not all anticlerical exposés are full-fledged folktales. Many are anecdotes belonging (because of their structure) in VII—anecdotes about the supposedly blasphemous Bektaşi dervish, about the colorful Caliph Harun Reşit (Haroun al-Rashid), about the *kadı*, judge of Muslim canonical law. Altogether, 7 percent of ATON holdings could be considered anticlerical.

VII. Anecdotes are the most numerous (24 percent) and provide the most diverse ATON classification. This section has twenty-six subdivisions, some with only a few items, others with more than a hundred. Many anecdotes are humorous, some are satirical, and a few are doctrinaire. Some of these narratives feature individual characters—local, historical, or imaginary. Even more are based on group stereotypes—ethnic, regional, professional. Rarely does any of the anecdotes use any of the formulaic elements (opening devices, terminal devices, traditional descriptions, courtesy routines) found in other narratives. A plurality has a performance time of three to five minutes.

VIII. The section given to miscellaneous narratives is open-ended. Who knows what new subject or subgenre may emerge in the oral tradition? Thus VIII (19 percent of the total) presently contains accounts of buried treasure, creation myths, folk history, peasant wish-fulfillment fantasies, saints' legends, tales derived from or explanatory of religious beliefs, and unusual personal experiences.

Tellers on Location

One or another kind of story might be told almost anywhere, almost anytime, but some contexts are especially propitious for both narrator and audience. The most obvious of these is the child/parent, child/grandparent relationship existing within the home. Oral narratives may be acquired from many different sources, but most committed Turkish storytellers first savored and first memorized choice tales at an early age. Mothers and grandmothers are the patron saints of the genre in Turkey, and perhaps elsewhere.

After the home the coffeehouse and its ambience may well provide the most congenial setting for the raconteur and his listeners. More than a mere purveyor of refreshments, the Turkish coffeehouse is a center of male social life. Purchase of a cup or two of coffee or a glass or two of tea secures a comfortable seat for an afternoon or evening in this open club. When village men are unoccupied or lack the will to be occupied, they automatically gravitate toward the coffeehouse. There, along with card games and backgammon, yarnspinning is a cherished pastime. Until fairly recently a large urban coffeehouse might employ a *meddah*, a professional entertainer who was a comedian, a pantomimist, a mimic, and a storyteller (see Nutku 1977). The coffeehouse is also a base of Turkish minstrelsy. Not only does the individual minstrel perform there; so, too, do whole groups of minstrels during periodic contests in sung repartee. One-upmanship in lyrics sung and insults flung has long been an exciting activity in parts of Europe, where it is known as "capping" or "flyting," and in Turkey where it is called "stoning." Given widespread advance notice, these *âşık* competitions still pack coffeehouses in eastern Turkey, especially in Erzurum and Kars provinces (see Erdener 1995).

At least 20 percent of ATON holdings were taped in coffeehouses. But there is a negative side to village coffeehouses as sites for collecting: they are primarily male institutions. In some conservative areas in Turkey the roof would collapse if a woman walked into a coffeehouse! (Many of our very best tales were told by women, but not in coffeehouses.)

Where, then, would one be likely to hear female storytellers outside their own homes? Urban Turkish women regularly enjoy afternoon teas devoted initially to conversation. They gossip. They hazard political opinions. They speculate about future events revealed by the configurations of grounds left in tiny coffee cups. They recount family experiences. Any or all of these routes of verbalization may lead into a favorite folktale. Some of our older informants at such gatherings in the mid-1960s recalled an earlier kind of social occasion that also sometimes produced folk fiction: Ladies' Day at a public bath. There ablutions were accompanied by refreshments and stories.

A rural setting congenial to oral narrative is the *yayla*, the summer pasture to which sheep, goat, and cattle raisers take their flocks. A *yayla* is a section of open range on a high plateau or mountain slope where grazing fees are usually very low. Entire families move up to their respective *yayla*s where, with their livestock, they will camp for three months. With no ready-made entertainment available, these isolated herders while away their time with folk dance, folk song, and folktale.

The holy month of Ramadan (*Ramazan* in Turkey) also indirectly fostered storytelling. During that month devout Muslims fast from dawn to dusk, ingesting neither a morsel of food nor a drop of water. After the firing of the sunset gun, they break the fast with a ritual meal (*iftar*), and they may continue to nourish their famished bodies intermittently throughout the night. Various kinds of entertainment maintain their wakefulness and relieve the ascetic mode of the daylight hours. Until the middle of the present century men were wont to go to a neighborhood coffeehouse to watch shadow puppetry projected through a silk screen, the *Karagöz* Theatre (see And 1975), named after the leading character.[2] Successful puppeteers had a repertoire of thirty plays, one for each night of Ramadan. These dramas contained much Punch-and-Judy slapstick, political satire, and humor based in part on ethnic stereotypes. There is evidence that some of this comic scenario later reappeared in stories told by members of the audience.[3]

Another narrative context, not limited to any specific time or place, may be created by the practice of using parabolic rather than direct communication. An exemplum may provide an apt and unmistakably clear answer to a question. A woman of our acquaintance was seriously ill in Turkey with hepatitis. When she asked how long it would take for her to recover sufficiently to travel, the Turkish physician responded with this brief folk anecdote.

> One day while Nasreddin Hoca[4] was working in his garden, he was hailed by a man walking along a nearby road: "Hoca, how long will it take me to reach the next village?" When he received no answer, the traveler moved closer and shouted, "Hey, Hoca! How long will it take me to reach the next village?" When there was still no response, the annoyed stranger went to the edge of the garden and bellowed, "How long will it take me to reach the next village?" The Hoca said not a word, and so the man hurried angrily down the road.

---

2 *Karagöz* means literally Black Eye. The character so named is a country bumpkin who repeatedly falls into arguments and fights with his city-slicker friend Hacıvad.

3 See, for example, "You Shouldn't Say That, *Karagöz*!" (Walker and Uysal 1966:159-61).

4 Turkey's most beloved comic folk character. A *hoca* (pronounced *hodja* in English) is a Muslim preacher.

> After the traveler had taken only a few steps, Nasreddin Hoca called after him, "It will take you half an hour!"
>
> "Well, why didn't you tell me that when I asked you about it?"
>
> "Ah, friend, how could I tell you how long it would take until I saw how fast you were going to walk?" (Walker and Uysal 1966: 232-33).

The use of folk narrative in such a pointedly contextual way is not uncommon in Turkey.

Behçet Mahir (1909-1988)

Behçet Mahir, narrator of *Hamzai Sahip Kıran*, may well have been Turkey's greatest storyteller of the twentieth century. His skill in oral composition, his unique performance, his extensive repertoire, and his devoted following all point toward that distinction. Although tradition could have made predictable some aspects of his career as poet and teller of tales, both his professional and his personal life were marked by striking anomalies. The son of a mason, Behçet Efendi[5] was born in Erzurum, for many centuries an important city of eastern Turkey. That he never attended school and remained illiterate all of his life was typical of folk poets and not uncommon for the poorer classes of the area at that time.

The great formative event of his life occurred when he was just thirteen years old. It was the sequence of dreams in which he was informed of his destined occupation. To be understood, this visionary experience must be compared to and contrasted with the spiritual initiation of the *âşık* (described above and in Note 1). Like a future *âşık*, Mahir met three aged spiritual figures in a dream, one of whom was Summani, generally considered to be eastern Turkey's preeminent *âşık* during the early years of this century. But because young Mahir awakened too soon from that first dream, he was denied the ability to play the *saz*, and he failed to be granted the status of *âşık*. These unfulfilled potentials were probably symbolized by the absence of Summani from his subsequent dreams. (Although Behçet Efendi never saw the real-life Summani—that elder poet died during World War I—he frequently celebrated his momentary mystical affinity with that dream patron by reciting lines from Summani's poetry, as he did in *Hamzai Sahip Kıran*.)

[5] *Efendi*, meaning roughly *sir*, is an honorific following the first name of a male. During much of the Ottoman era it was used to show respect to men of distinction, but in the twentieth century its status has been so eroded that it is now generally applied only to children and servants. Yet during the years that I knew him, Mahir was almost invariably addressed as *Behçet Efendi*. Perhaps this was a result of his lower-class origin and the menial job with which in his later years he supplemented his performance income.

From the initiation that went awry, Behçet Efendi received only one award, and that was the honorific *mahir* (a talented person)—hence the surname *Mahir*.[6] Unlike the *âşık*, therefore, he was committed neither to searching for a predestined lover nor to creating predominantly love poems. He was to become a poet, however, and he was to become a storyteller.

At the end of the seven dream sessions Mahir was cursed with blindness for having broken a taboo: revealing to others too much of his visionary venture. He remained totally blind for three months, recovering his eyesight only after being counseled by a local clairvoyant. He then became an apprentice of *Hafiz*[7] Mugdat, an Erzurum minstrel and *meddah*. Until the time of his own death, Mahir continued to extol the training and good influence of "my master." In time Behçet Mahir had his own apprentices, some of whom, like *Âşık* Reyhan, drew national attention.

A storyteller to the end, Behçet Mahir was, long before his death, forced by the decline of the narrative stage in Turkey to take supplementary employment. Radio invaded the coffeehouses, and by the 1950s battery-powered transistor sets had reached even those in isolated areas. The 1960s brought television to Turkey, and many coffeehouse proprietors felt constrained to mount large video screens in their establishments. There were still—indeed there are yet—here and there, some owners willing to give priority to the programs of minstrels and tellers of tales, but clearly the traditional markets for these arts had declined. Behçet Efendi became a janitor at Atatürk University (Erzurum) by day and, when opportunity afforded, a ready raconteur during the evening hours. A kindly disposed and culturally sensitive administration at the university made his custodial duties nominal so that he could, whenever he wished, narrate on campus for visiting folklorists and student groups.[8]

The Style Is the Man

Behçet Mahir had considerable stage presence and a narrative technique that commanded attention. His was a powerful voice, a sine qua non for storytelling in the come-and-go stir and constant clatter of any coffeehouse. Because he was so small physically—barely five feet tall—the unusual volume and timbre of his voice often came as a surprise to those hearing it for the first time. Almost all of his recitals included some poetry,

[6] One unacquainted with Turkish social history might well wonder how a person could acquire a surname so easily. Until 1935 most Turks did not have last names. In that year a reform law required that every Turkish citizen must have a family name.

[7] *Hafiz* is an epithet which identifies a person who has memorized and can repeat verbatim the entire Koran.

[8] For much of this information about Behçet Mahir I am indebted to Ahmet E. Uysal (see Uysal 1983a).

but even his prose lines moved with steady, pronounced rhythm. Despite his frequent digressions, asides, and interpolations, there was no sense of meandering in his delivery. He marched sturdily toward his goal in measured strides. His manner of presentation was so distinctive that, having heard him once, even a person who knew not a single word of Turkish could recognize it unmistakably thereafter. A consistent graphic element of his programs was his posture. He insisted on standing as he spoke, because, as he said on numerous occasions, that position allowed his 366 veins to vibrate more effectively. (No one, to my knowledge, ever pressed him about the anatomical implications of the matter.) Even in his 70s he stood throughout his public appearances, though then supported by a heavy walking staff.

One element of Behçet Efendi's style which we could not reproduce was the rhyming of his verse lines. Because Turkish verbs, which usually come at the ends of sentences, are inflected, and because Turkish is an agglutinative language which may add one or more suffixes to a given word, rhyming is much easier in Turkish than it is in English. Rather than torture the sentence structure to produce all too often only forced rhymes, we have reluctantly forgone all efforts to recreate this attractive sound effect. We have, however, maintained some of the rhythm of the Turkish original.

Differences between tradition and the individual talent are not, of course, limited to the technical but are often—perhaps more often—substantive in nature. What did Behçet Mahir add? Compare his rendition of a given tale with that of another storyteller, and one is likely soon to become aware of Mahir's enrichment.[9] In most instances Behçet Efendi gives greater detail in character motivation, social setting, and description. This is not mere padding but an attempt to flesh out the often stark skeletal structure of the story. When a tale passes through a succession of hasty narrators, there is a tendency for it to become plot-ridden. Mahir left no narrative vulnerable to such critical accusation! He also made much more extensive insertions which are arguably valid contributions. (In all fairness, it must be acknowledged that the temporary stalling of the narrative flow might be deemed by some to be unjustifiable authorial intrusion.) Like his long-removed bardic forerunners, Behçet Efendi periodically had a compulsion to advise, exhort, criticize, and warn his people. He did this in seemingly impromptu moralistic passages and carefully selected parables. On occasion

---

[9] For specific examples of this contrast, see two sets of tales—one simple, the other complex. On the same day in August 1970, and in the same section of Erzurum, we recorded renditions of "Behlül Dane's Good Advice Ignored" by İshak Kemali and Behçet Mahir. The two men were of approximately the same age, and both had lived all of their years in Erzurum. Kemali's version (ATON No. 1603) was completed in ten minutes; Mahir's ran to twenty-two minutes. In 1990 Nüriye Yalvaç (a resident of Kilis in Gaziantep Province) performed in thirty-two minutes her variant of the complex tale "The Adventures of Hatemi Tey" (ATON No. 1179). In a 1974 storytelling session Behçet Mahir took two hours and fifty minutes to complete his narration of the same tale (ATON No. 559).

these judgmental sections are clearly aimed beyond the coffeehouse audience immediately facing him. He sometimes began these insertions with such a vocative expression as "O Turks" or "O young men!"

Like many other storytellers, Behçet Efendi performed at his best before a receptive and sizable audience. His stage was sometimes the classroom but more often the coffeehouse, and the time was usually evening. During workaday hours the makeup of a coffeehouse crowd is more or less accidental, and from day to day its composition changes, but following the evening prayer service, the steady patrons, the old habitués, can be counted upon to return. These are the listeners who await with eager anticipation each succeeding installment of a serial production. Theirs were the ears that received Mahir's *Hamzai Sahip Kıran* over five evenings between January 9th and 13th of 1977 at the Gölbaşı Coffeehouse, a short way from Erzurum.

Audience participation is not uncommon at Turkish storytelling sessions. Listeners sometimes pose a question, ask for clarification of a passage, or dispute a statement made by the narrator. In this particular tale there are few such interjections. This apparent reticence to interrupt may have prevailed out of respect for Behçet Efendi or reverence for the near-sacred nature of some of the contents of his tale.

A Flexible Repertoire

It is doubtful that anyone can establish definitively the canon of Behçet Mahir's works. He himself was inconsistent in indicating the tales he could tell. Lists that he dictated to us in 1974 and 1976 differed, and both omitted some of his tales that are among ATON holdings. He was apparently reluctant to cite his briefer tales—ATON has sixteen of them—for his métier was the long and involved story akin to the minstrel *hikâye*. Before I was aware of this, I unwittingly offended Behçet Efendi in 1974 by asking if he could tell us a Behlül Dane[10] anecdote. After a pregnant pause, he responded proudly but patiently, "*Anyone* can tell a Behlül Dane anecdote!"

There is also uncertainty about the length of some of his narratives. As he enumerated their titles, he claimed performance times of six, eight, ten, twelve, and even twenty hours. Although I do not wish to suggest that he was incapable of extending them to such lengths, the taped versions we have of several of those tales are considerably shorter. Our evidence indicates

[10] Behlül Dane was the supposedly mad half brother of Harun Reşit, most colorful of the Abbasid caliphs—so much so, in fact, that he appears in several tales of *The Thousand Nights and a Night*. Behlül was sane and saintly. His madcap antics (like those of Shakespeare's fools) provided a "cover" that enabled him to satirize with impunity the high and mighty of this world, including his "brother."

that, excepting the epic about Köroğlu[11] (No. 8 below), his oral romances average four to five hours in length. Even so, few indeed are the twentieth-century storytellers who can match such a narrative time span without the aid of written script. Interestingly the extreme length of his rendition of the Köroğlu epic has itself become legendary. While one source estimated a total taping span of seventy-two hours for that masterpiece, another extended the purported time to ninety-five hours. It can be demonstrated, however, that the published text, edited by a team of competent scholars (see Mahir 1973), probably could not have required a recording time of more than forty-five hours.[12] This is not, of course, to deny the marathon proportions of Mahir's achievement!

While some of the subsequent tales in Mahir's list (given below) contain love elements, the first four are primarily amatory romances. They are to a degree similar to orally transmitted love stories of the past several centuries in the Middle East and Central Asia, as well as in Turkey. Usually initiated in a dream, the relationship between the principals retains throughout their love a transcendent or spiritual quality. The plots are as familiar to Turkish audiences as are those of Puccini, Verdi, and Wagner to opera fans, and suspense is not of crucial importance. Suspense there is, of course, first generated in the quest of the dream-betrothed couple to find each other in the real world, and then renewed in their struggle to overcome the obstacles which block their progression toward consummation of their love in marriage.

1. Emrah and Selvi
2. Ferhat and Şirin*
3. Garip and Senem
4. Tahir and Zühre
5. Blood Castle
6 The Cunning Züleyha
7. Ebul Halis, Ebali Sinan, and the Handsome *Helva* [Candy] Maker*
8. The Epic of Köroğlu

---

[11] A noble outlaw who fought against the oppression of the Turkish peasantry. His name, which means "Son of the Blind Man," reflects the all-too-frequent persecution by those in powerful positions. His father had been cruelly blinded by Bolu Bey (Baron of Bolu). His fierce championing of the downtrodden was often lifted to a lyrical tone by his frequent communication sung in verse lines accompanied by a *saz*. Westerners inevitably likened him to Robin Hood, but the similarity is limited.

[12] Although we do not have the tape recordings, we do have the 585-page book transcribed from them. Having timed frequently the speed of Mahir's narration, one can with reasonable accuracy estimate how long it took him to deliver the 234,000 words of the epic. Additional time could conceivably have been consumed by repetitions or by Mahir's personal insertions, which in this context might have been deemed inappropriate for inclusion.

9. Firdevs Shah
10. The Green *İmam* [prayer leader]
11. Hamzai Sahip Kıran*
12. Hatemi Tey*[13]
13. Havarı Zemin
14. The Heroic Slayer
15. The Iron Wrestler
16. Kirman Shah*
17. Nimrod Caravansary
18. The Ordeal of Lâtif Shah and His Family*
19. Rüstem, Son of Zal
20. Seyfülmülük[14]
21. Solomon, Son of David, and the *Anka**[15]
22. Wounded Mahmut
23. Wrestler Mıkdat

Only the seven starred entries on this list are presently available in English, although several other Mahir tales which he did not claim as being among his oeuvre have also been translated into English. It seems appropriate, therefore, to indicate in one place the accessibility of all of his narratives that have been Englished.

Title	ATON No.	In Print	Record. Time Hours	Mins.
1. The Three Princes	330	----	1	38
2. The Stonecutter (retelling in 1971 of No. 4 below)	334	(Walker, Barbara 1990)	----	44
3. The Adventures of Padishah Hatemi Tey	559	(Walker and Uysal 1992)	2	50
4. The Stonecutter (original telling, 1964)	591	----	----	37

[13] Those interested in the language of Mahir's "Hatemi Tey" may find of value Tuncer Gülensoy's study (Gülensoy 1979). This is a linguistically scored and annotated transcription of the tape recording of the tale in ATON.

[14] Seyfülmülük had the head (and upper torso in some variants) of a woman, but the remainder of her body was serpentine. She was one of the legendary figures referred to as the Queen of Snakes. A popular version of this tale, shorter than that of Behçet Mahir, was published in 1958 in Istanbul by the firm of Ayıldız Kitabevi. Unfortunately, the source was not identified.

[15] The *anka* is one of the legendary giant birds of Old World folklore. It was capable of carrying human beings great distances on its back. Similar huge birds are the phoenix, the simurgh, and the roc (rukh). It was a roc which provided transportation for some of the travels of Sindbad in *The Thousand Nights and a Night*. The *anka* also appears in *Hamzai Sahip Kıran*.

5. The Ordeal of Lâtif Shah and His Family	672	(Walker and Uysal 1992)	5	20
6. Sultan Murat and the Lunatics	936	----	----	11
7. Behçet Mahir as Young Poet	937	----	----	12
8. Habik Father and Sultan Murat	945	----	----	9
9. Hızır on Wisdom	946	----	----	6
10. Habik Father on Virtue	947	----	----	12
11. Behlül Dane Remains Cool in Hell	1008	----	----	2
12. Solomon Teaches a Friend Animal Languages	1556	----	----	7
13. The Immutability of Fate	1572	----	----	2
14. The Behavior of Hasabi-Kep's Daughters Betrays Their Origins	1583	----	----	6
15. Sultan Mahmut and the Wise Sewer Worker	1584	----	----	6
16. The Horns of Alexander the Great	1604	----	----	5
17. Behlül Dane's Good Advice Ignored	1606	----	----	22
18. Solomon and the Giant Bird's Fate	1607	----	----	2
19. Ebul Halis and Ebali Sinan	1637	----	1	37
20. Lokman Understands a Remedy Which He Cannot Administer	1639	----	----	11
21. Kindness Interpreted	1641	----	----	7
22. Kirman Shah	1698	----	4	----
23. Hamzai Sahip Kıran	1700	present volume	9	42
24. Ferhat and Şirin	1701	----	2	48

"Linkéd Sweetness Long Drawn Out"
"L'Allegro"—John Milton

Hamzai Sahip Kıran is not one story but two that share the same protagonist. In the first he is the male lead in a hectic, star-crossed romance.

In the second this uncle of Mohammed is a hero in the founding of Islam. As the two plots crisscross, he sometimes plays both roles simultaneously. This ambivalence is a key structural factor.

Like love, a lengthy tale told by Behçet Mahir is a many-splendored thing. What better evidence can be offered than that of *Hamzai Sahip Kıran*, which had a performance time of nine hours and forty-two minutes? It subsumed in its composition history, legend, myth, miracle, magic, Judaic and Muslim literary works. While other storytellers may blend in their narratives seemingly disparate elements, rarely do they incorporate so many.

Such a range of contents is not only a matter of subject but also one of structure. It militates against the simple linear progression assumed by some to be the inherent sequence of events in any folktale. Behçet Efendi does not often merely refer in passing to, say, an historical incident, a moral position, or a literary parallel. He usually proceeds to elaborate upon the item, to rehearse its details, and while he is doing so, the central narrative is placed on hold. In other words, the time line in a Mahir performance is not unalterably longitudinal but is occasionally vertical. During this kind of time warp one thing may lead to another via association, as it does in the digressive episodes of the two gardens at the beginning of the narration of January 12th. Having recently learned from Mohammed that he is fated to kill a giant which is ravaging a nearby land, Hamzai sets forth to carry out this mission. En route he comes upon the Garden of Solomon, where he finds a message and instructions inscribed to him 1,500 years earlier by the historical Old Testament monarch. One of Solomon's orders takes Hamzai to a second garden, an allegorical one called the Garden of Allah's Wisdom. There he witnesses several curious little dramatic actions, all of them morally symbolic (affording Behçet Efendi a convenient opportunity to expatiate upon some of his cherished values). Shortly after Hamzai leaves the two gardens, we learn the relationship between his mission and Solomon, and we learn it from the words of the ancient ruler himself as he talks to the giant many centuries earlier: "I could have killed you and torn you into pieces, but it is not my fate to do so. You will die at the hands of Hamzai Sahip Kıran. The appointed hour when Hamzai will kill you has already been set." The point to be made here is that instead of an expository prologue for the slaying of the giant, we are introduced to it by means of a 1,500-word scenario of live action and dramatized doctrine in the present, all of which is, however, projected from an allusion to the Solomon of long ago (see Walker, Warren 1987).

It is the multiplicity of interwoven elements that is to a large extent the making of this work. The greatest critical misjudgment of *Hamzai Sahip Kıran* would be to consider it an historical document made more attractive by the addition of superficial decorative features. The simple fact is that all of the unquestionably reliable historical information about Hamzai can be expressed in very few sentences. Even the massive and authoritative *Encyclopaedia of Islam* devoted only one brief paragraph to the biography of this heralded

Muslim hero (Meredith-Owens 1971: 152). Hamzai (usually referred to by others as *Hamza* or *Hamzah*) was born in Mecca in 567 A.D. He was the paternal uncle of Mohammed, though only three years older than the Prophet. Initially opposed to the new religion enunciated by his nephew, Hamzai soon became one of its most zealous converts. At a time when Islam was struggling to survive in a region predominantly polytheistic, Hamzai was one of its staunchest supporters.[16] He distinguished himself in single combats against enemy warriors in the Battles of Badr (622-624), but in 625 he was killed in the Battle of Uhud.

If few were the known facts about Hamzai, many were the fictions that succeeded them. One cluster of fictive motifs was used to develop *The Message* (1977), a 170-minute religious film which is now broadcast annually on Turkish television during two successive evenings of Ramazan.[17] Coalesced—probably in part by Mahir, partly by a long line of predecessors—were numerous other factors contributing to the Hamzai fantasy. Although it would obviously be impossible to trace most of these images, actions, and ideas to their origins, one can tender some hypotheses about a few potential influences.

The earliest identifiable input into the cumulative Hamzai legend resulted from a case of mistaken identity. Not quite two centuries after the death of Hamzai of Mecca, another Hamzai, son of Adharak of Sistan, Persia, led an insurrection of the Kharijite sect against the authority of the Abbasid caliph Harun Reşit between 793 and 798.[18] Both his resistance to the caliphate and his subsequent military expeditions to India and Ceylon demonstrated a kind of valor that appealed to contemporary imagination (see Caroe 1958: 103-07). The confusion of the two Hamzais in the folk memory aggrandized the legendary reputation of both men.

No later than the 11th century a Persian romance titled *The Epic of Hamza* began to circulate orally and in manuscripts (attributed to various writers). Hamzai of Mecca is now called Amir Hamza. The action occurs in the same Sassanian court that is the site of part of *Hamzai Sahip Kıran*, and similar too are some of the references to mythic Rüstem. The romance describes at some length the destruction of Zoroastrian idols by adherents of monotheistic Islam. It would be too simplistic to suppose that this attack on

---

[16] In his 10th-century universal history—thirty-eight volumes in the English edition—al-Tabari cited one brief reputed episode that attests to Hamzai's efforts to protect Mohammed. But since all of al-Tabari's sources were oral—at best usually fourth- or fifth-hand reports—even that one episode may be apocryphal (see al-Tabari 1988:103-06).

[17] *The Message* was directed and produced by Moustapha Akkad in both Arabic and English. Anthony Quinn starred in the role of Hamzai in the English-language version. Turkish was dubbed into the English edition to accommodate viewers in Turkey. The films are still available, as is an inexpensive video format in English (see Akkad 1977).

[18] The Kharijites were an unusually deviant and aggressive sect of early Islam, dating from the 7th century during the last two years of the caliphate of Ali (see Frye 1975: 108-09, 510-12).

the icons of polytheism was a direct source for the denigration and smashing of idols that was described during Mahir's narration of January 11th, but it may have contributed to the flow of quasi-history that filtered down through the centuries to the present (see Virolleaud 1958-59: 3-10). A medieval Georgian redaction of the romance, attributed to Mose Khoneli, retains this iconoclastic action.[19] The honorifics that Behçet Mahir added to Hamzai's name[20] may possibly have been derived from the title of an anonymous 16th-century poetic work, *The Legend of Sahib-kıran* (see Meredith-Owens 1971: 153).

Whatever usable raw materials the broad cultural heritage may have afforded, it was Behçet Mahir who selected and metamorphosed the components of the final narrative production. His was the artistry that created *Hamzai Sahip Kıran*, and his was the breath that gave it life.

---

[19] For the most readily accessible edition of this work at present see Khoneli 1958.

[20] *Sahip Kıran* is a Persian epithet meaning "Lord of the Auspicious Conjunction [of planets]." Jupiter and Venus were considered to be benevolent planets, and their conjunction was especially propitious.

The Legend of Hamzai Sahip Kıran

First night; narration of January 9, 1977

The Antagonist, Nuşirvan, and His Heritage

Today I shall begin the story of Hamzai Sahip Kıran, but before talking about him, I wish to make some comments about Nuşirvan,[1] and it will be through these comments on Nuşirvan that we shall come to Hamzai Sahip Kıran.

Gentlemen, the name of Nuşirvan's grandfather was Key Kubat,[2] and it was from this grandfather that Nuşirvan inherited his throne while he was still quite young. Key Kubat had his men build a palace for Nuşirvan in Ani,[3] a city which Key Kubat had earlier founded. There is an old proverb which says, "If the rest of the world were ever to be destroyed, Ani could rebuild it, but if Ani were ever to be destroyed, the rest of the world could never replace that city." Key Kubat, the grandfather of Nuşirvan, founded that city and then later built Nuşirvan a palace there.

(People come to and depart from this world continuously, for we are here really only as guests. Allah gives a different life to every person, and thus everyone has his own form of livelihood and his own part of the soil. We must realize that we are given only a limited number of breaths, and we cannot draw even one more breath than that.

Allah did not create anything superior to Adam. As you know, when Adam was created, all of the other creatures prostrated themselves before him—all, that is, except Satan. Satan refused to show Adam this respect, saying, "How can I prostrate myself before a creature made of clay when I was made of fire?" Because of this refusal to honor Adam, Satan had a curse

---

[1] *Nuşirvan* is not really a name but a title or honorific attached to a name. It is variously translated as "happy soul" or "of immortal soul." Behçet Mahir is not alone in using the title as a proper name, for it is so used by Farid al-Din Attar in his *The Ilahi-Nama* [Legend], *or Book of God* (Attar 1976: 53, 193-95, 232, 280). *Nuşirvan* here refers to Khusraw I, the most illustrious king (531-579) of the Sassanid or Sassanian Dynasty of Persia (3rd to 7th centuries). His name is also spelled in several other ways: *Kasra, Kusra, Khosrow,* and *Chosroes*. He is referred to extensively in Ferdowsi's *The Epic of the Kings: Shah-Nama, the National Epic of Persia* (Ferdowsi 1967: 99-130).

[2] Key Kubat here but King Qobad in *The Epic of the Kings* (Ferdowsi 1967: 114) and Kavad in *The Cambridge History of Iran* (Yarshater 1983: 148-57). He was not Khusraw's grandfather but his father. He was not the founder of Ani, which was not built until the 9th century.

[3] Ani was not a Persian city but an Armenian city. Ruins of Ani lie in Kars Province, extreme eastern Turkey.

placed upon him.[4] As a result of this, I am always led to think, "Do not consider what you are but rather what you might become." Allah created us from nothing and can return us to nothing. He can send you to bed as a rich man but awaken you at dawn as a pauper. The power is His. Let me remind you that there are some people who complain about their lot and say, "Fate, may your wheel[5] break; may your house be demolished!" Such words achieve nothing but making the speaker feel even more rebellious. Isn't Fate like an angel who gets orders from Allah? Is it possible that Allah's order will be canceled by your saying, "May the wheel of Fate be broken!"? No, it will not be canceled. Because of that fact, there is no point in our being rebellious. Speak more wisely than one using angry words! As our forefathers instructed us, "Speak with a good tongue." Train your tongue to speak wisely. Those who do not may speak falsely even about unimportant things; they spend curses upon trivial matters. This is a mistake. Speak only the truth, the plain truth.)

Key Kubat built the city of Ani, and he built a very big palace for Nuşirvan. Nuşirvan was a very merciless man. A traitorous man has no compassion and no faith.[6] Before the time of Key Kubat or Nuşirvan, there had been people living in this world for six or seven thousand years. Then came Rüstem,[7] son of Zal.

Have a look, take a glance
At those who come and go.
Look at Rüstem, son of Zal,
Who slew the tens of thousands,
A madman and a padishah.
Look too at the Prophet David,
And Solomon, that David's son,
Who ruled the nations from his throne.

---

4 Throughout this work references to the Bible do not always reflect the Judeo-Christian canon. They are often old and well-established Muslim interpretations.

5 The wheel here is the Wheel of Fortune, a widely distributed image that appears in numerous contexts, including that of the Tarot cards.

6 This is counter to the reputation given to him by Attar (Attar 1976: 53), where Nuşirvan is pictured as a just and kind ruler. Furthermore, the honorific *Nuşirvan* indicates that he had a "happy soul," hardly the epithet for a traitor and an infidel. There is no denying, however, that in Mahir's tale Nuşirvan is deceptive, merciless, and even vicious.

7 A mythical hero of ancient Persia, he is featured in tales that extend over the reigns of several rulers and almost three centuries. The Persian name is *Rustam*, but we are here using the Turkish form, *Rüstem*.

The fourth grandson of Rüstem, son of Zal, became the grand vizier of Nuşirvan. He had been a blacksmith originally, but he was an unusual man in that he understood the language of birds.[8]

The name of Rüstem's grandfather was Dal,[9] and this Dal was a padishah. His son, named Zal, was not only a very handsome man but also a very strong man, for he was a wrestler. Dal said to himself, "I shall go forth and find a bride who will be a match for the admirable qualities of my son. I wonder if there has ever really been produced such a girl?" But Dal did find such a suitable wife for his son, and Zal married that girl.

Rüstem was the first child to be produced by that marriage. He was born prematurely, two months before the full term of gestation. But he had threatened to be even more premature than that. When his mother was only five months pregnant, she began to shake and was unable to walk. The doctors and astrologers were consulted, and they said, "This child cannot be born in a normal way. We should cut her belly just below the rib cage and remove the child at once. If we do not do that, the mother will die."

But others said, "A baby carried by its mother for only five months will not be able to live."

Then Dal intervened saying, "No, the child must survive whether or not the mother lives." The woman remained in her bed on her back for another two months, often crying out in great distress.

Observe the work of Allah here. What had Dal said? "My son is very handsome, and his wife is a great beauty. The offspring of two such people should be even more attractive than they are." But no one can interfere with the work of Allah. He can create an attractive child from a pair of beautiful parents, but He can also create a very ugly one, if He wishes.

Allah had placed a very awesome child in the womb of this woman, and eventually the doctors did have to cut the mother's belly just below the ribs in order to deliver the child. Those who caught a glimpse of the child were quite amazed by its size, for Allah had produced a really enormous baby. Dal grew quite furious. He said, "Take this child to the wilderness and leave it there for the wolves and the birds to eat! I said, 'Let us see how

---

[8] The notion that selected human beings learn to understand the languages of birds and/or animals may come close to being universal. It was a quality attributed to such culture heroes as Siegfried and Hiawatha. In Turkish folklore Solomon is the person most frequently credited with such unusual linguistic ability. The popularity of this bit of folk fantasy in the Middle East is suggested by the fact that it is the basis for one of the opening stories of *A Thousand Nights and a Night* (Burton 1934: 16-22). It is not surprising, therefore, that Behçet Mahir finds occasion to include it subsequently in this tale. It is very close to folktale Type 670 (Aarne and Thompson 1961). Other related Aarne-Thompson types are those numbered 517, 671, 671B*, 672, and 673. In Stith Thompson, *Motif-Index of Folk Literature* (Thompson 1955-58), Motifs B210-217 distinguish among aspects of Knowledge of Animal Languages. Motif C245—Tabu: Revealing Knowledge of Animal Language appears in Type 670 and in some variants.

[9] *The Epic of the Kings* (Ferdowsi 1967: 135-37) gives his name as *Sam*.

beautiful the child of two beautiful people can be,' but see this child! Anyone would become frightened just looking at this baby!" (Long before that, Solomon, the son of David, had been informed that in a distant land there would be born a boy who would someday succeed him to the throne.[10])

Gentlemen, the power of performing miracles is in the hands of Allah, but often Allah has human beings enact the events which lead up to miracles. They left the child of Zal in the wilderness with no name attached to it or any other indication of its origin, but the child was nevertheless rescued.

While an emerald-green *anka*[11] was flying over that area, she heard beneath her the crying of a baby. The *anka*, who was the padishah (ruler) of birds, swooped down, picked up the baby, and took it to her nest in a great cypress tree. Knowing the source of the baby, she named it Rüstem, son of Zal. She gave it that second name so that the child would grow up knowing who its father was. The *anka* reared Rüstem with her own children. Seven years passed, and the bird had just finished nursing Rüstem as she had her own children.[12]

But after fifteen years had passed, Rüstem was able to repay her for all of her kindness. Whenever in the past the *anka* had reared a brood of nestlings to the age of fifteen, she had begun to teach them to fly. But always in the same fifteenth year a large dragon had appeared and devoured her brood of children. This had always occurred at times when the *anka* was away from the nest working to find food for her family's livelihood. (Even she,

---

[10] This is apparently a folk interpretation of *1 Kings*, 11-12. Because of the idolatry in his court (imported by his numerous foreign wives), Solomon received divine warning that the son, Rehoboam, who would normally succeed him would be deposed and replaced by a servant, Jeroboam. Solomon's situation is not really apposite to this context. The child of Zal would pose no threat to Dal, for it would be Zal, not Zal's child, who would be his immediate successor. This may be an echo from *The Epic of the Kings,* in which Zal's father, Sam, casts Zal into the wilderness because Zal was born with white hair, which Sam thought very ugly. Thus in *The Epic* Sam/Dal is attempting to get rid of his putative successor. In a sense this royal fear of deposition anticipates Nuşirvan's concern about Hamzai Sahip Kıran.

[11] In its frequent appearance in Turkish folktales the *anka* is almost always female and almost always strongly maternal. The bird/human relationship, however, is usually played out in different order. Here the bird serves as Rüstem's surrogate mother and is later repaid by the boy (at age fifteen) when he rescues the *anka*'s brood of chicks from a dragon. More frequently the fully grown hero quite gratuitously saves the nestlings from destruction, thereby placing the indebtedness upon the bird. She settles her obligation to him by carrying him either out of danger or back to his distant homeland. For examples of this syndrome see *Tales Alive in Turkey* (Walker and Uysal 1966: 19-20) and *More Tales Alive in Turkey* (Walker and Uysal 1992: 177-78). Further information about giant birds in Turkish folklore can be found in Mehmet Önder, "Kubâd-Ârad Sarayı Harpi ve Simurg'ları," (Önder 1967-68).

[12] Here is still another similarity to *The Epic of the Kings*, in which Sam casts his son Zal into the wilderness where that abandoned infant is reared by an equally huge bird, a *simurgh*. When Zal has grown to young manhood, he repays the bird's kindness in the same way that Rüstem does here.

the huge bird so powerful that she could lift ships from the sea, had to work for her daily food! Therefore, I say to you, "Work, O sons of Turks! Work!")

Every time the *anka* children were fifteen years old, the dragon came and ate them. Well, another brood of chicks were fifteen years old, and Rüstem, son of Zal, was also fifteen. The chicks had taught him the language of birds. Therefore, Rüstem, son of Zal, understood the language of human beings[13] and the language of birds. One day the chicks asked the emerald-green *anka*, "Mother, why can't Rüstem, son of Zal, fly like us?"

The *anka* answered, "Oh, my children, he comes from the race of human beings. He has two arms instead of wings. You can fly, but he cannot. Allah created him as one of a race which is superior to our race."

When the emerald-green *anka* left the nest that day to find food for her family, the dragon appeared, grinding his teeth. The chicks were now fifteen years old, and Rüstem was also fifteen. Both he and they had been nursed for seven years by the *anka*. When the dragon appeared, the chicks were frightened and immediately flew away from the place where they were playing to the cypress tree. Rüstem was also frightened, but he was unable to fly up into the cypress tree. Instead, he hid himself behind the trunk of that tree.

(The chicks and Rüstem were fifteen years old, an age which is a quarter of our present life span of sixty years. Human life span was once much greater, but people then often thought about their lives in the same way that some people now think. They thought, "Why should I take the trouble to build a house when I shall be here for only seven hundred years? We are here today and gone tomorrow."

Didn't they have any brains? Were they not capable of building an apartment house? Of course they had brains! And of course they were capable of building an apartment house or a palace. But they said, "We are mere guests here, where we shall live for only seven hundred years. It is pointless to build an apartment house or palace in this mortal world where we shall remain so briefly. We shall be dead in seven hundred years!"

But what are we doing now? We are constructing buildings of many stories and they are supported with steel beams. We do not look back to where we have come from, and we do not look forward to death. Yes, have such buildings, O sons of Turks! Have great buildings! I am not saying that you shouldn't construct such buildings. Work, O sons of Turks! Work! Beautify your own country! In later times, even if the country were conquered by enemies, people will admire you and thank you for raising such buildings.)

The dragon intended to eat the chicks of the *anka*, and Rüstem understood this. As the dragon was beginning to climb the tree slowly, Rüstem gripped the section just behind its head very tightly with his bare

[13] Within the framework of Behçet Efendi's tale there is no way in which Rüstem could have learned any human language by this time.

hands. He kept squeezing more and more tightly until he finally strangled the dragon. Even after the monster was dead, Rüstem continued to squeeze its neck with all his strength.

Later in the day the *anka* returned from her search for food. She saw at once that her chicks were still alive and that the dragon was dead. She called to Rüstem, "Relax your grip now, Son! Drop the dragon, for it is dead! Bravo! The milk with which I nursed you I now make *helâl*.[14] I have long wished to see a brood of my children flying about, but every brood that has reached the flying age was devoured by the dragon. You have made it possible for me to attain my greatest desire. I shall now see my children fly unmolested."

Yes, gentlemen, the fourth grandson of Rüstem was the grand vizier of Nuşirvan. After having spoken briefly of some of those who preceded him, I now wish to talk about Hamzai Sahip Kıran himself.

One day Nuşirvan and his grand vizier were walking together. Because the grand vizier was a grandson of Rüstem, he understood the language of birds. But now that I have said that—O respected listeners—an anecdote comes to my mind which I must tell you.

The Speech of Birds and Animals

Solomon, the son of David, knew eighteen thousand languages. The grand vizier's knowing two languages—that of human beings and that of birds—was insignificant alongside Solomon's understanding of eighteen thousand. Among the people he knew, Solomon had an especially close friend. (See here! Human beings cannot be without friends of some kind. Some are friendly only with their tongues while within their hearts they are really enemies.) One day this friend of Solomon asked him, "Can you teach me some of the animal and bird languages?"

"Yes, I can do that," answered Solomon, "but you must never reveal to any other human being that you know these languages. If you do make such a disclosure, you will die at once."

---

[14] The principle of *helâl/haram* is an important Muslim religious concept. What is *helâl* is that which is permissible and debt-free according to canonical law. That which is *haram* is forbidden. There is no obligation or restriction or penalty for doing or accepting whatever is *helâl*, but there will be punishment assigned on Judgment Day for having done or taken whatever is *haram*. A dying or endangered person will ordinarily declare *helâl* everything he has given or done for another, always with the tacit understanding that the absolution of indebtedness will be reciprocal. The granting or refusal of *helâl* status to human interaction can be used as a power play. If a mother has a difference of opinion with any of her offspring, for example, she can reduce the recalcitrant child, of whatever age, to immediate and total submission by declaring that she will not make *helâl* the milk with which she nursed him or her. What more damning evidence of unworthiness could be presented at the bar of divine justice than the fact that even one's mother will not absolve one of guilt?

"No, of course I shall not reveal that," answered his friend. "I shall not tell anyone."

Solomon taught that friend the languages of several domestic animals and fowls—the languages of donkeys, oxen, dogs, cats, and chickens. After he had finished teaching these languages, he again warned his friend, "Now remember! Do not tell anyone of your ability to understand the speech of any of these animals!"

"No, of course not," said his friend once more. "I shall not tell a soul."

The man who had just learned these languages began to enjoy listening to the animals on his farm talking to each other. Not knowing that his owner now understood their languages, the donkey one day said, "Oh, brother ox, if you wish to avoid going to hard labor in the field again tomorrow morning, don't eat your food tonight. Then our owner will conclude that you are ill, and as a result of that he will not have you do any plowing tomorrow."

The ox replied, "That is an excellent idea, brother donkey. I am glad that you told me about it."

But their owner overheard their conversation. That evening he said to his son, "Son, go and give food and water to all of our livestock."

The boy went to the barn and fed and watered the animals as his father had directed. After a while, however, he noticed that one of the oxen was not eating. When morning came, the boy saw that that ox still had not touched its food or water. He went to the farmer and said, "Father, one of our oxen is sick. He has not eaten any of the food or drunk any of the water which I gave him last night."

The farmer knew perfectly well why the ox had not eaten food or drunk water, but he could not explain this to his son, for he knew that revealing that information would cost him his life. He therefore simply said to the boy, "Son, get the donkey and harness him to the plow with the other ox."

"All right, Father," answered the boy, and he did exactly what his father had ordered him to do.

The donkey worked very hard that day from early morning until the time that they returned to the barn at night. As soon as he was back in the barn, the donkey said to the ox who had been there all day, "Alas, brother ox, you had better eat your food tonight, or our owner may sell you to the butcher." Of course the donkey was worried about himself and not about the ox. He knew that if the ox again failed to eat its food, he himself would again be harnessed with the other ox to do another day of heavy field work.

The farmer had been listening to the conversation between the donkey and the ox, and when he heard the donkey's remark, he could not keep himself from laughing aloud. His wife, who just happened to come along, heard the farmer laugh and asked, "O, my husband, why did you laugh just now?"

"It was not for any reason, Wife. I just felt like laughing."

But the woman did not believe that, and she insisted on having an answer to her question. "But why, Husband? No one is here but you, I, the donkey and the ox. So, why did you laugh?"

"Oh, I laughed for no reason at all," said the farmer.

"Oh, no, no! You laughed at me! I know!" said his wife.

The man found himself in a helpless situation. To gain time, he said, "Oh, Wife, I did not laugh at you, but if you insist on knowing what caused me to laugh, I shall tell you tomorrow morning." He was, however, greatly concerned about this matter, and he began at once to think of some excuse that he could give his wife in the morning.

While he was deep in thought about this, he overheard a conversation between the cat and the dog. The cat said, "Our master will die in the morning. Well, I like *helva*[15] very much."

The dog replied, "Yes, I know that he is going to die. Well, I like meat very much."[16]

The rooster then joined the conversation. He said to the dog and the cat, "I do not understand this situation. I have forty wives here, and although I am only one rooster, I can make all of those forty hens obey me perfectly. But here is our owner, who has only one wife, but he cannot make even that one woman obey him. If I were he, I should get a stick. Then when she demanded to know why I laughed, I should strike her with that stick and say, 'That is the reason I laughed.' If he did that, she would not ask him that question again."

Hearing the rooster's comment, the man said to himself, "Ah, yes! Now I know what I shall do tomorrow morning!"

When morning arrived, the woman asked the farmer, "Husband, why did you laugh yesterday? Tell me now!"

Striking his wife with the stick, the man said, "This is what I laughed at. I laughed at the thought of striking you with this stick!" In this way the farmer saved himself from death.

---

[15] *Helva*, a candy, is used synecdochically here to represent a ritual at which it is served. Named *Mevlüt* or *Mevlit*, this ritual is a memorial service in the form of a requiem cantata, usually first performed forty days after the death of the person being honored. It may thereafter be repeated annually. Composed by Süleyman Çelebi at Bursa in the 15th century, it celebrates the birth of Mohammed and selected episodes of his life. It may be Turkey's most notable contribution to religious music.

Mevlüt is an expensive event for the family of the deceased both because of the number of musicians and singers required and because of the traditional refreshments accompanying it. Sherbet and other nonalcoholic beverages and a variety of sweetmeats are served to all in attendance. Small bags of the confections are usually given to departing guests. *Helva* is the favorite candy at a *Mevlüt* performance. Although there are various recipes for *helva*, all of them have in common these ingredients: sesame flour, butter, and honey.

[16] The dog here is probably anticipating a portion of the funeral banquet.

While the grand vizier was walking with Nuşirvan, he overheard a conversation between an owl and a sparrow. The grand vizier was able to understand the language of birds because he was descended from Rüstem. The sparrow said to the owl, "Oh, brother owl, let us have our children married to each other. Give your daughter to my son in marriage."

The owl responded, "Oh, brother sparrow, there is no way that you could pay the bride-price[17] for my daughter. I want forty houses for my daughter, and there is no way that you could provide them."

"There would be nothing easier than doing that," said the sparrow. "Sahip Kıran will one day invade this country and possess all of the realm of Nuşirvan. Everything will then be so changed that I could get not just forty but even a thousand houses for you."

When the grand vizier heard this, he laughed. Nuşirvan asked his vizier, "Why did you laugh just now?"

The grand vizier answered, "My padishah, there was no reason for my laughing. I just laughed."

"No, I do not believe that," said Nuşirvan. "If you do not tell me why you laughed, I shall send you to the executioners."

Then the grand vizier said helplessly, "My padishah, I shall tell you why I laughed if you will first promise not to kill me for anything that I say."

After Nuşirvan had given his word not to harm his vizier for anything he said, the vizier explained his reason for laughing. (Yes, I should advise you never to lie. I have been advising this now for forty years. O sons of Turks: never lie! Speak only the truth!) The grand vizier said, "O my padishah, I was listening to the conversation between an owl and a sparrow. The sparrow wanted to have the owl's daughter become the wife of his son, but the owl said that the bride-price of forty houses would be more than the

---

[17] *Başlık* (bride-price) is defined in most Turkish dictionaries as the sum of money paid to the father of a bride by the bridegroom or his family. This applies to the conventional marriages arranged by the families of the principals, not to those (usually urban) decided upon by the young couple themselves. Villagers sometimes object fiercely to the term *bride-price* because it implies that a sale is involved, though they regularly use the verb *satmak* (to sell) when discussing this transaction.

Whatever it may be called, the custom provides a practical solution to an economic problem. Weddings are financed by the parents of the bride, and the expense can be devastating for a low-income family. Although real-life weddings do not last for the forty days and forty nights of folktale nuptials, they may last for several days, during which time room, board, and entertainment for large numbers of guests (often hundreds) are paid for by the bride's family. Villagers give accounts—some perhaps apocryphal but others we know to be accurate—of fathers who plant a row of trees when a daughter is born; eighteen or twenty years later the wood of these trees will be of sufficient value to help defray the cost of the girl's wedding. The transfer of wealth does not always move in just one direction, for the bride usually takes with her to her new home a large and valuable dowry. Many Turkish girls begin accumulating a trousseau at the age of ten or eleven. As one scholar has aptly observed, "Nowadays the bride-price is often regarded . . . as a quid pro quo for the trousseau" (Sterling 1965: 185-86).

sparrow could afford. The sparrow then replied that such a price would be no obstacle, for after Sahip Kıran had invaded and conquered all of Nuşirvan's territory, everything would be so changed that he could afford to pay a thousand houses for the girl. It was that bird conversation that made me laugh."

"Aha! Then this means that Sahip Kıran will conquer my country?"

"Yes, my padishah. Your injustice will eventually make it possible for Sahip Kıran to conquer your country."

The Coming of Hamzai and His Companion, Ömer

They then returned to the palace, and Nuşirvan began immediately to change his whole behavior. Instead of basing his decisions on injustice, he now began to base them on justice. In fact, he became a very righteous man. One day soon after that, he said to his grand vizier, "Cast *remil*[18] and discover where Sahip Kıran is located. I want to be a righteous and just man. Justice will help me to protect my country from seizure by Sahip Kıran. Unless I am just, I shall not be able to withstand the sword of Sahip Kıran." (Oh, gentlemen, even if there were a thousand Nuşirvans, they could not stand before the sword of Sahip Kıran! But Nuşirvan's turning to justice protected him from the sword. Oh, honorable gentlemen, he who is just has power.)

The grand vizier cast *remil* and received some information about Sahip Kıran. He then said, "My padishah, Sahip Kıran has not yet even been born, but he will soon be born at Mecca, the center of the world." He then predicted the exact time—the month, the day, and the hour—when Sahip Kıran would be born.

Nuşirvan then said, "Go to Mecca and when Sahip Kıran is born, put him immediately upon a salary from me. If he grows up eating my bread, his sword will never kill me."[19] (O people gathered here, nobody can survive

---

[18] *Remil* is a type of geomancy used to obtain information about the present and to predict future events. It is carried out by means of several small cubical objects (like dice) on the facets of which are inscribed coded numbers, letters, and signs. Each of these markings has been assigned a meaning. After the cubes have been cast upon the ground, the sides turned upward are read and their meanings related to each other. Sometimes repeated castings are required in order to elicit intelligible communication. In rural areas the cubes are often made of sheep's knucklebones. Such a knucklebone is known as an *aşık* , not to be confused with *âşık* (lover poet or minstrel).

In one of the two basic plots for Turkish oral detective stories *remil* is used to pick up successive clues with which to solve the crime. See Eberhard and Boratav (1952)—Type 347—*Die Detektive I.* For examples of this folktale type, see ATON tales numbered 198, 335, 416, 447, 651, 660, 956, 1328, and 1834.

[19] In many societies acceptance of food from another person commits one to what might be called a kinship of hospitality. This idea is especially strong in Turkey where the gift of food

without food in his stomach, and so do not deny the hand that gives you bread. If you do so, then sooner or later you will be punished. If you are not punished in this world, then you will be in the next. Therefore, do not look with malice upon anyone who has helped you.)

Before the Blessed Hamzai Sahip Kıran was born, the grand vizier of Nuşirvan arrived in Mecca. But it has been said that Hamzai Sahip Kıran had been acting in this drama forty years before our Prophet was born. We are telling this story just as it was told to us, but if we were to give the actual dates here, we should have to say that there were only three years' difference between the ages of Hamzai Sahip Kıran and the Blessed Mohammed. Hamzai Sahip Kıran was born just three years before the Blessed Mohammed, but we shall say here that the difference was forty years because that is the way that people before us told the story, and we are following in their footsteps.[20]

In Mecca at that time there were two notable clans. One of them was the clan of Haşimi, and the other, the clan of Hurişi. Abdüzalüllahim[21] was of the Hurişi clan, and Hamzai Sahip Kıran from the Haşimi clan.[22] These two clans were not entirely distinct, for they were related to each other.

Allah can make a person blind if He wishes, but He can also give a person powerful vision if He wants to do that. When the grand vizier of Nuşirvan arrived in Mecca, the noble families there welcomed him with great respect. The grand vizier said to these nobles, "On such and such a date a certain boy will be born in this city; you are to inform me about this event when it occurs, for Nuşirvan has ordered me to put that boy on a royal salary from the moment that he enters this world." As we know, Nuşirvan wanted to do this so that the sword of Hamzai Sahip Kıran would never slay him. Well, gentlemen, a baby boy was born at precisely the time that the grand vizier had predicted. It was in the middle of the night that Hamzai Sahip Kıran entered this world, and news was taken at once to the grand vizier that this boy had been born in the Haşimi clan. The grand vizier put this boy on a royal salary immediately, just as he had been instructed to do by Nuşirvan.

But just two hours after the birth of Hamzai Sahip Kıran, Ömer Ümmiye also was born, and thus on the same night two baby boys had

(or lodging) automatically binds the recipient into reciprocity. Furthermore, during the time that one is a host, he or she benefits from a halo effect. This is reflected in ATON tale No. 1269, "A Host Can Do No Wrong," and in No. 679, a variant.

20 The conflict in time here may be the result of Behçet Efendi's or some predecessor's confusion of the names of Hamzai Sahip Kıran and Nuşirvan. It was Nuşirvan who had been active for approximately forty years before the birth of Mohammed. Nuşirvan's reign began in the year 531; Mohammed was born in 570.

21 Unidentified.

22 Both Hamzai Sahip Kıran and Mohammed were descendants of the family of the powerful Meccan leader Abd al-Muttalib of the Haşimi clan. That clan ruled Mecca, with few interruptions, from the 4th to the 10th century (Rentz 1965).

entered this world. The father of this second child went to the grand vizier and said, "O vizier, a son was also born to me tonight. You told us that you would at once put on royal salary any boy who was born here tonight. You have already placed the heir of the Haşimi clan on royal salary, and you should also place my son on such a salary—something which we really need, for we are poor."

When the grand vizier heard this plea, he again cast *remil* and studied the signs that were given. He discovered from these signs that Ömer Ümmiye would become even more powerful than Hamzai Sahip Kıran, and he therefore immediately put him on royal salary, too. These two boys grew up together. For fifteen years their lives were uneventful, and they grew up in comfort, for they had during all of that time drawn a royal salary. When they were old enough to do so, they spent time together hunting in the nearby mountains.

When they reached the age of fifteen, Hamzai became interested in wrestling. He soon became such a good wrestler that no one could throw him to the ground, neither boys his own age nor even adults. Not only was he very strong, but he also exercised and trained day and night. Of course it was Allah, Creator of Hamzai Sahip Kıran, who caused him to practice wrestling so steadily. Wrestlers from Mecca and the surrounding area kept coming to Hamzai Sahip Kıran's arena, but none of them was able to defeat him. Was there any possibility that a wrestler, regardless of what family he had come from, could throw Hamzai down on his back? Of course not. Hamzai Sahip Kıran won every contest, and he continued to improve his skill every day.[23]

Divine Gifts for Hamzai and Ömer

Hamzai Sahip Kıran and Ömer Ümmiye went everywhere together. They always ate and drank together. They had always worn the same kind of clothes. And both of them received money to support themselves from royal

---

[23] It is not surprising that Hamzai should have chosen to excel in wrestling rather than, say, fencing, archery or horseback riding. Turks have long produced excellent wrestlers, some competent enough in recent years to win awards in international competition. In their own country they also engage in an unconventional form of the sport known as "grease wrestling," which requires that combatants coat their bodies and scant clothing with olive oil to make them more difficult to grasp.

But the champion wrestler is more to many Turks than just another athletic hero. He is the quintessential strong man, a symbol of physical prowess. In Turkish tales and legends wrestlers are protagonists almost as frequently as are giant killers, tricksters, or saints. Their exaggerated prestige becomes patent subsequently when the backbone of Hamzai's army is an elite corps of wrestlers! While it is probably true that before the advent of firearms in combat, brute force was an important factor, it would seem most unlikely that mere muscle could prevail in any major battle.

salaries. They liked each other very much, and each was the other's best friend.

One day while the two boys were hunting, a colt began following Hamzai. Since the colt was only an animal, without human mouth or tongue, it could not speak, and as a result it was unable to tell Hamzai whose it was and why it was there. Although Hamzai Sahip Kıran inquired everywhere in an effort to find the colt's owner, he was unsuccessful in his search. But apparently this colt came from a noble line of horses.[24] It was Allah Who made it follow Hamzai Sahip Kıran. It was Allah Who gave Hamzai Sahip Kıran that fate. Hamzai not only searched personally for this colt's owner, but he also sent messages about the colt to more distant places. All such efforts were in vain, however, and there seemed to be no way that he could discover the owner of that colt.

By the time that two years had passed, the colt had become a very fine horse, but Hamzai Sahip Kıran hesitated to ride it. He said repeatedly, "How can I ride on a horse that isn't mine? It belongs to someone else, and it would not be proper for me to use it." It was the fear of Allah that made him feel that way.[25] (How different it is in our time! If you turn your back now, someone is likely to take something that belongs to you! We may say that we can do this or that forbidden thing because nobody will see us do it. But there is still Allah, Who sees everything that we do. Our minds do not always realize that nowadays. There are always eyes that see you when you are taking what is not yours.)

Then one day Hamzai Sahip Kıran heard a great voice speaking: "The horse came to its owner. O Hamzai Sahip Kıran, this horse has been following you for two years. It is yours! Now take the horse which belongs to you." Hamzai looked around for the source of the voice that he heard, but all he could see were the rocks, the mountainside, and Ömer Ümmiye. He heard the voice speak this way three times, and Ömer Ümmiye heard this voice, too. Therefore, Hamzai Sahip Kıran took the horse, and when they returned home that night, he put it into his stable.

But Ömer Ümmiye ignored the message that they had received from the great voice. He said, "We were born on the same day; we have grown up together, and we have always shared everything that we have had. We should, therefore, share this horse, too."

Hamzai Sahip Kıran answered, "But, Ömer, this horse is not like other kinds of goods. We cannot divide this horse. If we did, it would die."

But Ömer Ümmiye did not accept this statement. He insisted that they should share the horse equally. Hamzai tried very hard to change Ömer's mind about this, but he was unable to succeed in doing that. He said,

---

[24] The term used by the narrator is *askeri devzade*.

[25] This is an application of the *helâl/haram* principle discussed above in Note 14.

"Ömer, everything that belongs to me also belongs to you. Everything which is mine is yours too."

While they were arguing about this, they heard the great voice speaking again. It said, "Oh, Ömer, your fortune is in the nearby cave. Go to that cave, and there you will find a sheepskin hanging on the wall. Take that hide, and it will enable you to get whatever you want."[26] It was the skin of the sheep that Prophet Abraham had sacrificed to Allah instead of his son Ishmael.[27] The skin of that sheep had been waiting there for Ömer Ümmiye since the time of Abraham. The sheep had originally been sent by Allah to replace Ishmael as sacrifice. Ömer went to the cave, took the sheepskin, and made a pouch[28] for himself from it.

Oh gentlemen, observe the working of Fate in this matter. Ömer went to Hamzai Sahip Kıran, who was sitting astride his horse, Askeri Beyzade.[29] He said to him, "O Hamzai Sahip Kıran, you refused to share the horse with me, but Allah has provided me with a fortune that is of far greater value than a horse."

Hamzai asked, "But what is it? It looks like only an old leather pouch."

Ömer answered, "You may see only an old leather pouch. Aha! See what I can get from my old leather pouch. I shall now put my hand into my pouch and draw forth some *helva* so fresh that it is still hot."

Hamzai Sahip Kıran did not believe that. He laughed, thinking that Ömer must have gone mad. He said, "Ah, Ömer, it is really nothing but an old leather pouch. You must be joking!"

Ömer replied, "Just wait a moment, Hamzai. Just wait and see." Ömer reached into the pouch, drew out two large pieces of *helva*, and began eating one of them.

Hamzai Sahip Kıran said, "Oh, Ömer, give me some too. Don't eat all of it yourself."

Ömer answered, "Oh, Hamzai, that horse belongs to you, but this pouch belongs to me." He did, however, give some of the *helva* to Hamzai Sahip Kıran.

---

[26] It will be through the use of this supernaturally potent skin that Ömer will hereafter frequently play the role of trickster.

[27] In the Muslim version of God's preventing Abraham from sacrificing his son, the son is Ishmael, not Isaac (as in the Old Testament). Ishmael is considered to be the progenitor and patriarch of the Arab people. *İsmail*, the Turkish form of *Ishmael*, is a very popular male name throughout Turkey.

[28] The term used by the narrator here is *dağarcık*, usually defined as *a leather pouch carried over the shoulder by shepherds and hunters.*

[29] The name means literally *Prince of Warriors*.

As Hamzai was eating the candy, he realized that its flavor was better than that of any *helva* that he had eaten previously. He said, "This is the best-tasting *helva* I have ever eaten."

Ömer Ümmiye then said, "Well, Hamzai, whatever you may wish can be gotten for you from this pouch." Then Hamzai began asking for all sorts of things that no one else could possibly provide, but Ömer produced every one of these things from his pouch. Gentlemen, behold all of the buried treasures that have been discovered across this whole land.[30] Most of them were placed underground by Ömer Ümmiye. Allah made him gold-mad and silver-mad. When he withdrew from his pouch the gold and silver objects he had acquired, he buried them on moonlit nights for safekeeping, but then he usually forgot where he had buried them. His pouch never seemed to be without at least some gold and silver, but no matter how much he put into that pouch, it was never completely full. It was a magic pouch, the result of its having been made of the skin of the sheep sent by Allah as a substitute for Ishmael in Abraham's sacrificial offering.

Soon we shall see how Ömer Ümmiye stole gold and silver dinner plates from Nuşirvan's dining table and hid them in his pouch. Nuşirvan's guards examined the pouch but were unable to find anything in it because it was a magic pouch. They searched and searched inside the pouch, but they were unable to find any of the gold and silver plates.

Now I am beginning my main story. Listen very carefully in order to learn about some of the people who lived in this world before our own time. Gentlemen, all of the residents of Mecca heard about Ömer Ümmiye's magic pouch. They also knew that in some ways Ömer Ümmiye was superior to Hamzai Sahip Kıran, for if he wished to do so, he could deliver a thousand heads to Hamzai. When he told this to Hamzai Sahip Kıran himself, Hamzai

---

30 That the old artificer Behçet Mahir knew well how to captivate an audience is illustrated throughout this tale. Here is an example of that narrative acumen. Nothing—absolutely nothing—appeals more to the imagination of a rural Turkish audience than treasure hunting. It is for many of them a covert part-time occupation and a full-time preoccupation. An exciting hobby for some, it may for others become a compulsion, even an obsession, with potentially tragic consequences. All too many seekers after buried hoard (*define* in Turkish) impoverish themselves to support what turns out to be a futile quest. But not all such ventures are futile, for occasional treasure troves are still being uncovered—just often enough to inspire more digging (most of it illegal) and add yet more to the already large body of treasure lore. Over millennia many different peoples have occupied Asia Minor and then been forced to leave by succeeding invaders. The necessity for hasty departures (according to the treasure-hunting mystique) led refugees to bury their wealth so that later, in safer circumstances, they might return and recover it. Such a scenario existed even into the present century. After World War I there was an exchange of populations arranged between Turkey and Greece which required Turkish Greeks to return to Greece and Greek Turks to return to Turkey. Later, in somewhat more amicable times, Greeks making sentimental journeys to their hometowns in Anatolia were suspected of having returned to unearth their assets. See Ahmet E. Uysal's illustrated study of Turkish treasure hunting (Uysal 1983b).

said, "Don't ever do such a thing! We have grown up together fed by Nuşirvan's bread. I have not requested a thousand heads from you, and it would be embarrassing for me if you were to deliver them to me. People would say, 'Hamzai Sahip Kıran kills as many men as he can, but those he cannot kill he has slaughtered by Ömer Ümmiye.' This would be a great disgrace for me, for it would be viewed as a sin in the eyes of Allah. Don't kill innocent people." If Hamzai had not compelled Ömer to swear that he would not slaughter the innocent, Ömer might actually have brought a thousand or more heads every night. Why? Because he did not have complete religious faith. How could he have managed to catch so many people? Because he did not have ordinary legs, and he could run faster than anyone else.

Ömer Extends His Life Span

Because Ömer Ümmiye did not have any kneecaps, he was able to run very swiftly. He could race with the wind. Hills and mountains were as easily crossed by him as flat plains were by other people. He could cover two days' distance[31] in two hours. That is the reason that he lived forty years longer than he was supposed to live.

Azrail[32] was unable to catch him to take his soul because of Ömer's great speed. He could run even faster than Azrail could fly. Unable to carry out his duty, Azrail appealed to Allah for advice. "O my Allah, I am not able to catch Ömer Ümmiye to take his soul. What should I do?"

Allah replied, "Azrail, get a golden pickaxe and a silver shovel and place them in a newly dug grave. Ömer Ümmiye will come to get that golden pickaxe and that silver shovel. When he climbs down into the grave to get them, you can trap him there and thus catch him." Because Ömer Ümmiye was, by the will of Allah, passionately fond of gold and silver, he was unable to resist the lure of such metals whenever he saw them. He would do anything to get them and put them in his pouch. Then in the moonlight he would bury these precious objects. Most of the buried treasures that people find were placed in the earth by Ömer Ümmiye. He lived forty years longer than he should have.

While Azrail was digging a grave with the golden pickaxe and silver shovel, Ömer Ümmiye detected the presence of those precious metals nearby. Some feeling within him drew him to the grave to get those precious

---

31 Until recently many Turkish peasants measured distances in terms of the time it would take them to travel there on foot.

32 In both Jewish and Muslim mythology Azrail is the angel of death. He it is who is sent by Allah to take the soul of a person whose life span has expired. Despite his great power, Azrail is sometimes met with resistance from human beings reluctant to die. ATON tales which present variations on this theme are Nos. 486, 1040, 1107, 1156, 1315, 1480, 1558, 1705, 1795. (See also Boratav 1951.)

tools. When Ömer arrived there, Azrail said to him, "Oh, Ömer, come here and lie down in this grave."

"Why?" asked Ömer.

Azrail answered, "Someone died today, and he was just your size. If you will lie down in this partly dug grave, I shall be able to tell how much more I shall have to dig." Ömer was so eager to get the golden pickaxe and the silver shovel that he did as Azrail had requested. Once Ömer was lying in the grave, Azrail jumped on his chest and said, "That is enough! You have not allowed me to take your life for the past forty years, but now it is time for that to happen." Having said that, Azrail took Ömer Ümmiye's life.

(Gentlemen, no matter how long you may live, the last stopping place is the grave. We must all go there. Let me now tell you something about that last stop, the grave.

Some go on foot and others may ride upon mounts.
If a loved one departs, you must then bear all the grief.
Arise in the dawn with all of your relatives.
Whoever comes into this world must leave again.

They come on the road that leads away from Kirman.[33]
Clear hearts will see and steady hands will write
That the last of our homes upon earth will be called the grave.
Whoever comes into this world must leave again.

Though the nightingale flies, escapes at the end from its cage,
May it leave not the way of Allah, the path of the just,
The path that is clearly shown in the mirror of Fate.
Whoever comes into this world must leave again.

Avoid the curse of innocence betrayed;
Avoid revolt against authorities;
Avoid a life of sin upon this earth.
Whoever comes into this world must leave again.

Meaningless is the inn you entered here,
For what is water, what, besides, is air?
What the sorrows felt by Solomon?
Whoever comes into this world must leave again.

One day it will be said, "Mahir has gone."

---

33 Kirman (or Kerman) is a middle-sized city in eastern Iran. Why Kirman, rather than any other city, should be referred to in this context is not clear.

An hour above is worth a thousand here.[34]
Up there my grief will quickly pass away.
Whoever comes into this world must leave again.

Yes, one day you will speak about me, saying, "Once there was a Behçet Mahir. He used to tell us stories and entertain us, but now he has gone." May Allah give us all well-being! May Allah give us all our daily bread! We long for those who have departed, but we should continue to work hard and perform good deeds so that after we have departed, people will remember us favorably. What we do here should cause them to say, "Though he has gone, we have been saved." We should cause them to say, "May Allah have mercy upon him, for he was a very good person." It is only that which keeps this world from being a meaningless place, for we are here today and gone tomorrow.)

Exhortation on Work and Study

Hamzai Sahip Kıran trained to be a wrestler, but he also strove to be a good hunter. (Hard work can make you whatever you want to be, but laziness achieves nothing except to make you lazier every day; it makes you an unhealthy person. Why is that? Because your body becomes accustomed to not doing anything. After a while you can reach the point at which you cannot pick up a small stone. That is one of the reasons why I keep saying, "Work! Work!" Those who preceded us in this world accomplished what they did by means of hard work. Nowadays people have their children educated all the way from elementary school through the university, but unless the child has good sense, all of his education may come to nothing. You must have not only great mental capacity but also good judgment. One must be clever in order to benefit from the ideas of his predecessors. Just being able to read and write is not enough. You must have cleverness and a willingness to work hard.

Gentlemen, we now see and hear about universities being built in every city in the land.[35] Because of that every young person can learn a

---

[34] This may possibly be a distant echo of Biblical lines. *Psalms*, LXXXIV, 10 reads, "For a day in Thy court is better than a thousand elsewhere." *Psalms*, XC, 4 presents the same idea from a different perspective: "For a thousand years in Thy sight are but as yesterday when it is past." For Bible texts see May and Metzger (1962). Two ATON anecdotes about the legendary mystic Behlül Dane are based on this concept: No. 816 and No. 1475.

[35] Although this is an exaggeration, it is indicative of the boom in university construction during the past half century. In 1950 there were no more than a dozen institutions in Turkey that could claim university status; the number has increased sixfold since that time. In 1995 there were fifty-eight state-supported universities plus another twelve provided for by law but not yet built. There were also six private universities. We are indebted to the Turkish Educational Attaché at the United Nations for these figures.

foreign language without even leaving home. In former times one had to go to a foreign country in order to learn a foreign language. Then one was sent to Europe or elsewhere, at great expense to one's parents, and at great anxiety to those same parents who were, as a result, unable to see their child for long periods of time.

Now everything has changed. We have a valuable education system in which well-qualified instructors can teach our children everything. Our money need no longer go elsewhere to provide that education. This change was made possible by Atatürk,[36] who started a program of university construction which continues to this day. It takes an intelligent person to realize the value of this system. Unless one has a clever brain, one cannot change. I have a poem about universities which I shall now recite to you.

> Our Atatürk built universities.
> His friends applauded; foes resented this.
> His goal would dim the eyes of enemies.
> Great stature has a university.
>
> Beneath the colors of their country's flag
> Houses of science dot the campus scene.
> Keep all their hearths aglow with steady flame!
> Great stature has a university.
>
> Your classes well attended bring success.
> Your teachers offer knowledge to the wise,
> For wisdom by itself is functionless.
> Great stature has a university.
>
> Your learning adds a finger to each hand.
>
> > [The narrator inserts this amplifying comment in the very midst of a quatrain!] Before, we could not help strangers in this country because we could not understand them when they asked for tea or asked for bread. And when we ourselves went abroad, we were cursed for being unable to understand the languages there, but now we have the words to throw the curses back at such people. They claimed that the book of

[36] Mustafa Kemal Atatürk (1881-1938) was the father of present-day Turkey. He was largely responsible for the modernization and Westernization of the country after the deposition of the sultanate and the founding, in 1923, of the Republic. In the new democratic order Atatürk served as Turkey's first President from 1923 to 1938.

Jesus and the book of Moses[37] were theirs and not ours, but they are ours too.—Now let me finish my quatrain.

May all of us appreciate your worth;
May Allah add His blessing to that worth!
Great stature has a university.)

Ömer Steals Gold, but Hamzai Steals a Heart

Gentlemen, Nuşirvan had only one child, a daughter who was very dear to him—the apple of his eye. She was a very beautiful girl, and her name was Mehli Nigâr. Hamzai Sahip Kıran and Ömer Ümmiye did not know about her when they decided that they had an obligation to visit Nuşirvan.

Hamzai and Ömer said to each other, "Nuşirvan has now been supporting us and feeding us for fifteen years. We should go to his country and visit him." Hamzai and Ömer, along with ninety-seven wrestlers who had by this time gathered around Hamzai, went to visit Nuşirvan.

When he discovered that these men had set out for his country, Nuşirvan's grand vizier traveled half the distance between the two lands to welcome them. He then conducted the visitors into the presence of Nuşirvan. Hamzai Sahip Kıran was greatly excited by this visit, for Nuşirvan was the wealthiest and most powerful man of his time. His treasury was filled with jewels, gold, and silver. He was the ruler of seven countries.[38] History says that first he was a shah and later a padishah. He had complete control of Shiraz[39] and supreme authority over all of its shahs. All of the lands up to the very borders of India were in his domain. Nuşirvan had control of all these armies for his use at any time. The soldiers were all his.

Nuşirvan's daughter and Hamzai Sahip Kıran were of the same age: fifteen. As I said, Mehli Nigâr was the only child of Nuşirvan. When Mehli Nigâr saw Hamzai Sahip Kıran, as he entered the palace with his wrestlers and Ömer Ümmiye, she at once fell madly in love with him and wished that she could throw herself from the balcony to be down where he was, but the iron bars on the windows prevented her from doing so. The servants of Mehli Nigâr also restrained her, saying, "O beautiful lady, what are you trying to do?" Mehli Nigâr fell madly in love with the handsome Hamzai Sahip Kıran. It was love that was sudden but also very deep. Hamzai's face was not only handsome but also beatific, like the face of a saint. (Even if a Muslim person reaches the age of one hundred years, his face may remain lighted with a

[37] In Turkey this is a common way of referring to the New Testament and the Old Testament respectively.

[38] It is uncertain whether the reference here is to seven distinctly separate countries or to seven sections of the then extensive Persian domain.

[39] A city of eastern Iran which became an important commercial center during the Sassanid era.

divine glow. His face may look the same as it had when he was in his twenties. It keeps its fresh and saintly appearance. It may gleam continuously. The faces of infidels are not preserved as well as the faces of Muslims. They change with age and grow dark, lacking any gleam.)

Hamzai Sahip Kıran stole Mehli Nigâr's heart during her first glimpse of him. In that same instant Hamzai Sahip Kıran glanced at the girl on the balcony and fell in love with her. He was astonished by the incredible beauty of her face, a beauty as great as that of the fourteenth of the moon.[40] Gentlemen, their Fate had been written before they were even born.

(Now let me speak briefly about Fate. Listen, and he who wishes to understand will do so. A word to the wise is enough. The words that I am uttering here do not belong to me; they were spoken by those who came along before our time.

If the world were mine, why should it all be sad?
From soil of endless sadness was I formed.
The Author of my life wrote, "Endless grief."
The same pen wrote Creation and all Fate.[41]

Gentlemen, before Allah created anything else, He said to the pen, "Write, pen! Write!"

The pen asked, "What should I write, my Allah?"

"Write the Muslim confession of faith, 'There is no god but Allah.'"[42]

Having written that, the pen prostrated itself before Allah. As it did that, three beams of divine light burst forth from the pen. One went to heaven; one went to the arch above heaven; and one remained there. Before He created all of the other creatures and things, Allah created the spirit of the Prophet Mohammed.)

Just the brief moment during which Hamzai Sahip Kıran and Mehli Nigâr saw each other was time enough for them to fall madly in love. As I said, Allah had written their Fate before they were born, and no one can escape that Fate once it has been written.

---

40 Throughout the Muslim Middle East the moon is greatly admired as a symbol of beauty. Both oral and written literature testify to this. To compare a woman's beauty with that of the moon is to flatter her greatly. But why the fourteenth rather than any other day in the moon cycle? Since fullness rather than slenderness is commonly a key criterion of female pulchritude in the Middle East, it is appropriately compared with that point on the lunar calendar when the moon becomes full.

41 Turkish poets and storytellers often speak of Creation, Fate, and Divine Will not as things established or achieved but rather as realizations of previously enunciated ideas. In a way they parallel the Biblical line which reads, "In the beginning was the Word . . ." *John*, I, 1 (May and Metzger 1962).

42 *Lailahe illallah* is the transliterated Arabic for this important expression.

Hamzai Sahip Kıran and Ömer Ümmiye were brought into Nuşirvan's presence, but neither of these men could understand the language of Nuşirvan. There were, however, interpreters who could communicate the meaning of what each said to the other. Hamzai Sahip Kıran, Ömer Ümmiye, and all of the wrestlers were seated.

Nuşirvan called his grand vizier to his side and said, "Oh, vizier, all of your predictions have become reality. Hamzai Sahip Kıran is a very strong and honest man."

The grand vizier answered, "O my padishah, you must observe him from now on so that you will understand what kind of a person he really is." Nuşirvan looked at Hamzai Sahip Kıran and his ninety-seven wrestlers with great admiration.

After a short while the dinner tables were set with golden plates and golden knives, forks, and spoons. Everywhere one looked there were expensive pieces of jewelry to be seen, all of which had been provided by Key Kubat. Hamzai Sahip Kıran was astonished at so much wealth and luxury. Servants then brought great quantities of food to the table and began to serve it to everyone and to pour wine for them. Hamzai Sahip Kıran, Ömer Ümmiye, and the ninety-seven wrestlers were seated at tables all around Nuşirvan.

Everything seemed to be proceeding very pleasantly, but, alas, there was a serious problem. This was Ömer Ümmiye's irrepressible lust for gold and other precious things. He took three of the golden plates and put them inside his magic pouch, but he was observed doing this by Nuşirvan's grand vizier. The vizier reported this to the servants, saying, "The man seated by Hamzai Sahip Kıran has stolen three golden plates." The servants at first did not believe this, but when the dinner was finished and they counted the golden plates, they discovered that three were indeed missing. The servants then informed Nuşirvan about this situation. The ruler was shocked by what he heard, but, upon second thought, he refused to believe what he had been told. (Now listen to what is going to happen as the result of a rift between Hamzai Sahip Kıran and Nuşirvan caused by two devils.)

Nuşirvan had the servants who had reported the theft bound hand and foot, but the grand vizier intervened on their behalf. He said to Nuşirvan, "Why have you had those servants tied up? I also saw what happened. I saw Ömer Ümmiye steal three golden plates and put them in his pouch. Examine that pouch, and if you do not find the golden plates inside, then turn the servants over to the executioner."

Nuşirvan replied, "Go back and sit down, Mehdi,[43] and do not talk too much." Mehdi went back to his place, sat down, and remained silent. But

---

[43] In the Persian context of this tale *Mehdi* quite appropriately appears as a personal name meaning *right way* or *true path*. Seldom used that way in Turkey, the word more frequently seems to refer to the Muslim Messiah, a figure whose predicted arrival is awaited with the same anticipation as that for the Second Coming of Jesus Christ. Over the years several people

then Nuşirvan called him back and said to him, "Go and tell Hamzai Sahip Kıran that I forgive Ömer Ümmiye and that I do not want the plates back. But tell him also that Ömer Ümmiye must never repeat such a deed in my presence."

When he received this message, Hamzai Sahip Kıran turned toward Ömer Ümmiye and glared at him angrily. He then stood up and said to Mehdi, "I do not want Nuşirvan to forgive Ömer Ümmiye! He should instead order someone to examine the inside of Ömer's pouch. If the plates are found inside, then he may, if he wishes, kill or punish Ömer right now. I am not responsible for that kind of bad behavior." Inasmuch as Hamzai Sahip Kıran was aware of the secret of the magic pouch, he knew that he could safely speak in a tone of anger.

Hearing Hamzai's loud remarks but not understanding them, Nuşirvan asked his interpreter, "What is it that he is saying so loudly?"

The interpreter explained: "He said that he was not responsible for whatever bad behavior his men committed. He said that you should have the pouch searched and that if the plates were found within, you should punish Ömer Ümmiye in any way you wish."

(Gentlemen, no one can be responsible for a thief. Neither father nor mother nor brother can control the behavior of a thief. They may be able to influence the actions of a murderer but not those of a thief. Gentlemen, if you try to help a thief, then you too are, in a way, a thief. Whether one steals a chicken or a cow, it amounts to the same thing. The punishment for stealing either a chicken or a cow is six months in jail. Now if you wish to buy a chicken, the price is only thirty liras, but if you wish to buy a cow, the price is 40,000 liras. Why, then, should the punishment for both crimes be the same? What is the reason for that? It is because of the fact that if a man steals a chicken today, he is likely to steal a cow tomorrow. Or he may go from stealing a chicken to stealing a goose to stealing a cow. Therefore, gentlemen, no one can account for the behavior of a thief; no one wants anything to do with him; no one even wants to sit near such a person. People hate thieves that much. On the other hand, one may be willing to talk with a murderer and perhaps even find some justification for his crime. Theft is a very low and evil act. The worst crime is taking something that does not belong to you.)

They searched and searched the pouch of Ömer Ümmiye, but they were unable to find anything in it. Ömer arose in great fury and said, "Now go ahead and search my pouch again! Can you find anything in it?" So they searched the pouch again, and again they found nothing.

---

have claimed to be the Mehdi. Probably the most notable of these was Muhammad Ahmad (1843-1885) of Sudan, a radical religious reformer whose followers carried on a "holy war" throughout the 1880s and 1890s until the movement was destroyed in 1898 by General H. H. Kitchener and an Anglo-Egyptian army. The concept of a Muslim Messiah is not Koranic.

The guests remained in Nuşirvan's palace for eight days and eight nights. Nuşirvan ordered his men to give gold to Hamzai Sahip Kıran and his wrestler friends. When the ninth day arrived, Nuşirvan instructed his men, "Take these wrestlers and Hamzai Sahip Kıran on a tour of the city. Show them my army with all its soldiers, and show them too my great prosperity."

Hamzai Sahip Kıran and his ninety-seven wrestlers were taken through the whole city. It took three days and three nights to show the guests everything. Hamzai Sahip Kıran observed all of this, including Nuşirvan's soldiers and his great prosperity. Hamzai was all the while thinking, "What I really want is Nuşirvan's daughter. If he is willing to give her to me, that will be very pleasant, but if he is unwilling to give her to me, then I shall have to get her by means of my sword."

The Pangs of Love

Because Hamzai Sahip Kıran and Mehli Nigâr had fallen madly in love with each other, there was a pathway between the hearts of the two. Mehli had wished to throw herself from the balcony in order to be with Hamzai Sahip Kıran, but the servants had restrained her.

Well, gentlemen, on the twelfth day Hamzai Sahip Kıran, Ömer Ümmiye, and the ninety-seven wrestlers left the city of Nuşirvan, the city of Ani. As they were departing, Hamzai Sahip Kıran realized, "I shall never be able to capture this city by means of power of the sword." This city was built in such a way as to make it very secure. Ani had been built, as I told you earlier, by Key Kubat, the grandfather of Nuşirvan. As I also told you, there is a proverb which says that if the rest of the world were destroyed, Ani could reconstruct it, but if Ani were destroyed, all the rest of the world could not rebuild it. What finally destroyed the city of Ani was a curse.

Gentlemen, Nuşirvan said farewell to Hamzai Sahip Kıran and wished him a safe journey home with all of the gold that had been given to him. Yes, he left Nuşirvan's country. But all of the way back to his own land of Mecca his three hundred and sixty-six veins were aflame with love for Mehli Nigâr. It was a fire that no water could quench. No one in the world could make him forget his love of Mehli Nigâr, for that love was larger than anything else, larger than anybody else.

(Now I should like to recite for you a poem which I composed about love. I have passed the age of sixty, and now I am seventy.[44] I have faced

[44] Turks in the audience would have agreed with Behçet Efendi's statement about his age. Had there been foreigners among the listeners, however, there might have been differences of opinion about the matter. In some countries, including the United States, a person would not be considered to be seventy until he or she had completed seventy years. In Turkey a person is said to be seventy beginning the day after his or her sixty-ninth birthday. One is then in one's seventieth year and hence is called seventy.

many difficulties and have overcome all troubles that I have encountered, but I in turn was overcome by love. I was young and strong, but love defeated me.

Great pain not caused by any battle wound,
A pain no judge or *şehit* [45] understands,
Love's pain for beauty that the heart desires.
I know it is a thing more felt than said.

I know my heart's pain, and Allah knows it too, for He created me and my Fate. But if a person has not had this experience himself, then how can he understand what I am saying?

I cannot tell what I have seen of love.
I saw but cannot say just what I saw,
Nor yet deny the love that you confessed.
It is a thing, I know, more felt than said.

My hair grew white—yes, whiter than the snow—
But still my heart will boil if I think, "Girl!"
Whether that one is dead or still alive.
Ah, yes, it is a thing more felt than said.

I learned love's sorrow while I was asleep,
A vessel newly launched upon the sea.
I was reduced to skin and bones and brain;
A curious thing that is more felt than said.

Gentlemen, a person lost in love can soon become no more than skin and bones, a body almost lacking flesh. If it were not for his skin, his bones would fall apart and scatter. Only his brain is left intact.

Now listen well to what I have to say:
Your head must function well and not in vain.

[45] A martyr—one who has died either in a religious cause or in defense of his country.

Fieldwork in November 1961, near the village of Nallıhan, Ankara Province. The narrator, Tellâl Mehmet Çavuş, had been a town crier (*tellâl*) until newspapers and P.A. systems replaced him. He then became the village herdsman, taking to and from the community pasture residents' various kinds of livestock. We caught him (with hat in hand) en route home with his mixed flock. Ahmet Uysal is holding the microphone.

Field trip in the Taurus Mountains in February 1962. Ahmet Uysal is shown with his motor scooter. At high altitudes the gasoline of the tiny vehicle sometimes froze.

I gave my beauty to the cold grave stone—
A thing more known through feeling than through words.

How will Mahir survive upon this earth?
Well yesterday, today much less than well.
I came tonight but may not see the dawn,
And this one knows without the use of words.

There is a chance of not awakening. Love is a misery for which the pharmacy has no relief, the doctor has no cure. You cannot halt love.)

Why have I been talking about love? Because Hamzai Sahip Kıran's heart had been set on fire by a single glance at Mehli Nigâr. By the time Hamzai Sahip Kıran reached his own country with his wrestlers, all three hundred and sixty-six of his veins had caught fire. He thought, "I have arrived here, but where is Mehli Nigâr? I could not bring her here. If she is not here, I cannot be Hamzai! I cannot tell what I am eating or where I shall sleep." But love does not permit a person to sleep because of longing for the endeared one. You do not eat, nor do you wish to eat. Your condition will grow worse and worse with every day that passes, and after a while you may have no wish to live at all. When Hamzai Sahip Kıran reached Mecca, his three hundred and sixty-six veins were in flames and were scorching him. What are they saying? They are saying, "If that whipped bird had any hope for this world, it would not be singing in the ruins." They are saying that the end of the world is ruin. "If the moth were not in love with the fire, it would not circle around it, eventually throwing itself into the flames."

When Hamzai Sahip Kıran went to his palace, he called his wrestlers to him and said, "I want you to know that I am going to write on my own behalf to Nuşirvan. I shall tell him that I wish to marry his daughter, Mehli Nigâr. If he decides to give her to me, everything will go satisfactorily. If he decides not to give her to me, then he should think about the consequences of his decision. I shall either marry her or die in the attempt to do so."

Mehli Nigâr had fallen just as madly in love with Hamzai as he had with her. Burning with love for him, she said to herself, "What could I ever do with my father's crown? What could I do with my father's wealth and his sovereignty over many people? What are such things to me? But if Hamzai Sahip Kıran's hand and mine were joined, it would mean more than the whole world to me." The Writer who inscribed their Fate wrote in such a manner. This writing could not be changed or set aside. It was written by the powerful One.

Many important people in the past wished to change the Fate that had been written for them, but they were unable to do so. This you should know.

Once Nurettin Arabî[46] found a means of examining the Great Book of Affairs.[47] When he located his own name in that Great Book of Affairs, he discovered written alongside it a statement that he would be killed at a certain time at a certain place. He was greatly surprised to discover such a statement, and he asked himself, "Why is this written here? And why should I be killed? I am, after all, the Commander of the Faithful! It cannot be!"

Nurettin Arabî put his finger in his mouth to wet it with saliva. Then he used his wetted finger to erase his name from the Great Book, but when he dropped his arm to his side, his name reappeared at the same spot. He very quickly erased it again, but once more it reappeared on the page. Then when he attempted to erase it for a third time, a voice spoke from above saying, "If you erase that for a third time, I shall erase you! You must accept your Fate." In the end he was killed at the time and place that had been written. So, if even Nurettin Arabî could not change his Fate, how can we?

Hamzai Sahip Kıran wrote a letter with his own hand to Nuşirvan. Handing it to Ömer Ümmiye to deliver, he said, "O Ömer, do not give this letter to anyone else. Take it directly to Nuşirvan and place it in his own hands. Otherwise it might be hidden by someone else and never reach Nuşirvan." What did he say in that letter?

"O Nuşirvan, after I had entered this world, I grew up with your support, receiving your salary and eating your bread. When I reached the age of fifteen, I wanted to visit you to thank you for this support. But I want you to know that I come from the family of Muttalib and the clan of Haşimi as did the Prophet, and I should not have been the one to travel in order to make our acquaintance. You should have come to my country to visit me. But because you were a very just ruler, and because you had supported me during my childhood, I went to you.

"While I was there, I walked about your city and discovered that you were a just person. I saw your large and well-trained army too, but that army can do no harm to me as long as I have the aid of my countrymen.

"I also saw a beauty while I was there, a girl standing on the balcony of the palace. Although no army in the world could defeat me, and no one could pin my back to the ground, the love for Mehli Nigâr overcame me. One glance at that girl caused me to fall in love with her. I wish to marry her. If you send Mehli Nigâr, accompanied by two women and provided with a

---

[46] Although he is described as the Commander of the Faithful, the caliph, there is no reference to him in the *Encyclopaedia of Islam*, the *Turkish Encyclopaedia*, *The Cambridge History of Islam*, or in a prominent history of the caliphate (Arnold 1965). The anecdote about him here would seem to suggest that he is an imaginary person.

[47] Even though much mythology and early religion were transmitted through oral tradition, Muslim narrators visualize philosophical concepts, provisions of Fate, and the will of the Deity as written doctrines. The writing seems not only to make the abstract graphic but also to insure its validity. See also Note 41 above.

dowry, all will go well. If you do not do that, however, I should confront you with my sword, which is powerful enough to defeat not just one Nuşirvan but even two Nuşirvans. Then after that I shall have Mehli Nigâr anyway. But ask your daughter if she likes me, for though I love her, our marriage would not succeed unless she loved me too. It is said, 'Love the person who loves you, but avoid the person who does not love you, regardless of how mighty his or her station might be.'"

If you try to arrange a personal relationship by force, the result will be unsatisfactory. But Hamzai Sahip Kıran already knew that Mehli Nigâr had some feeling for him too, for he had observed her efforts to throw herself from the balcony to him, and he had seen the servants restraining her only with great difficulty. Hamzai Sahip Kıran had observed all this, and he had concluded that his love for her was matched by hers for him.

"O Nuşirvan, ask your daughter if she cares for me. If she says, 'No,' then I shall desist. But if your daughter says, 'Yes,' and you fail to send her to me, then I shall come and take her with my sword." He then placed the letter in an envelope, handed it to Ömer Ümmiye, and said, "Take this letter and deliver it personally to Nuşirvan. Do not let any other person in his palace have it." Hamzai knew that Nuşirvan had fifty-two servants in his palace who did nothing but attend to visitors. They served the visitors, but they also scrutinized them carefully and kept them steadily under observation. These special guards were so clever that it seemed almost as if they had been taught by a devil.

Now we shall see some of Hamzai Sahip Kıran's fighting and Ömer Ümmiye's rescuing of Nuşirvan. Ömer departed and started toward the palace of Nuşirvan, and he will have arrived there by tomorrow when we return here. Although the mother gave birth to the son, I shall (*İnşallah*[48]) tell you tomorrow what kind of son that was. But for now Ömer Ümmiye is on his way to Nuşirvan's palace. Thus our story stops here for tonight, and tomorrow night (*İnşallah*) I shall continue telling the story, and you can listen to it.

---

[48] *İnşallah* means *if Allah wills*. It is a frequently used expression and one taken very seriously by Muslims. When a person describes some planned activity, he or she is supposed to qualify his or her statement with *İnşallah*. It is a safeguard against committing the sin of hubris. Later in this tale Hamzai's failure to say *İnşallah* at the appropriate moment costs him several years of otherwise needless delay. Some brief tales are devoted entirely to inculcating the importance of saying *İnşallah*. See, for example, ATON tales No. 373 and No. 1343.

Second night; narration of January 10, 1977

Poems by Mahir and Summani

Gentlemen, before we renew the telling of our story, we must have some introduction to the next part. As you know, if you wish to enter a building, you must first open the door; now the door of the story will be reopened by means of a poem. Storytellers who preceded us used this method of beginning a story, and we are following in their tradition. First I shall recite four quatrains of my own, and then I shall recite a long series of quatrains by a greater poet.[49]

Stay on the path of truth whene'er you walk,
The route on which no one will be betrayed.
Though sweat may pour forth from my limbs today,
May not my empty head still hold its course?

His patience is the brave man's greatest strength.
Regardless of the tears his eyes may shed,
The man endowed with patience will survive.
An air of patience calms my troubled head.

My lot in life is quite enough for me.
The pain that love first brings will later end.
What need for pity others may extend?
Will not this sleepless, empty brain endure?

Behçet Mahir recites his verses here.
Well has he done if he has told the truth.
Though pangs of love have driven him quite mad,
May not his empty brain give virtue voice?

If someone does not wish to listen to you, then even shouting will be of no avail. A word to the wise is sufficient. He who is wise will understand it.

---

[49] The greater poet was Summani, mentioned in the Introduction as Behçet Efendi's spiritual patron. He lived in Sami Kale village, part of Narman *kaza* (county), in north-central Erzurum Province.

Now I shall recite part of a long poem which probably no one now remembers in its entirety. I should like to repeat all of it that I know, and then we shall renew the telling of our story. This poem is about the Prophet Abraham and about the ram which was sent down to him from the sky.

Rely not on wealth you may gain in your time on this earth.
Of far greater worth is pureness of heart and faith.
Claim not sincerity as yours alone.
Bully not, nor bluster in the courts.

Be not extremist in the goals you seek.
Don't strive for the utterly perfect here in this world.
Where went all the wealth and the power once held by
Harun?[50]
It all was seized and passed to the hands of Burhan.[51]

If you wish to possess any realm that will shatter and pass,
If you wish to exist in a place that is lacking in air,
If you wish to discover the secrets regarding this world,
Go and ask Solomon, ruler from north to the south.

Not even his throne could Solomon keep very long.
Whoever comes into this world must leave it again.
Even the mightiest king, this sovereign of sovereigns,
Had no other choice but to leave when his time had expired.[52]

Once Abraham prayed, "O Allah but give me an heir,
And I'll sacrifice even my dearest possession for You.

---

[50] Harun Reşit was the most powerful and well known of the Abbasid caliphs at Baghdad. He reigned from 786 to 809.

[51] The luxury and extravagance of the Abbasid caliphs became legendary. When Harun Reşit died, he was succeeded by his son Amin, whose brief reign was followed by that of another son, Ma'müd. When Ma'müd married Buran (here pronounced *Burhan*), the eighteen-year-old daughter of his vizier, in 825, the celebration occasioned ". . . such fabulous expenditures of money that it has lived in Arabian literature as one of the unforgettable extravaganzas of the age." (For details of this orgy of conspicuous consumption, see Hitti 1945: 91-93.)

[52] The reference here is clearly to the Biblical Solomon, previously identified in this tale. There is, however, always the need for caution while considering a Turkish folktale containing an historical or legendary person with the name *Solomon* or *Süleyman* (the Turkish form). Peasant narrators sometimes confuse Süleyman, the son of David, with Süleyman the Magnificent, the Ottoman sultan who ruled from 1520 to 1566.

Narrators discussing the ephemeral nature of human life often cite the case of Solomon. If this king of Judah, with all his power and all his wisdom, could not escape mortality, then how could any ordinary person expect to do so? See "Solomon and the Vulture" (Walker and Uysal 1966: 181-83) or (Walker and Uysal 1981: 52-54).

This I shall promise to do if You'll give me a child."
He said this while lifting his hands in respect to his God.[53]

Neither neighbors nor friends of the patriarch knew what took
place.
Not even the scholars or wise men of Abraham's time
Grasped the full meaning of Hagar's[54] conceiving a child.
Behold the full beauty of Allah's communion with man!

Divine was the aid conferred in response to his prayer,
Divine the reward for Abraham, prophet of Allah.
When the pregnancy ended, nine months and nine days from
its start,
A prince of great promise was born to a life in this world.

People from far and from near came to gaze at this prince,
Abraham's son, divinely bestowed upon him.
And what did they call the child they received in this way?
They called the child Ishmael. Long may the name be revered!

The pity that Allah had felt for His Abraham
Prompted good fortune to hover above the man's head.[55]
Till Ishmael reached the age of seven years,
The promised sacrifice had been forgot.

But the prophet one night was called from the world beyond,
Was called in a dream to remind him of something he owed:
"You once vowed to sacrifice even your heart's delight.
Now Ishmael must on the altar be slaughtered for me."

The prophet said, "Go bathe our son, Hagar,
And comb his hair and henna both his hands;[56]
Kohl-shade his eyes; dress him attractively.
He'll be with me today while I cut wood."

---

[53] While Christians often clasp their hands in prayer, Muslims usually extend their arms and open their hands, palms upward.

[54] Muslims call the Biblical Hagar *Hacer*, pronounced *Hadjer*.

[55] When someone in Turkey is unexpectedly lucky, he or she is likely to say, "The Bird of Fortune [*Talih Kuşu*] must have fluttered above my head!"

[56] Henna is a reddish-brown dye used to color the hands (and sometimes feet) for ceremonial occasions. It is customary for a bride (and often her attendants, too) to have hands hennaed the evening before the wedding.

Hagar then bathed and dried their Ishmael.
Hair combed, hands hennaed, his eyes made dark with kohl,
He was clad for the day in the finest of raiment he had.
Then father and son, holding hands, departed from home.

When the two of them started their trip, holding hands,
En route to fulfill a promise the father had made,
The curséd Satan sped to Hagar's side
To foster grief within the mother's heart.

That devil told her how her son would die.
But Hagar said, "Your evil mouth lacks truth!
My son, whose hair is musked and ambergrised,
Is with his father, Allah's prophet, now."

When Satan heard the words that Hagar spoke,
His hands and feet were tangled hopelessly.[57]
In the length of a breath he flew to Ishmael
And said, "Now halt, *civan*,[58] and hear my words!

"I'll tell you something that you do not know:
Your father means to sacrifice your life.
Upon an altar he will slaughter you.
Ah, what a pity for a handsome youth!"

"Get out! Do other work!" said Ishmael,
"Or I shall cause your eyes to flow with tears!"
Throwing a stone, he injured Satan's eye,
And powerful Satan feared this little child.

In truth, the demon suffered more than fright,
For Ishmael's stone had made that eye go blind.[59]
Before they reached the mountain Arafat,[60]
The son asked, "Father, whither are we bound?"

---

[57] A figurative expression to indicate confusion.

[58] A word meaning *a handsome youth*. We have kept the Turkish here because the translation would be too long to fit into the metered lines.

[59] The blinding of one of Satan's eyes by Ishmael is a common folk belief in Turkey. See, for example, ATON tale No. 1518.

[60] That the alleged injury to Satan's eye should have occurred on the approach to Mount Arafat, near Mecca, was not a matter of mere happenstance. One of the stages of the pilgrimage to the Holy City is the symbolic stoning of the (now invisible) Satan. This ritual takes place on Mount Arafat.

"Oh, Son, my bosom grieves," said Abraham.
"The mountain Arafat itself should moan
To see you slaughtered by your father's knife,
To see my hands both reddened with your blood."

"My father, will you do this thing to me?
How can a wise man act in ignorance?
How can a father be his son's fell foe?
Have mercy, Father! Slaughter not your child!"

But Abraham replied, "What can we do?
It is our Fate, by Allah's will required.
I made to Him a promise in the past,
When blessed Allah sent you to this world."

"Had I known this before," said Ishmael,
"I should have cleansed my erring heart of sin
And sought forgiveness for my mother's gifts,[61]
But now we shall not meet till Judgment Day.

"Let my poor mother shed hot tears of woe.
For loss of me her liver soon will ache.[62]
Father, first tie my arms before you strike.
Life is so sweet, I might resist your hand."

When Abraham bound both of Ishmael's arms,
The son upon the altar sighed and moaned.
Above, the angels witnessed from the sky.
"Release my arms so I can speak to God."

With open hands the pious boy declared,
"I now accept whatever Fate is mine.
My father, whet your blade and flex your arm.
Then strike with force before I can rebel.

---

[61] This is related to the *helâl/haram* concept described in Note 14. The "mother's gifts" are her milk and her years of tender care. By Judgment Day, the time will have expired for securing his mother's forgiveness.

[62] Body organs associated with various emotional problems vary from culture to culture. In Turkish lore, for example, fright is not thought to have potential danger for the heart but for the gall bladder. Similarly, grief does not always affect the heart but often causes severe liver pains.

"I was not fooled by words that Satan spoke,
For Allah's love had flowed into my heart.
View not my face lest sadness halt your hand.
An offering foiled will comfort only Hell."

"You are the orchard of my heart, O Son!"
"But give that now no thought," the boy replied.
"What's happened to the power of your arm?
Now send me into sacrificial death."

He loved his son upon the altar laid.
Angels in ranks gazed on him from above.
Then Allah sent this message to the knife:
"Don't cut him! Do not harm a single hair!"

The whole community of man now wept,
While angels in the sky sang out their prayers.
Then, chanting thrice, the father struck a blow,
But, lo! the useless blade left not a mark.

Amazed was Blessed Abraham by this.
The angels contemplated in the sky.
Then Abraham struck at a nearby stone,
And split it cleanly with a single slash.

Great is the sin of shunning Allah's rules.
What earthly being dares to disobey?
Then Gabriel brought a ram through Allah's will.
He said, "Our Allah is Omnipotent!"

If there had been no miracle performed,
If All-Wise Allah had not sent release,
And if the ram had not arrived in time—
How great a human loss by sacrifice!

Now hear the lesser words of Behçet Mahir speaking once again.

In serving Allah Summani felt joy,
But sorrow is my lot in vain attempt
To reproduce an epic so divine.
Mahir relays it weakly to the world.

That long poem was left to us by the late senior poet Summani. My part is simply to retell the poem in order to keep it alive, to prevent its being forgotten. I want such poems to be remembered. If there is only a single green leaf left on a tree, there is still hope for that tree; but if all its leaves are yellow, know then that there is no hope left for its survival. Even a very light wind may send it crashing to the ground. Human beings are like that, except that instead of getting yellow leaves, they get white hairs. Yes, today is the day; this is our hour; and once we depart, we shall never return! That is the way it is! No one has ever come back so far. Once you are gone, you are gone!

Ömer as Love's Ambassador

The story that I was telling you yesterday was about Hamzai Sahip Kıran. Yesterday we had reached the place in the story where Hamzai had sent a letter to Nuşirvan, a letter which was to be delivered to that ruler by Ömer Ümmiye. Ömer placed the letter in his sash and raced faster than the wind to Nuşirvan's country. He went all the way from Mecca to Nuşirvan's land in one night. (As you know, everything can happen very quickly in stories. In the words of the storyteller, forty male babies can be born and can grow into manhood in their respective countries all in one night!) Ömer went directly to Nuşirvan's palace and placed the letter in that ruler's hands. Nuşirvan took the letter, read it, and then said, "He wrote first the words which should have been written last."

What did Hamzai Sahip Kıran say? As I told you last night, he said, "O Nuşirvan, the padishah of all the world, I went to visit you because we had long been eating your bread. If I had not been supplied in this way by you for fifteen years, I should not have come to pay my respects to you, but the bread that you gave me took me there. During my visit I fell in love with your daughter, Mehli Nigâr, who was looking down at me from the balcony of your palace. She saw me at the same time that I saw her, and she, in turn, fell in love with me. We experienced the same feeling at the very same moment. We were wounded without the shooting of any arrows. We received deep heart wounds without having been struck by any shafts. By the will of Allah and with the consent of the Prophet,[63] I want to have Mehli Nigâr as my wife. If you will give your daughter to me, everything will go well; but if you should refuse to give her, then swords, pikes and shields will go into action between us, and much blood will be shed. However, I do not want your

---

[63] Until recently most Turkish marriages were arranged by matchmakers; in rural areas many are still arranged that way. In requesting the hand of the girl X for the boy Y, the matchmaker always says—in fact it is his/her opening gambit—"I have come by the will of Allah and the consent of the Prophet to ask for the hand of X for Y, the son of so-and-so, who lives at such and such place." There is no evidence about the will of the Deity or the consent of His Prophet. It is almost as if the wish is father to the thought. The declaration of the matchmaker is made, as it were, in the optative subjunctive mood.

daughter unless she consents to our marriage. If she does not want me, then that will be that, but if she does desire me as much as I desire her, then she will be mine. If I am not wanted by her, then I shall not take her by force." These were the words written in the letter.

Hamzai Sahip Kıran had given this order to Ömer Ümmiye: "Do not steal a single thing at the palace of Nuşirvan." Had he been free to steal there, he could have found all sorts of very valuable objects to take. Nuşirvan's crown alone was worth a whole fortune. But Ömer Ümmiye took nothing because of his fear of Hamzai Sahip Kıran. He behaved himself very well.

After Nuşirvan had finished reading the letter, he handed it to the commanders in chief of his two armies. Regardless of what the issue was, these two military leaders influenced the decisions that Nuşirvan made. After reading the letter, they looked into Nuşirvan's face and said, "O our padishah, you fed this boy for fifteen years, and now he announces that he will take by force your daughter whom he has seen just once. He says that much blood will be shed if you refuse to give Mehli Nigâr to him. He has behaved in a shameful way! Does he not know that ten Hamzai Sahip Kırans of his type could not defeat the armies of Nuşirvan?"

But the grand vizier could not tolerate their aggressive comments. He said to Nuşirvan, "We should make no decision about the letter right now. It is not possible to do so. We should send the letter to Mehli Nigâr in order to discover her feeling about it. She is the one who should judge what Hamzai Sahip Kıran has written. She is the one who should have the last word about it. If the girl wants him but you say, 'No!' to him, then your word will be wasted. We should discover Mehli Nigâr's opinion on this matter. We should listen to her response."

Those around the ruler asked, "By whom should this letter be taken to her?"

Ömer Ümmiye spoke up then and said, "Order me to do so, and I shall take the letter to Mehli Nigâr."

But the two commanders in chief, Zohru and Mehdi,[64] interfered again, saying, "No, our padishah, we should not send the letter to Mehli Nigâr by Ömer Ümmiye, for he is likely to influence her response to it. We should have the letter taken to her by one of our own men." The letter was therefore given to a man named Cive for delivery to Mehli Nigâr.

Nuşirvan said to him, "Cive, take this letter to my daughter, Mehli Nigâr. Let us see what she will say about it."

Cive took the letter and went to Mehli Nigâr's palace. The female servants took the letter to Mehli Nigâr and said, "O Mehli Nigâr, from your father's palace a man named Cive has brought a letter for you."

---

64 In the small cast of characters in the court of Nuşirvan there are two men named Mehdi: the grand vizier and this military commander in chief.

"All right," the princess answered. "Give it to me." It seems that Mehli Nigâr had been awaiting news of some kind from Hamzai Sahip Kıran. Her heart had been beating rapidly in her hope for a letter from him. As I told you yesterday, "Beauty resides in the one you love." Even if you were presented with the most beautiful girl in the world, she could not replace the one you love. When Mehli Nigâr saw the name of Hamzai Sahip Kıran on the letter Cive had brought, her tears began to fall. She said to herself, "This letter was written to my father, but the writer wanted me." Hamzai Sahip Kıran had written in the last sentence of his letter, "If your daughter wants me, I shall do anything to get her, but if she does not want me, I shall search for another beauty." Cive stood by, watching the tears flowing from Mehli Nigâr's eyes.

The girl first wrote her name, *Nuşirvan's daughter, Mehli Nigâr*, in her message to her father. She then wrote, "I fell in love with Hamzai Sahip Kıran during my first glance at him. I am his, and he is mine. It makes no difference whether or not my father gives me to Hamzai, for I shall never give him up." Then she continued, "Everything that Hamzai said in his letter was true. I saw him from the balcony and fell in love with him at that very moment. Even if there were forty Nuşirvans like my father, they could not take Hamzai away from me nor take me away from Hamzai. Even if my father should have me chopped into tiny bits, every piece would cry out, 'Hamzai!'" Having written this, she said to Cive, "Take this letter and give it to my father."

Nuşirvan read her letter just as soon as he received it. Then his daughter's answer was circulated about the room so that everyone who was gathered there could also read it. Most of those present were impressed by Mehli Nigâr's final words: "Even if my father were to chop me into tiny bits, every piece would cry out, 'Hamzai!'"

As Nuşirvan was watching the faces of those reading the letter, his two military commanders, Zohru and Mehdi, arose in one corner of the room. These two were the kind of men who sow discord among people. They said, "O our padishah, your daughter's mind was stolen and influenced by our enemies. How can you even consider giving your daughter to Hamzai Sahip Kıran? Do not be deceived and do not be misled, O our padishah. Mehli Nigâr does not deserve being married to someone like Hamzai Sahip Kıran! She deserves someone ten times as good as he is. He is nothing compared to our Mehli Nigâr."

Speaking in this way they hoped to influence Nuşirvan's decision on how he would handle this problem, and it became obvious almost at once that their hope was realized. Nuşirvan wrote his response on the back of Hamzai Sahip Kıran's letter.

"Oh, Hamzai Sahip Kıran, I fed you and supported you for fifteen years, during which time I never mentioned swords and shields. I do not have a daughter to give you. Don't you even know that there are hundreds of thousands of Hamzai Sahip Kırans like you who cannot challenge me or defy me?"

After Nuşirvan had finished writing, he gave the letter to Ömer Ümmiye. Ömer took the letter and left the palace, but he was soon aware that he was being followed by soldiers. Nuşirvan had ordered these men to follow Ömer Ümmiye to show him the way to the city limits. After proceeding for a way along the city streets, Ömer Ümmiye turned to the troops behind him and said, "Gentlemen, you do not know how to carry out your assignment. Inasmuch as I am a stranger to your city, I should be following you, and you should be leading me." And so thereafter Nuşirvan's men led the way.

When they reached the fountain just beyond the city limits, the leader of the soldiers said, "Ömer Ümmiye, we have brought you this far, but from now on you must continue on your way by yourself. Our work has been completed."[65]

"Thank you very much for your help," answered Ömer Ümmiye. "To show you my appreciation, I should like to give you a small present—only a shepherd's present."[66] Saying this, he reached into his magic pouch and withdrew a tray of *helva*. He handed this to Nuşirvan's soldiers, saying, "Take this and eat it. It is very tasty." The soldiers accepted this *helva* and ate it, but immediately afterwards they collapsed and lay upon the ground like dead men. Then Ömer stripped the uniform from one of the soldiers and dressed himself in it. Using this disguise, he turned back toward the palace.

At the palace Nuşirvan mistook Ömer for one of his own soldiers and asked him, "Did you lead Ömer Ümmiye to the edge of the city?"

The disguised Ömer answered, "Yes, my padishah, we took him there, and then he continued his way to Mecca alone."

Now we shall see what Ömer Ümmiye will do after this point. By walking very slowly and stealthily, he was able to get very close to Mehli Nigâr. When no one noticed him there, he took the opportunity to bite the girl's ear quite viciously. In pain Mehli Nigâr fell to the floor. By this time everyone realized that the man in the military uniform was not one of Nuşirvan's soldiers but was Ömer Ümmiye instead.

The palace people shouted, "Catch him! Kill him!" but it was too late for that. Ömer Ümmiye had by then fled like a bird.

When Nuşirvan heard of this, he asked, "Oh, my grand vizier, can you catch Ömer Ümmiye?"

---

65 This little episode of the troops' guiding Ömer Ümmiye to the outskirts of the city is rather pointless, except that it provides Ömer with a way to purloin a military uniform for his own purposes. This is the second time he has come to and departed from the palace, and this time he reached the palace unassisted.

66 *Çoban armağanı çam sakız* (a shepherd's present of pine pitch) is an expression of modesty used when presenting someone with a gift. It is equivalent to saying, "Oh, it's not much!"

The vizier answered, "My padishah, if he was able to come back here and injure Mehli Nigâr's ear, he must first have done something to the soldiers too." When they rushed to the fountain, they saw the three soldiers lying on the ground there as if they were dead.

In the meantime, Ömer Ümmiye returned to the palace still dressed as one of Nuşirvan's soldiers. He said to himself, "I cannot go back to Hamzai without having seen his Mehli Nigâr. If he should ask me whether I had seen her, I simply could not afford to answer, 'No.' I must, therefore, find Mehli Nigâr and talk with her."

When the girl's servants saw Ömer Ümmiye approaching, they said to Mehli Nigâr, "One of your father's men has come."

After he had been admitted into the room, Ömer greeted the princess and then asked, "O Mehli Nigâr, do you recognize me? Who am I?"

The girl answered, "You must be the best friend of Hamzai Sahip Kıran. You must be Ömer Ümmiye."

"Oh, delicate beauty, how did you know that I was Ömer Ümmiye?"

"I recognized you in your greeting," she said. "My heart told me that you were Ömer Ümmiye."

(Yes, gentlemen, when Padishah Hatemi Tey arrived in the distant court of the Padishah of Winter Land clothed as a dervish, his host saw through his disguise at once. He said, "Efendi, you look like a dervish because you are wearing dervish clothes, but your demeanor reveals that you are of much higher status than that of a dervish. What was the reason for your leaving your own country and traveling to this remote land?"

Hatemi Tey answered with these words:

Who'd choose to travel to a distant land?
Some greater force assigns us to such tasks.
'Twas Allah's will, not mine, that sent me here.
Our life and death and Fate are in His hands.
His was the compass pointing out my way.
He gave me strength for rigors of the road.")

Now I recall the part of the story we interrupted to speak of Hatemi Tey. Ömer Ümmiye had asked Mehli Nigâr, "How did you know that I was Ömer Ümmiye?"

And Mehli Nigâr had answered, "My heart told me who you were when I heard your greeting."[67]

---

67 The recognition of Ömer Ümmiye here reminded Behçet Mahir of an identification scene in his "The Adventures of Hatemi Tey." Actually the two occasions are not entirely similar, for while the first results from a kind of intuitive perception on the part of Mehli Nigâr, the latter is produced by the close observation and deduction of the Padishah of Winter Land. The narrator's associative outreach was not far off the mark, however, for just nine lines later in

And Ömer Ümmiye had then said to her, "Oh, delicate beauty, when your father read the letter from Hamzai Sahip Kıran, he became very angry. He said, 'He wrote first those words which should have been written last, and he wrote last the words that should have been first.' He will not consent to your becoming the wife of Hamzai Sahip Kıran."

Mehli Nigâr asked, "Did my father really utter those words?" She grew sad and began to cry.

Kneeling before her, Ömer Ümmiye said, "O beauty, do not cry. I am willing to sacrifice my life for you and Hamzai. Tell me everything that is in your heart."

Mehli Nigâr said to him. "Oh, Ömer, inasmuch as you would sacrifice your life for us—for me and Hamzai—I entrust in your hands everything that I own: my life, my honor, my chastity. Give my greetings to Hamzai Sahip Kıran. Kiss his hands for me. Tell him that my life is his. If you want to take me to Hamzai right now, I am willing to go with you."

But Ömer Ümmiye said, "O Mehli Nigâr, Hamzai did not give me an order to bring you to him. If he had given me such an order, I should take you to him at once without even consulting Nuşirvan. For now, you should remain here in your palace. I shall go and deliver your father's letter to Hamzai Sahip Kıran. Then if he orders me to do so, I shall return and take you to him—a task which would be very easy for me to accomplish."

Mehli Nigâr gave him many valuable presents to take to Hamzai Sahip Kıran. Among these were two precious jewels. She said, "Take these as gifts from me to Hamzai Sahip Kıran." Placing all of these gifts in his pouch, Ömer Ümmiye departed. Running very swiftly all the way, he reached his own country in twenty-four hours.

Now let us return to the three soldiers of Nuşirvan. They were asked, "What happened to you?"

They answered, "We do not know. Hamzai Sahip Kıran's man, Ömer Ümmiye, gave us three lumps of *helva* to eat, and we cannot remember anything after that." Some other soldiers who had by then arrived there laughed loudly when they heard that.

In the meantime, they had taken Mehli Nigâr to a hospital. There doctors had restored her ear to its former shape.

Gentlemen, in twenty-four hours Ömer Ümmiye reached Mecca, where he delivered Nuşirvan's letter to Hamzai Sahip Kıran. As he handed over the letter, Ömer said, "My heart will not permit me to bring myself to tell you the news. Read it with your own eyes. Everything is written in this letter."

"Hatemi Tey" occurs a passage (not quoted in the present tale) that Mehli Nigâr would have appreciated. Once Hatemi Tey's royal status has been detected, he and his host begin a cordial conversation. In response to a remark made by his guest, the Padishah of Winter Land ". . . bowed his head and listened with his heart" (Walker and Uysal 1992: 97).

Hamzai Sahip Kıran read the letter to the end, where Nuşirvan had written, "Even if there were many, many men like you, they could not do any harm to me or my country. I do not have any daughter to give you. If you still think that you can take my daughter, let us see how you will do so."[68]

Ömer Ümmiye then asked Hamzai Sahip Kıran, "O my shah, do you have any wishes for me to fulfill?"

Hamzai asked him, "Ömer, did you see Mehli Nigâr?"

"Oh, yes, my shah. Look! Here is something in her own handwriting."

"That may be in her own handwriting," said Hamzai, "but did you actually see the girl?"

"Of course I did!" answered Ömer. "With Allah as my witness, I declare that I could not have returned to you without having seen her. My own two eyes observed the fact that Mehli Nigâr loves you deeply. I knelt before her when the tears were flowing from her eyes as a result of her having read Nuşirvan's letter to you. She recognized me at once. I can say that however much you may love *her*, she loves *you* three times that much. She said that she was ready to have me bring her here, but I told her that I feared to do that without first having had your orders to do so."

"Oh, Ömer, may your tongue be cursed!" exclaimed Hamzai Sahip Kıran. "Go back and bring Mehli Nigâr here at once!"

Before Ömer could leave, however, Hamzai stopped him, saying, "No, Ömer—wait! Wait! Anything achieved by consent will be a crown on one's head that will last to the end of one's life, but that which is gained with ill will may turn evil in the middle of one's life. I know that if I order you to bring Mehli Nigâr here, you would do so very quickly, but this gain of mine could also easily bring disgrace upon me. People would say, 'Oh, yes, Hamzai Sahip Kıran is a great man, but he flies beneath the wing of Ömer Ümmiye. He has a man whom he uses to do all of his very difficult tasks!'" Hamzai Sahip Kıran therefore ordered Ömer not to go.

At this time our Prophet, Mohammed, was not yet born. I told you something about this yesterday when I was starting this story. As I said then, people before our time set many good examples for us to follow, and we can be more effective if we do indeed follow them. Hamzai Sahip Kıran was only three years older than the Prophet, but even so, he was Mohammed's uncle. Hamzai and our Prophet were actually just three years apart in age, although here we are pretending that they were forty years apart, because that is the way we heard it.

Gentlemen, while speaking about Ömer Ümmiye, I was reminded of two other men named *Ömer.* Our Prophet once said, "If even one of those other two Ömers accepts our religion, it will become much stronger." Who

---

[68] As the reader will have recognized by now, when Mahir repeats something previously spoken or written, he does not always duplicate it verbatim. He gives the general sense of the original statement, sometimes slightly compressed.

were these two Ömers? One of them was Ebu Cellidahi, whose name was also *Ömer*,[69] and the other was the Blessed Ömer.[70] (Neither the Blessed Ömer nor the Blessed Ebu Bekir[71] was in Mecca at this time, for they were both traveling in other parts of the world.)

Hamzai Invades the Land of Nuşirvan

Hamzai Sahip Kıran's army marched into Nuşirvan's country. Nuşirvan had been expecting this invasion, and he had stationed guards along all of his borders. He had given them these instructions: "Watch everyone and everything closely. If you see Hamzai Sahip Kıran or any of his soldiers, inform me of this immediately."

When the army from Mecca had gone half the distance to Nuşirvan's country, Hamzai called Ömer Ümmiye to him and said, "Ömer, we have reached the midpoint of our journey. Without revealing your identity to anyone, go to Mehli Nigâr and give her the good news that I am coming."

"I shall do so with great pleasure," answered Ömer Ümmiye, and he set out for Mehli Nigâr's palace through the lines of Nuşirvan's border guards.

Riddling Questions Unresolved

(Gentlemen, ten years ago I presented a question to a group of minstrels. That question just came to my mind, and so I shall repeat it to you. I did not ask that question of *molla*s,[72] nor did I ask it of common people. Here is the riddle that I asked:

> Something I saw that lacked a human look.
> [This line is unintelligible on tape recording.]
> Though full two hundred and ninety years of age,
> It has no more than six months left of life,
> But still it is complete and wanting naught.

Yes, I gave them ten years to solve that riddle, and now seven of those years have elapsed without their having answered it. Even distinguished

---

[69] The reference here may be to Ebu Cehl (554-624), an influential contemporary of Mohammed, but we have no record of his ever having been called *Ömer*.

[70] The Blessed Ömer was the second caliph, who was the Commander of the Faithful from 634 to 644.

[71] The Blessed Ebu Bekir, the first caliph, reigned from 632 to 634.

[72] *Molla* may refer to a student of theology or to a specialist in Islamic doctrine.

teachers have been unable to solve it.[73] Why can't they solve it? Well, gentlemen, can a sleeping baby be nursed? No! The baby is asleep.

Last year I was told that Karabey was going to test a student,[74] and I said to myself, "I shall go to that examination to see whether the questions are difficult or easy." His eye was inside my eye.[75] May Allah not withhold the minds of such people from us!

When I entered the room, the student said, "Test me! Come and test me! Is all this about gold or silver or just about a poor man? Come and test me!"

I asked, "Why?"

Gentlemen, I have been working at Atatürk University for the past sixteen years. The pay may not seem to be very much, but the job is most gratifying to me. They have respect for me here, and they do not meddle in my affairs. May Allah make respected those people who have shown respect to me. But the work that I do is not worth even the small pay I am receiving. Therefore, the money that I get is not *helâl* for me. I do not deserve that much for the small amount of work I am asked to do.

Recently no one has asked me, "O poet, what more do you have to tell us?" I am here now, but soon I may be gone. May there be some people after my time who will still be gleaning some benefit from my words.

So the minstrels to whom I presented the riddle ten years ago have only three more years to answer it. Four years ago I posed the same question to some teachers of literature. They looked into each other's faces, but they found no answers there.

If someone were to ask you how many components the *kible*[76] has, the answer is five, like the number of daily prayer services. The first one is

---

73 If indeed this riddle went unsolved by intelligent people for several years, it is unlikely that it will ever be understood—especially in view of the fact that it is incomplete. It does not appear in the standard reference work on Turkish riddles (Başgöz and Tietze 1973).

74 Taken literally, this passage would seem to suggest that the narrator had been indirectly involved in an academic examination; the suggestion is strengthened by his subsequent expression of gratitude for respect shown to him by university personnel. Bear in mind, however, that Behçet Mahir was an illiterate janitor. One can speculate that Karabey (who is given no last name nor any academic title) may have been a minstrel or storyteller who was examining an apprentice.

75 This figurative expression can refer to either inference or insight.

76 From beginning to end this riddling question and its purported answers are obscure. Outside this context the word *kible* or *kibla* has documentable denotations: 1) the direction of Mecca, 2) the *mihrab* (niche in a mosque wall which indicates the direction of Mecca), the Kaaba (the small building which houses a sacred black stone at Mecca) (Weinsinck 1986: 82-83). But the connotations suggested here elude all objective source study and analysis.

arş.[77] The second is *küş*.[78] Following this, the third is *Beytülezelî*,[79] and the fourth is *Beytülmanur*.[80] The fifth and final component is *Kabeibeytullah*.[81] If anyone should ask you what these are made of, you should answer that the first is made of rubies, the second of emeralds, the third of gold, the fourth of silver, and the fifth of stone.[82]

If someone should ask you why the *ezan*[83] that is chanted five times daily is not also chanted before a requiem service for a dead person, you should answer, "If a baby is born and enters this world, the *ezan* can enter its ear, but although the *ezan* cannot enter the ear of a corpse, the death service must be conducted for it anyway."

I can give accounts of many other perplexing questions similar to those I have been presenting to you. I spent seven years with Hafız Mugdat and was his apprentice for all that time. Now I should like to be the kind of master storyteller that he was and teach others. He used to say to me, "Here, son! Take this piece of information and store it in your brain. I shall leave this world one day, and so you should learn what you can from me now and learn it well." But that long tradition has now been lost, and things do not happen as they did even as recently as when I was young. We cannot bring up young people that way anymore. Young people whom I used to help in that way now place watermelon rinds beneath my feet. There are very few of the young people I taught who still appreciate me. They mistakenly thought that I taught them all I know, but they did not realize that I had taught them only about half of my knowledge. I suspected that one day they might even become my enemies, and what I suspected has become a reality in several cases. One day when I entered a room, there were four poets who had been students of mine sitting on chairs as they sang and played their *saz*es. One of them—I shall not mention his name, though he is well known now—saw me and said, "The slave of the dean has just arrived."

---

[77] The highest (seventh) level of heaven.

[78] The word *küş* often refers to killing. It may possibly refer here to the widespread slaughter of sheep for the *Kurban Bayramı* (Sacrifice Holiday), an important ritual occasion for Muslims.

[79] It is difficult to be certain about the meaning of this word. *Ezel* and *ezelî* refer to eternity, and thus *Beytülezelî* may possibly mean *House of Eternity*.

[80] A small palace at the seventh level of heaven.

[81] This is clearly a reference to the Kaaba.

[82] Because the components of *kible* (*kibla*) are not held together by any discernible pattern, it is impossible to assign symbolic values to the materials of which they are reputedly composed. Inasmuch as the building materials are listed in descending order of their preciousness, they may indicate the relative importance of the five components.

[83] The call to prayer is chanted five times daily by a mosque official known as a muezzin. It is usually chanted from the balcony of a minaret.

Storytelling in July 1970 at Abulyont (Greek Apollonius). The village has since been given a Turkish name, *Gölyazı* (*Summer Lake*) by the Ministry of the Interior. The chief narrator here was İsmail Doğan (wearing cap, at center). The man with the microphone was, at 94, the village's oldest resident. Although he was not an apt raconteur, it was socially strategic to include him in the taping session. Warren Walker is at right side of picture.

"Stop, my son!" I said. "You have gone a little too far this time." That was the way in which I responded to him. He thought that he had obtained from me all that I had to offer, but in fact I had taught him only part of what I knew. To himself he probably said, "Behçet Mahir is old now, but I am young and I can surpass him easily." He was incapable of realizing that even forty men of his ability could not surpass me. On that occasion I recited this quatrain to him:

My wish is that you know the human heart.
Work hard to learn the secret of its ways.
Look sharply while the caravan still moves,
And learn the lesson life alone can teach.

The former student immediately came to kiss my hand, but it was by then too late. He said that he was sorry, but the damage had been done already. He realized then that the weight of that stone would not easily be lifted. He had mistakenly thought that I had poured forth all my thought for him and left myself quite empty. But then, all masters are that way. They do not reveal all of their knowledge and skill, for they realize that if they were to do so, they might someday have to compete with their own apprentices.)[84]

A Parable of Ingratitude

Now I shall tell you a story about ingratitude. One day when a young man was traveling along his way, he came to a wooden trunk from which he heard a voice coming. That voice was saying, "Is there no human being nearby who can rescue me from this trunk?" But as soon as the young man opened the trunk, a snake sprang out and began to coil itself around his neck.

The young man was greatly confused by what had happened. As the snake began to squeeze more and more tightly, the young man said to it, "What did I ever do to you that would cause you to treat me in this way? You were imprisoned in that trunk, and I released you from it. Will you kill me as my reward for saving you?"

The snake answered angrily, "Was it your business to save me? You should mind your own business."

The young man became even more confused now, and so he said, "O snake, let us go and get advice from someone else about this matter."

"Very well," said the snake. The two of them proceeded along the road until they met an ox.

---

84 The section ending here constitutes one of Behçet Mahir's most regrettable lapses in the art of storytelling. Maundering, filled with self-pity, and often lost in obscurity, it breaks the narrative line to contribute nothing functional to the overall design.

The young man addressed the ox: "O brother ox, this snake was trapped in a trunk until I rescued him from his imprisonment. But the moment he was released from the trunk, this snake coiled about my neck and tried to kill me. Did I do something wrong in opening the lid of the trunk and saving him from imprisonment?"

When the ox heard this, he said, "O brother snake, human beings drink a great amount of our milk. Don't hesitate to strangle this young man. My master forced me to work very hard for fifteen years. I was whipped and made to suffer throughout all that time. But when I grew old and could no longer work as hard as I had in former times, my master decided to kill me so that he could eat my flesh and make shoes from my hide. He is having me graze here now so that he will get more meat from my carcass."

When the young man heard these remarks, he became even more frightened. He said, "O brother snake, stop! Let us go and consult someone else about this matter."

"All right," answered the snake.

After they had traveled together for some distance, the young man and the snake met a fox. The young man called the fox to his side and explained the situation in which he now found himself. After he had described everything that had happened, the young man said, "Now tell me, brother fox, do I deserve to be strangled by someone whose life I had saved?"

Speaking to the snake rather than to the young man, the fox said, "Human beings drink much milk. If you have the opportunity to strangle him, do not miss the chance to do so. These same human beings cause greyhounds to chase us. Then they kill us, give our flesh to the dogs, and wear our furs as coats. The human being is an ungrateful creature. Strangle him!" But after a few moments the fox took pity on the young man and called to the snake, "Stop, stop, brother snake! I want to ask you something before you kill him. I just cannot believe that a creature your size could possibly have gotten into so small a trunk as the young man is carrying."

The snake answered, "It was not so difficult to do. I just coiled up very tightly in order to fit inside that trunk. Here! I shall show you."

After the snake had unwound itself from the young man's neck, it coiled up very tightly and squeezed into the trunk. As soon as it was completely inside the trunk, the fox closed the lid tightly. In this way the snake was once again imprisoned.[85]

Yes, sometimes a person may suffer as a result of his kindness, but kindness also has its rewards. It is not so bad if a person you have helped

[85] This simple fable is of ancient origin, and variants of it are very widely distributed. It is listed in Aarne and Thompson, *The Types of the Folktale*, as Type 155—*The Ungrateful Serpent Returned to Captivity*; in Eberhard and Boratav, *Typen Türkischer Volksmärchen*, it appears as Type 48—*Die Schlange und der Mann*. ATON variants are tales numbered 341 and 727.

does not appreciate your kindness, for eventually a helpful person will himself receive help when he needs it. There is a proverb which says, "Do a good deed and throw it into the ocean. Even if the fishes do not recognize it, Allah will."[86] Help others without expecting any reward. Allah will know about the good you have done. Your good deed as well as your evil act will be recorded in the Great Book of Affairs, and sooner or later you will be rewarded for the good things you have done. Don't leave the right way during your life. Be compassionate. Allah knows that your kindness is often unappreciated. After the Last Judgment you will be rewarded in the other world.

Hamzai Victorious in Fifty-Six Duels

Now we should continue with our story. The soldiers of Nuşirvan's large army were everywhere. Nothing seemed able to pass safely through that area, nor could birds fly over it without being killed. But what could stop Ömer Ümmiye? Dressing himself as a priest, he pulled a lute from his magic pouch and proceeded toward Nuşirvan's forces singing and playing songs based on episodes in the Bible. The soldiers welcomed him, and their commanders asked him, "From where have you come?"

Ömer Ümmiye answered, "Jesus sent me here. He wants you to know that Hamzai Sahip Kıran's army is approaching but that He will always be with you. He will never cease helping you. He sent me as an ambassador to tell you this good news." Nuşirvan's troops were very pleased to know that Jesus would help them in the coming battle.[87]

Ömer Ümmiye then left the soldiers and went on to the palace of Nuşirvan. There the ruler said to him, "O priest, come and stay in my palace so that I shall be able to hear your songs from the Bible."

But Ömer Ümmiye replied, "No, my pasha,[88] no. I am a wandering priest who cannot remain at any one place. I must travel. I came here only to bring you a message from Jesus. He sent me here to inform you that Hamzai Sahip Kıran's army is approaching this city."

After leaving Nuşirvan, Ömer Ümmiye went to Mehli Nigâr's palace, where he was shown into the presence of the princess. When she saw him, she asked, "Oh, Ömer, have you really come?"

"Yes, I have really come, and I bring some good news for you. Hamzai Sahip Kıran is on his way here. He sent me ahead to inform you of

[86] This is a very well-known Turkish proverb: "İyilik yap denize at; balık bilmezse, Halik bilir" (Yurtbaşı 1993: 478).

[87] This episode should not be considered either sacrilegious or anti-Christian. Like the wind, the wiliness of the trickster is licensed to blow with impunity "where it listeth."

[88] Today the word *pasha* (*paşa*) means simply *general*. In earlier times it referred to the military governor of a large area, perhaps a province or two. *Pasha* would not, therefore, be an entirely inappropriate title for Nuşirvan.

this. He has by now covered half the distance to this place. It will not be long before swords begin dancing. O beautiful lady, what do you have to say now about that?"

"I want only one thing now, Ömer. Just tell Hamzai Sahip Kıran that he should show his full power to my father."

"All right," answered Ömer Ümmiye, and he then immediately left Mehli Nigâr's palace. He returned to Hamzai Sahip Kıran's army not only with a message from Mehli Nigâr but also with information about the size of Nuşirvan's army, for he had been sent to Nuşirvan's country partly as a spy.

When Hamzai Sahip Kıran was told of the safe return of Ömer, he was meeting with his wrestlers. He said to the messenger, "Bring Ömer Ümmiye to my tent at once." And when Ömer arrived there, Hamzai said, "Oh-h-h, Ömer Ümmiye, have you indeed returned safely?"

"Yes, I have returned well in every way."

"Did you see my Mehli Nigâr?" asked Hamzai.

"Yes, Hamzai Sahip Kıran, I did see her, and she sent her greetings to you."

"Did you manage to go to Nuşirvan's palace?"

"Yes, I went there too, and while I was there, I sang him a song about something that happened in the Bible."

"Were you also able to learn how many soldiers Nuşirvan has ready to meet our attack?"

"I was there, and I saw his soldiers, but they were so numerous that there was no way in which they could be counted. O Hamzai Sahip Kıran, you could more easily count every single star in the sky than you could count his troops. They were everywhere. They were already lined up in ranks awaiting our arrival."

"Oh, Ömer, do not worry. The decision about the outcome of our war will be made by Allah. I have been an honest person all my life. I shall never depart from the right path, Allah's way. Allah's words are the right words, and nothing can happen unless He has said that it will happen." He then ordered his troops to continue marching day and night until they reached Nuşirvan's city.

Soon the guards of Nuşirvan reported to that ruler, "The troops of Hamzai Sahip Kıran have now come into view." They were all afraid that Ömer Ümmiye might be somewhere in their country as a spy. They did not know that he had already been there, had spied on them, and had by now been gone for some time.

Gentlemen, Hamzai Sahip Kıran rode his horse into the open field between the two armies. Lifting his right hand, he gave a mighty shout. It was so loud that it terrified many of Nuşirvan's soldiers, causing them to let their swords fall from their hands to the ground. Then Hamzai Sahip drew his sword from its scabbard and shouted at Nuşirvan's soldiers, "Is there any brave man among you?"

A very strong man rode out from among Nuşirvan's troops. He was a wrestler and the strongest man that Nuşirvan had. This man asked Hamzai Sahip Kıran, "Are you the man who let forth that strange yell?" Without waiting for an answer, this man rode straight at Hamzai.

Hamzai said, "The first blow is yours. Prepare to make your first attack." The wrestler galloped his horse straight ahead and swung his sword at Hamzai Sahip Kıran. Warding off this blow with his shield, Hamzai grabbed the wrestler by the collar with his other hand and lifted him right out of his saddle. Holding that wrestler aloft with his one hand, Hamzai Sahip Kıran said, "Oh, wrestler, the Last Prophet [Mohammed] will soon come, and he will lead everyone along the path set by Allah. Come to Allah's path now and join my religion. Otherwise I shall not free you, and no one can save you from my hand."

The wrestler answered, "Oh, Hamzai, stop! No one else could pick me up with one hand. No one else has ever taken my sword away from me, and I know that you will be the last one to do so. I have killed more people than the number of hairs in my head, and I killed each with only a single stroke of my sword. Oh, Hamzai, put me down, and I shall accept your religion. Your religion must follow the right way."[89]

Hamzai Sahip Kıran then called Ömer Ümmiye and said to him, "Pierce this man's ear and hang a circular earring from it, for he is now on our side." After Ömer had done as he had been directed, the wrestler knelt before Hamzai Sahip Kıran and kissed his hand.

Nuşirvan's soldiers had watched all that had happened, and they were amazed at what they had seen. However, one of Nuşirvan's commanders spoke to them, saying, "Soldiers, do not allow yourselves to be influenced by what you saw. That wrestler must have had a spell placed upon him."

The converted wrestler then spoke to Hamzai Sahip Kıran. He said, "O my shah, now that I have chosen the right way of religion, allow me now to fight for you."

"O brother," said Hamzai Sahip Kıran, "welcome to the battle! May Allah make you a great warrior!" Then Hazmai again shouted at Nuşirvan's army, "Is there any strong man among you who is willing to fight with me?"

When another strong wrestler came from the ranks of Nuşirvan's army, Hamzai grabbed him around the chest and lifted his feet off the ground. "Oh, wrestler, come to the right way and become a Muslim."

---

[89] Although Mohammed (570-632) was the prophet and founder of Islam, he was not, according to folk theology, the first Muslim. Because the Arabic word *muslim* can be defined as *one who surrenders to God*, it is often applied to earlier monotheists. See, for example, ATON tale No. 1522—"The Martyrdom of an Ancient Muslim Family." Thus many prominent figures in the Old Testament are considered to be Muslims. It is no anomaly, therefore, when Turkish storytellers refer to Abraham as Blessed Abraham and to Moses as Blessed Moses.

But that wrestler first began cursing at Hamzai Sahip Kıran, and then he shouted, "I shall never accept your religion, even if you cut me to bits!" When Hamzai Sahip Kıran heard this, he grew very angry. He threw his opponent up in the air, and as he fell back toward the earth, Hamzai cut him in half with one swing of his sword.

On that first day of battle Hamzai Sahip Kıran fought in single combat with fifty-six wrestlers, six of whom accepted the Muslim faith. When night came, the fighting stopped. Nuşirvan's men reported to their ruler what had happened. They said, "O padishah Nuşirvan, most of our strongest wrestlers have been killed by Hamzai Sahip Kıran. Six of them he did not kill because they accepted the Muslim religion and went over to the side of our enemy."

When Nuşirvan heard this report, he became very sad but also very angry. Taking off his crown, he threw it aside, saying, "Why doesn't the Fire God[90] help me?"

Ömer Intercepts Assassins

On the other side of the battlefield Hamzai Sahip Kıran called Ömer Ümmiye to him and said, "O Ömer, you are the only person upon whom I can depend completely. You are the only one whom I can always trust. I want you to sit on the top of that nearby hill and guard us tonight, keeping watch in all four directions. That will enable us to get a good night's sleep." Shortly after that everyone else went to sleep in his tent, but Ömer Ümmiye remained awake and watched carefully in all directions.

Meanwhile in the palace of Nuşirvan, that ruler was meeting with some of his advisors. He said to them, "We must find some way to kill Hamzai Sahip Kıran tonight. It is necessary to kill him if we expect to win this war. Send someone to kill him tonight!"

The two military commanders said, "Yes, our padishah."

While Ömer Ümmiye was standing on the hill doing guard duty, he observed a soldier leaving Nuşirvan's camp and heading for the tent of Hamzai Sahip Kıran. That soldier was trying to go unnoticed, but Ömer detected his movement before he had taken more than a few steps, and Ömer knew that the man's intentions were not good. He left the hill in order to intercept that soldier, and a few minutes later he confronted him. Ömer said to that soldier, "I was sent by Nuşirvan to tell you not to attempt to kill

---

90 This could refer to any of numerous fire gods in this part of the world, including the classical Prometheus or Hephaestus (Vulcan). Although he was not really a fire god, the deity in question here is probably Ahura Mazda, one of the two principal Zoroastrian divinities. Zoroastrians and their latter-day descendants, the Yezidis, are often mistakenly described as fire worshipers. This error can be attributed to two factors: 1) fire is used in some of their rituals, and 2) Ahura Mazda is associated with light, as his cosmological opponent, Ahrimanes, is associated with darkness. During the time of the Sassanid dynasty, Zoroastrianism was the state religion of Persia.

Hamzai Sahip Kıran but to let me do so. Wait for me here in this tent. I shall go to Hamzai Sahip Kıran, cut off his head, and bring it here to you. Then you may take that head to Nuşirvan."

But as soon as that soldier entered the tent, Ömer jumped upon him, knocked him down, and tied him very tightly to the tent pole. During the rest of the night Ömer captured three more of Nuşirvan's soldiers in the same way. Then when morning arrived—may Allah make every morning as good as this one—Ömer Ümmiye went to the tent of Hamzai Sahip Kıran and said, "Good morning, Hamzai."

"Good morning, Ömer—but why are you smiling so broadly?"

Ömer answered, "O Hamzai Sahip Kıran, during the night I captured four of Nuşirvan's men right here in our camp. Inasmuch as you did not give me permission to behead these men, I have come to ask what you want done with them."

Hamzai Sahip Kıran said, "Ömer, bring those men to me."

Ömer brought the four captives to the tent of Hamzai Sahip Kıran. The hands of all four of them were tied very tightly behind their backs. Hamzai said to them, "Soldiers, I am drawing my strength directly from Allah. Even if there were one hundred thousand soldiers like you, they would not be able to harm me in any way; they could do nothing to me. Come and accept the true religious faith, and then I shall set you free."

They answered, "Oh, Hamzai Sahip Kıran, we are soldiers of Nuşirvan, who is an extremely powerful man. How dare you tell us to accept your religion and join you—you who are a poor and unimportant person?"

When Hamzai heard these words, he said to Ömer Ümmiye, "Ömer, now you do have my permission to cut off their heads." Taking the soldiers from Hamzai's tent, Ömer beheaded them. Then he removed from their clothes all of the gold and silver they had and put it into his magic pouch.

Later that day the two sides clashed once more on the battlefield. As he had done the day before, Hamzai Sahip Kıran rode out into the open space between the armies to challenge combat with one of the enemy warriors, but as he did so, he was attacked on all four sides by soldiers of Nuşirvan. They came at him like a huge herd. But Hamzai Sahip Kıran's wrestlers, as well as the six wrestlers who had formerly been Nuşirvan's men, rode their horses onto the battlefield. It became a very fierce battle, with blood flowing from swords and foam flowing from the horses' mouths. The forces became so intermingled that no one could tell who was Hamzai and who was Ömer, who was Hasan or who was Hüseyin.[91] Heads were cut from bodies and fell to the ground.

---

[91] *Hasan* and *Hüseyin* might seem to be names almost randomly chosen (perhaps for their alliteration) for unidentified combatants. The matter is not quite so simple as that, however. In a Muslim society anywhere in the world, the juxtaposition of these two names strikes responsive chords that echo more than 1,400 years of strife between Sunnites and Shi'ites, the

This battle continued all day until night came, when the birds went to their nests and the sun returned to its home in the west. A horn was blown to signal the end of the hostilities for that day. When the soldiers of Nuşirvan returned to their tents, they were very tired but they were also mystified by something that had happened that day. They had repeatedly been struck by large stones which had fallen upon them from above. They did not know that these stones had been hurled by Ömer from the same hilltop where he had kept guard the night before. Back in their tents, Nuşirvan's troops kept saying, "Alas! Alas![92] During the battle stones seemed to rain from the sky! Where did they come from?"

The battle continued for another two days, and each night Nuşirvan's army was forced to draw back closer to the city. Hamzai's army kept advancing. Each night Nuşirvan received messages from his soldiers saying, "Stones were raining from the sky again today! What is happening to us?"

Nuşirvan gathered his council around him and said to them, "Why isn't the Fire God guiding us any longer? How can we stop Hamzai Sahip Kıran? We must find some way to do so very quickly."

One of the members of the council said to Nuşirvan, "O my shah, order me to bring Hamzai Sahip Kıran to you tonight, and I shall do that."

Nuşirvan answered, "My councilman, you are too valuable to me to be killed. Could you really bring Hamzai Sahip Kıran here?"

"O my shah, just order me to bring him to you tonight, and then you will see that I can do so."

Nuşirvan said, "If you can do that, I shall give you whatever you want. I shall fulfill your every wish."

While this was going on, Ömer Ümmiye was again in the palace of Nuşirvan. He came this time disguised as a sergeant. Since there were more than 150 sergeants in the army of Nuşirvan, it was easy for him to move around unnoticed in the uniform of a sergeant. When the member of Nuşirvan's council offered to capture Hamzai Sahip Kıran, Ömer Ümmiye stood up and asked for permission to speak. When Nuşirvan gave his approval, Ömer Ümmiye stood up in his sergeant's uniform and said, "O my

two major divisions of Islam. The split began as a result of Ali's having been made the fourth caliph instead of the first. Hasan and Hüseyin were the sons of Ali and the grandsons of Mohammed. Ali had expected his sons to succeed him as Commander of the Faithful, but they were cast aside by founders of the Umayyad dynasty of caliphs. Deposed soon after he had become caliph, Hasan (the older son) retired to private life and died under equivocal circumstances. His brother, Hüseyin, led a small band of zealous supporters against Umayyad forces, which quickly massacred all of them at Karbala (in present-day Iraq) on October 10, 680. The pathos of the sons' plight helped to earn them the status of martyrs. Behçet Mahir uses the names of Hasan and Hüseyin more casually here than he usually does, but no matter how lightly they may seem to be introduced, those two names in tandem proceed to speak volumes.

92 The Turkish word used here was *aman*, usually meaning *alas*, but occasionally it is a stronger exclamation.

shah, let me accompany your councilman to get Hamzai Sahip Kıran. Two of us working together can accomplish more than one."

Nuşirvan was so touched by this offer that he said to his men, "Look at this sergeant! What a brave man he is! Yes, you may go along to help bring Hamzai Sahip Kıran to me."

Ömer Ümmiye and the councilman soon left the palace together to get Hamzai Sahip Kıran. When they came to a fountain, Ömer reached into his pouch and withdrew from it a glass of liquid that was as clear as water. He said to his companion, "Councilman, let us take a brief rest at this place and drink some water. Here! Drink this, and you will feel refreshed." Speaking in this way, Ömer Ümmiye handed the drugged drink to the councilman. As soon as he drank it, the councilman lost consciousness.

Ömer Ümmiye decided to carry this unconscious man to Mehli Nigâr's quarters. Picking up the councilman, he put him on his back and took him to Mehli Nigâr's palace. After she had been awakened, the princess recognized Ömer Ümmiye at once. She asked, "Ömer, what are you doing here? Who is that man on your back? Is he dead? He seems to be."

Ömer Ümmiye replied, "O Mehli Nigâr, your father gave permission to this man to kill Hamzai Sahip Kıran and bring his body back to the palace. I received permission from your father to accompany this man and help him bring back the head of Hamzai. When we came to a fountain, I pretended to give this man water to drink, but I really gave him a sleeping potion instead. He is now sleeping very deeply. I brought him here to ask you what should be done with this body."

Mehli Nigâr answered, "Ömer, he is your captive, and you may do whatever you wish with him."

"No, my princess. I am going to leave him here so that you may dispose of him as you wish." Ömer Ümmiye then left her palace.

When morning came, the drugged councilman opened his eyes and was both amazed and embarrassed when he beheld Mehli Nigâr. She spoke to him, saying, "You were brought here by Ömer Ümmiye. Don't you remember that you and he were on your way to kill Hamzai Sahip Kıran? At midnight he brought you here unconscious. By doing so, he indicated that he had forgiven you and that you could return to my father."

By this time Ömer Ümmiye had reached the tent of Hamzai Sahip Kıran. Ömer said to him, "Hamzai, I captured one of Nüsirvan's men who was on his way here to kill you."

Hamzai Sahip Kıran asked, "But you did not kill that man—did you?"

Ömer answered, "No, Hamzai, I did not kill him. Instead, I took him to Mehli Nigâr's palace and left him there."

When Hamzai Sahip Kıran heard Mehli Nigâr's name mentioned, he became excited. "Did you see Mehli Nigâr?" he asked.

"Yes, I did, and she is well," said Ömer.

At the same time the drugged councilman of Nuşirvan gained complete consciousness. Mehli Nigâr directed him, "Go to my father's palace now and tell my father what happened to you. Tell him about Ömer Ümmiye, Hamzai Sahip Kıran, and their invincibility."

The councilman followed her directions. He went to Nuşirvan's palace, and when he had been admitted into the presence of the ruler, he told him about everything that had happened. When Nuşirvan heard this almost unbelievable account, he became very worried. He ordered that more guards be placed on duty at every door of the palace. "Be especially careful about any stranger that you may see," he said.

When morning arrived, both armies again went to the battlefield. As before, Hamzai Sahip Kıran rode forth into the open space between the armies, and as before, Nuşirvan's soldiers attacked him from four sides. The clash between the two armies raised a large cloud of dust. Men on both sides were fighting with a willingness to continue until they had shed their last drop of blood.

Third night; narration of January 11, 1977

Ten-Year Armistice Signed

We have all kinds of stories in this country. Some of them might make you cry, and others might make you laugh. That is the way life passes. We also have stories that teach lessons or provide good advice. We need all of these kinds of stories.

We left the forces of Hamzai Sahip Kıran fighting with those of Nuşirvan. It was a very bloody conflict. After twenty-eight days of such warfare, Hamzai Sahip Kıran was still fighting like a lion. Every day Nuşirvan's men brought back reports which displeased that ruler. He was disappointed with the results of the struggle engaged in by his troops. Again he called his council together and sought their advice. "What are your thoughts about this situation in which we find ourselves? We do not seem to be able to defeat Hamzai Sahip Kıran. Can you think of any solution to our problem?"

The wise men of the council said, "O our shah, you are very rich, but your great wealth does not help us to defeat Hamzai Sahip Kıran. We should call a halt to the fighting long enough to find some new strategy with which to overcome that man. We can trick him by proposing an armistice." They did not know, of course, that Ömer Ümmiye was again in the palace disguised as one of Nuşirvan's sergeants and was listening to everything that they said.

Nuşirvan responded to this suggestion quickly. He said, "I like that idea very much. Write a letter to Hamzai Sahip Kıran from me."

This is what they wrote. "O Hamzai Sahip Kıran, my astronomers warned me that you would attack me. Although you were reared on my bread, you are now using swords against me. But I forgive you for that. You want my daughter, Mehli Nigâr, as your wife, but you will never get her by fighting. Come to my presence, for we should talk together. Many soldiers have been killed on both sides. Let us keep alive those who are left. You make your preparations, and I shall make mine. After that I shall give Mehli Nigâr to you in a very large wedding ceremony." (All the while that this letter was being dictated, Ömer Ümmiye was listening to every single word.) The letter was given to Civaniayyar[93] with this direction: "Do not deliver this letter to any hands but those of Hamzai Sahip Kıran!"

---

[93] As indicated in Note 58, *civan* means *handsome youth*. The suffix *-ayyar* means *crafty*.

Civaniayyar took the letter and set off on his journey, but Ömer Ümmiye had left the palace ahead of him and was already well on his way to the tent of Hamzai Sahip Kıran. When he got there, he said, "Hamzai Sahip Kıran, Nuşirvan and his council have concluded that they cannot stop your sword by fighting. They said, 'We can stop him only by trickery.' They have, therefore, decided to offer you an armistice in order to gain time and reorganize their army. What do you want me to do now? I can get the letter from Civaniayyar, or I can kill him. Just give me your orders."

Hamzai Sahip Kıran laughed and answered, "Sit down, Ömer Ümmiye! Sit down and relax! Let him come here with it. Let us learn clearly what they want." After some time had passed, a guard informed Hamzai Sahip Kıran that Civaniayyar had arrived. By this time Hamzai's wrestlers had also come to his tent. "Bring the messenger into my presence," Hamzai ordered.

When Civaniayyar was brought into the tent, he saw Ömer Ümmiye sitting among the others there, but he did not know that Ömer had arrived there from the palace shortly before he himself had, and he did not know that Ömer had already informed Hamzai about the contents of the letter. Civaniayyar greeted Hamzai Sahip Kıran and handed him the letter. Hamzai read the letter, observing that its message was exactly the same, word for word, as Ömer had reported to him. It said, "O Hamzai Sahip Kıran, we must stop our warfare. Many people have died so far, and we must save those who are still alive. We can solve this problem by talking about it." Hamzai called his council together and read the letter to them. Although they all knew about the trick that Nuşirvan was trying to play on them, they all said that they were willing to accept Nuşirvan's offer of an armistice. When Civaniayyar heard this decision, he was very pleased, and he left very soon after that to take the message to Nuşirvan. But once again Ömer Ümmiye preceded the messenger and arrived first at Nuşirvan's palace. He wanted to learn what kind of welcome they were planning for Hamzai Sahip Kıran.

When Civaniayyar arrived at Nuşirvan's palace, the ruler asked him, "Hey, Ayyar, what is the news? Tell me the news!"

Civaniayyar replied, "O my shah, the news is very good. Your offer has been accepted by Hamzai Sahip Kıran, and he will be arriving here tomorrow with some of his wrestlers."

Nuşirvan was delighted with this news. He at once gave orders that preparations be made for the visit of Hamzai Sahip Kıran. While all of this was going on, Ömer Ümmiye was observing everything very carefully to determine whether or not they really planned to kill Hamzai Sahip Kıran. He decided that at this point they were being sincere and that their immediate intentions were not evil.

On the next day when dawn arrived—may Allah give everyone good mornings—Hamzai Sahip Kıran went to Nuşirvan's palace accompanied by forty of his wrestlers. The palace people greeted him with great respect and took him and his forty wrestlers into the presence of Nuşirvan. Almost immediately Hamzai noticed Ömer Ümmiye working among the servants, and Hamzai smiled at him. A short while later Ömer Ümmiye took from his pouch a lute and accompanied himself with it as he recited some verses from the Bible. Nuşirvan was pleased by this performance.

Now we are coming to the best part of our story, and that is the part which concerns our Prophet, the Blessed Mohammed. Eighteen thousand countries [sic] yearned for him. They loved his holy face and the light that glowed from it. It was not just his friends but also many of his enemies who came to love him. Love cannot be contained; it will have its way, and it is unpredictable. Love can make you behave insanely; it can make you jump into the ocean or into a fire. That is the reason why I am going to recite a poem about Mohammed for you.

Greetings, O my sultan and my love!
No one exceeds you in benevolence.
You give the intercession that we need.
Your ways are filled with beauty and with grace.

How fair and varied are your attributes!
Weary, I faltered on the course of life,
But you became my wings, replacing arms.
Your ways are filled with beauty and with grace.

Your mystic love pursued and captured me.
My wistful sadness groped aloft for *arş*.[94]
Does love within the heart commit offense?
Your ways are filled with beauty and with grace.

The love within my heart will never fade.
My words but echo what my heart has said.
Your hand alone can guide me heavenward.
Your ways are filled with beauty and with grace.

I squeezed a thousand hours into one.
I walked, felt weak, grew thin, and moved no more.
Know how your love affected my travail.
Your ways are filled with beauty and with grace.

Your hands are branches of the tree of joy.
Both sun and moon draw strength from you to rise,

---

94 See Note 77.

Coffeehouse at Ova Akça village, Bursa Province. The three narrators taped here were Şerif Mehmet Ceylan (with microphone), Mehmet Meşüt (to his left), and (at extreme right) Mehmet Özkan, village *hoca* (preacher). Warren Walker is next to the *hoca.*

Behçet Mahir (at right) with Ahmet Uysal in August 1974, taking a break from a three-hour taping session. They were in garden of Atatürk University, Erzurum.

And eighteen thousand lands reflect your face.
Your ways are filled with beauty and with grace.

Behçet Mahir speaks from a mortal world.
What's seen today tomorrow disappears,
With naught between us and the Day of Doom.
Your ways are filled with beauty and with grace.

Yes, gentlemen, everyone felt love for him, his enemies as well as his friends.

Nuşirvan welcomed Hamzai Sahip Kıran with great respect, and after that everyone was invited to be seated. Nuşirvan's council members went to Hamzai and said, "Hamzai Sahip Kıran, you know our proposal. We do not want any further fighting. We wish to resolve our differences in a more humane way. No resolution can be reached by force."

Hamzai Sahip Kıran replied, "If you are really sincere about this, and if you have no hidden intentions, then I shall favor your proposal and accept it."

Nuşirvan then said, "O Hamzai, we are not trying to deceive you. We have no hidden intentions. We are honestly asking you for time."

"Very well," said Hamzai Sahip Kıran. "How many days do you want?"

Nuşirvan answered, "Give us seven years. During that time I shall make my preparations."

Hamzai stood up and said, "O my padishah, you ask for seven years, but how can any of us know that we shall live that long? Only Allah knows how long we shall live. Nevertheless, I shall suggest that we add three years to your seven, which will give you an armistice of ten years."

When Nuşirvan heard this offer of a ten-year truce, he was delighted. He ordered his men, "Give gold and silver to Hamzai Sahip Kıran's wrestlers."

But Hamzai Sahip Kıran responded, "No, we cannot accept your gold or silver. We seek neither tribute nor alms." When Nuşirvan heard this remark, he realized how mature and wise Hamzai was.

They drew up a peace treaty and made it binding for ten years. They signed an agreement to maintain this truce. All of Nuşirvan's council members appeared to be satisfied with this arrangement. The grand vizier went to Hamzai and spoke softly into his ear, "Very soon our Prophet will arrive. In case I should fail to meet him, ask him on my behalf not to forget to intercede for me on the Day of Judgment."

"I shall be pleased to do that," answered Hamzai Sahip Kıran.

Hamzai and his wrestlers left Nuşirvan's palace, gathered the rest of their army, and returned to their own country. Before they departed, however,

Hamzai said to Ömer, "Go and see Mehli Nigâr and find out what she thinks about all of this."

Mehli Nigâr had already sent two maids to her father's palace to get news about whatever events had taken place. "Go and learn what has been decided and then bring news of that decision to me," she had said. Those two maids had returned to Mehli Nigâr with the news before Ömer reached her palace. They had reported, "Here is good news for you. A ten-year truce has been signed. Until that much time has passed, there will be no more warfare between the two forces."

Just a few minutes after that report had been delivered to Mehli Nigâr, Ömer Ümmiye arrived at her palace. Because her room was filled with servants, Ömer Ümmiye pretended that he was one of Nuşirvan's men. He said, "O Mehli Nigâr, inasmuch as this is a very fortunate day for our country, I have come to play my lute and recite some poetry from the Bible." He then began his recital.

After a few minutes Mehli Nigâr said to one of her servants, "Take the lute player to another room where I can ask him what he wants from me for his performance here." A few minutes later she went to the room where Ömer Ümmiye had been taken.

Ömer asked, "O princess, have you heard the news? There will be no more fighting for ten years, and I have been sent by Hamzai Sahip Kıran to discover what your feelings are about that ten-year truce."

Mehli Nigâr answered, "I have heard the news that is said to be good news, but I am now wondering if there is no compassion in the heart of Hamzai Sahip Kıran. Does his heart have any feeling at all? Does he not know that I cannot wait for ten years? I cannot repress my feelings for ten years! I cannot live without him for ten years!"

"I understand you, my princess, but be patient. Patience is a strong weapon even against sorrow over the death of someone. Even Allah exerted great patience in creating the universe in six hours, as some say, or in six days, as others say. He was capable of creating the universe in one second, but He took His time and showed great patience. I shall carry back and forth the news between the two of you every two or three days. I shall be your messenger. Hamzai really loves you more than you love him."

Mehli Nigâr then gave Ömer Ümmiye some gold and silver, which he immediately put in his pouch. As you already know, he was in love with gold and other precious things. When night came and the moon was bright, he would bury his treasure beneath the surface of the earth. But in the morning after the moon had disappeared, he could never locate the place where he had buried his gold and silver.

Leaving Mehli Nigâr, Ömer Ümmiye returned to his own country in the space of an hour. There he reported every word of Mehli Nigâr's comments to Hamzai Sahip Kıran.

The Arrival of Mohammed in This World

The coming of Mohammed[95] was now very near at hand. Hamzai Sahip Kıran and his army were now back in Mecca. They had not been there long, however, when suddenly the Kaaba was flooded with heavenly light. Three divine beams of light fell from the sky. One of them landed on the top of the Kaaba. Another was diffused from north to south.[96]

All idols but one were smashed to pieces on the night that Mohammed's soul arrived from heaven and he was born. On that night our mother, Emine,[97] saw the miracle with her own eyes. She realized that the last prophet was arriving, that the sultan of eighteen thousand lands was on his way.

Gentlemen, all idols were demolished on the night of Mohammed's birth except the idol of Satan which was on the wall of the Kaaba. Our Prophet let his name be known to everyone. He made the peoples of eighteen thousand lands hear his name. All intelligence, compassion, and awareness of justice were given to him by Allah.

(Gentlemen, we have to realize that it is a person's character rather than his handsome face which is important. Without character behind it, the handsome face means nothing. Moral qualities are of the greatest importance. Any lasting love for a person is based on that person's character and not on his appearance. Unless you have moral standards, neither your wealth nor your education will be of much use to you. They alone cannot raise you to the highest level attainable by a human being.)

In Mecca the Blessed Ebu Bekir, who was the richest person in the city,[98] went to the Prophet Mohammed's house. He was one of the first believers in Mohammed. But the supporters of Ebu Leheb[99] were throwing stones at the house; however, Ebu Bekir and his men confronted the stone throwers and protected Mohammed. Ebu Leheb, who was Mohammed's uncle, was the son of Abdül Muttalib, one of the wealthiest people then in the entire land. Why was Ebu Leheb throwing stones at the house of Mohammed? He was doing so because he was, in an important way, blind.

---

95 The narrator here refers to Mohammed as *Rahmet-ülühi* (Mercy of Allah).

96 Although the text does not say so specifically, the context would seem to suggest that the third beam of divine light bore to earth the soul of Mohammed, which had been waiting in heaven since the earliest moment of Creation.

97 Emine (*Amina* in the transliterated Arabic) was Mohammed's mother. The narrator here calls her "our mother," making her somewhat parallel in Islamic belief to Mary in Christian belief.

98 Although he did come from a well-to-do family, this is probably an exaggeration.

99 His real name was Abd al-Uzza b. Abd al-Muttalib, but in the Koran (Chapter 111, verse 11) he is designated as "Abu Lahab" (The Father of Flame). He was Mohammed's uncle but also one of his steadiest, fiercest, and most violent opponents.

He could not see the right way, even though the followers of Mohammed were increasing in number day by day. Those people who were able to see the right way became Muslims, and the Muslim religion gained strength every day.

Mohammed's mother became blind when he was seven years old.[100] She worried continuously, and that made her cry frequently. It was her crying that caused her blindness.[101] When Prophet Mohammed placed his fingers on his mother's eyes, she began seeing again. May Allah give us strength to endure all of our sorrows! Say three times, "My God of Gratitude," because one of the names of Allah is *Gratitude.*[102] The eyes of Mohammed's mother began seeing again, and everyone heard about that miracle. Ebu Leheb grew quiet about this, for he had by now grown afraid of Hamzai Sahip Kıran.

Time passed. One night another of our mothers, Sefiye,[103] had a dream. The following morning she went immediately to Mohammed and said, "O light of my life, I had a dream last night."

Mohammed responded, "May your dream be auspicious!"[104]

Gentlemen, the master barber of that whole area was named Selmani Taş. He had immigrated into Mecca from elsewhere, arriving there at a time before Ali was born. Selmani Taş became Mohammed's barber. One day when he was shaving the Prophet, he accidentally cut Mohammed's face with the razor. The barber immediately licked the blood of Mohammed. Mohammed said, "O Selmani Taş, I have good news for you. My blood has been mixed with your blood, and so you will be my neighbor in heaven."

Sitting to the left of Mohammed was a man named Mavyar. When Mavyar heard what Mohammed had said to the barber, he said quietly to Selmani, "Let me also cut his face." Taking the razor, he nicked the face of Mohammed and then licked the blood.

---

[100] According to the *Encyclopaedia of Islam*, Mohammed's mother died when he was six years old.

[101] It is a popular notion that crying will cause blindness. It appears frequently in Turkish folktales.

[102] Muslims speak of the ninety-nine names of Allah, but the word *name* here is misleading. They are actually referring to epithets which indicate qualities of Allah. The narrator here cites *Teşekkür Yarabbe* (*My God of Gratitude*). This epithet is *Al-Shakur* (*The Grateful*) in Arabic (Denny 1981: 93).

[103] This is, as the tale subsequently reveals, the mother of Ali (fourth caliph). Her actual name was Fatima (which, by coincidence, was also the name of Ali's wife). Ali's father was Abu Talib (another uncle of Mohammed).

[104] According to Turkish folk belief, it will cause bad luck to disclose the contents of one's dream until the person with whom the dreamer is speaking says, "May it be auspicious." This amounts to a taboo. There are several ATON tales in which the plot pivots upon the failure of the second person to make this ritualistic remark. See especially tales numbered 73, 417, 886, and 901.

Turning to his left, Mohammed said, "Mavyar, you have become my enemy."

Bursting into tears, Mavyar said, "Why, O light of my life? Why have I become your enemy?"

Mohammed said, "The first time I was cut, it was an accident, but you cut me deliberately. Therefore the people who are born to you will be enemies of my people." Mavyar was so shocked by this that he never married. He did not want to have children who would be the enemies of Mohammed.

Early Meccan Foes of Islam

Gentlemen, one day Ömer[105] said, "O Mohammed, give your people some dates. They are hungry." The women especially wanted dates from Mohammed, but he could not give them any, for there were none available. These people were very poor.

However, Allah created a very large date tree for Mohammed, and He sent the angel Gabriel to place it in position. Allah said, "I have created everything for you, Mohammed."

There was a large date palm tree in Mecca which had seemed to be dead for seven years. If a tree does not have any leaves or any fruit, it is useless. (And people are like trees. If they do not have children or work to help others or leave behind anything useful to humanity, they are dead trees. They are useless except as wood—like a dead tree.)

Many people had become followers of Ebu Cehl because he had control of much of the food supply in Mecca. After Mohammed had announced that he would provide the people with a great quantity of dates from the dead palm tree, thousands followed him to the tree to see if he could really do that. When Prophet Mohammed reached that tree, he touched its trunk and said, "O tree, with the permission of Allah, I want to see dates on your branches."

Ebu Cehl turned to the crowd and said, "People, watch this madman! He has lost his mind completely! He is speaking to a tree which has been dead for seven years and asking it to produce dates."

Gentlemen, that dead tree suddenly put forth leaves and became a green tree. It produced fruit. In fact, all of the branches of that tree were loaded with dates. All of Mohammed's followers were given great quantities of fruit. Then Mohammed said to the followers of Ömer, "Come! You too may have fruit. Come and take as much as you want. It is all Allah's fruit, and its supply is endless."

Gentlemen, at that time Muslim worship was carried on secretly. The prayer services were performed in hidden, underground places. Although the number of Muslims was increasing, they still worshiped secretly. Prophet

---

105 This is not the Blessed Ömer (second caliph) but Ebu Cehl, whom Behçet Mahir calls Ömer. He was an enemy of Mohammed and was killed later at the crucial Battle of Badr.

Mohammed had said, "If one of the Ömers is converted to our religion, we shall then be able to worship openly."

Besides the Ömer whose real name was Ebu Cehl, there was the Ömer now called Blessed Ömer. But at that time the Blessed Ömer had not yet become a Muslim. Instead, he was still an enemy of Islam, and many people were afraid of him, for at that time there were only two very powerful men in Mecca. One was Hamzai Sahip Kıran, and the other was this Ömer. This Ömer was at that time an ally of the other Ömer [Ebu Cehl]. That was the main reason why Muslims went into hiding to worship. Unknown to the man who would later become the Blessed Ömer, there were some Muslims within his own family. His sister and her husband and their children had seen Mohammed at a moment when his face was beaming with divine light, and they had accepted the religion of Islam.

One day Ebu Cehl called his followers together at his palace. He said to them, "We must terminate the activity of Mohammed very soon, because his religion is gaining strength every passing day." He said to [Blessed] Ömer, "If you will bring the head of Mohammed to me, I shall give you forty sacks of gold."

Ömer buckled on his sword and said, "I shall bring his head to you right away."

At that time when the Muslims were still worshiping only in seclusion, Ömer left Ebu Cehl's palace to behead Mohammed. But as Ömer set out, Gabriel appeared to Mohammed and warned him of Ömer's intention. He said, "O Mohammed, Ömer is coming to behead you."

While Ömer was proceeding in a great rush to accomplish this act, he was stopped by a man who asked, "Ömer, where are you going in such a great hurry?"

"I am going to behead Mohammed. Then I shall take his head to Ömer [Ebu Cehl]."

The man asked, "Why, Ömer?"

"Because Muslims are increasing in number and gaining strength every day."

"Oh, Ömer, this is very strange," said the man who had stopped him. "You are going to behead Mohammed, but your own sister is a Muslim." Ömer did not believe these words, and the man who had spoken them realized that. He added, "If you doubt that, kill a sheep and have your sister cook its meat for you. Then observe her to see whether she will eat any of the meat which you have brought."

"All right! I shall do that," said Ömer. He went to his sister's house, but before he could knock on the door, he heard his sister's voice as she was reading something aloud inside. His sister was reading from the Koran, and as she did so, all of the trees and all of the birds around the house had prostrated themselves at the sound of the words. Ömer listened to his sister reading for a while, and the more he listened, the more he wanted to listen. A great emotion passed through his three hundred and sixty-six veins.

Finally he knocked on the door. When his sister discovered who it was that had knocked, she quickly hid the Koran before opening the door. He said to her, "Sister, bring me a lamb." When the lamb was brought to him, he slaughtered it and told his sister to cook it.

"All right, Brother," she said.

After she had cooked the meat and prepared the table for dinner, Ömer said, "Sister, come and eat with me."

She answered, "Thank you, Brother, but I have already eaten and I am very full."

"But can't you eat even one small bite?" he asked.

(Yes, gentlemen, the meat that is slaughtered by Muslims can be eaten by everyone, but Muslims cannot eat the meat that is prepared by non-Muslims. That meat is forbidden to them by Muslim religious law. But if you are on a journey and that is the only meat you can get, then you are allowed to eat it. Or if you are in a restaurant and unknowingly eat that kind of meat, it is all right. Our religion is a very convenient religion. It has no rules that are hard to comply with. It accommodates to human needs. For example, if you are on a journey during Ramazan, you are permitted to eat even though it is a time of fasting. Then after your journey has ended, you are to fast the number of days you failed to fast during Ramazan itself. Such easy conditions cannot be found in any other religion.

[*Unidentified man in audience*: But some people eat ham while they are in Germany. What will happen to them?]

Behçet Mahir: If they eat it without knowing that it is ham, then it is no sin; if they eat it knowingly, then it is a sin. One has to go wherever necessary to earn a livelihood for one's family. You have to go anywhere in the world, with the permission of Allah, to do that. If Allah does not grant your bread to you, your hard work will not mean anything. You may work and work, earning money—even great amounts of money—but Allah can take it all away from you in a minute. We can see examples of this every day—even among people close to us.)

Now we must return to our story. When the sister of Ömer said, "I will not eat," he realized that the man he had met along the road had told him the truth about his sister. He said, "Very well, Sister. If you do not wish to eat, do not do so." He ate all the meat he could, and then he said, "Sister, when I arrived here, I listened from behind the door to what you were reading. What was it that you were reading? Where is it? Bring it to me. I should like to see it."

The woman was frightened now, and she tried to deny what she had been doing. She said, "I wasn't reading anything, Brother."

"Don't be afraid, Sister. I should like to read it myself."

"Oh, Brother, please do not kill me!"

"Sister, I shall not harm you in any way. Bring it to me so that I can read it." When his sister brought him the book,[106] he began to read it. As he read more, he began to cry. Tears were pouring from his eyes.

As this was happening, Gabriel went to Mohammed's house again. This time he said, "O my Prophet, Ömer will very soon be coming to see you. When he arrives here, you should open the door to him yourself."

"Very well," said Mohammed.

Gentlemen, love is a very powerful emotion. It can make you jump into the ocean or into a fire. It can make you sacrifice your life. After Ömer had read more of the Koran, his three hundred and sixty-six veins became filled with love of Mohammed and love of Allah. He went weeping to Mohammed's door. When he knocked on that door, Mohammed's followers were startled, but Mohammed advised them, "Don't be frightened. Sit down. I shall open the door." Bilâl the Ethiopian[107] and Ebu Bekir both wanted to go to the door and open it, but Mohammed would not permit them to do so. He said, "Sit down! I shall open the door myself, for Ömer has come to accept our religion." It was, therefore, the Blessed Mohammed who opened the door for Ömer.

When Ömer entered the building and saw the divine light shining from Mohammed's face, he cast himself, weeping, at the feet of the Prophet. He said, "Please forgive me, O light of my life."

After making Ömer rise, the Blessed Prophet hugged him tightly and took him into his heart. Holding Ömer by the hand, he guided him in taking the ritual ablution. Ömer knelt before Mohammed and said, "O Blessed Prophet, O light of my life, I did not know myself until today. Not until today did I become fully aware of what it meant to be a human being. Only today did I discover who I really am."

Mohammed said, "Oh, Ömer, from now on you will experience that same feeling every day."

Crying again, Ömer said, "Alas! All of my life until today was wasted. I used my days for nothing."

---

[106] Neither Ömer nor his sister could have been reading from the Koran in book format, for that did not exist during the lifetime of Mohammed. They could have been reciting passages then in the oral tradition, or they could possibly have been reading fragments of revelations written by Muslims listening to the Prophet. (Mohammed himself was illiterate.) The revelations which constitute the Koran began in 610 and continued into the year of Mohammed's death, 632. These were subsequently collected and put into written text around 650, during the reign of Uthman, the third caliph. "This Uthmanic recension gave the Qur'an the form in which we now have it" (Watt 1967: 9).

[107] A slave who was one of the earliest admirers of Mohammed, he was persecuted severely for his support of Islam. Ebu Bekir purchased Bilâl at a high price and then gave him his freedom. He died in 641.

"Don't cry, Ömer," said the Blessed Mohammed. "Allah will forgive a thousand bad hours for one good hour."

(Yes, gentlemen, Allah can pardon you. If you find yourself in a situation where you cannot succeed no matter how hard you may try, the only advantageous step that you can take is to extricate yourself from the whole matter as soon as possible.)

Time passed, and the hour for the morning prayer service was approaching. Ebu Cehl kept thinking that it would not be long before Ömer brought to him the head of Mohammed.

When the hour arrived for the morning prayer service, Bilâl the Ethiopian prepared to go underground to chant the *ezan* and call the worshipers together. When Ömer saw him starting to do this, he asked, "Where are you going?" Bilâl explained the situation to him. After listening carefully to this explanation, Ömer said, "There is no longer any need for you to go underground. There is no longer any need to hide. Come with me to the roof, and you can issue the call to prayer from there."

"If we do that," said Bilâl, "they will throw stones and shoot arrows at us."

"Don't worry, Bilâl, for I shall be with you, and as a result, no one will find the courage to harm you." Ömer drew his sword and stood close to Bilâl the Ethiopian so that nobody would be able to get very close to him. On that morning Allah gave Bilâl the Ethiopian a uniquely beautiful voice. No one had ever heard anything like it before. Bilâl's heart was filled with love of Allah as he sang the *ezan*.

People of the tribe of Huriş were awakened that morning by the sound of the *ezan*. They poured forth from their houses in great confusion. Once outside they saw Bilâl the Ethiopian singing on the roof, and they heard his divinely inspired voice. They also saw Ömer standing beside him with his sword drawn. No one dared approach them to do them any harm because of the fear of Ömer. A few people threw stones at the house, but only from a great distance.

As you will remember, gentlemen, Mohammed had said earlier, "If one of the Ömers accepts the Muslim religion, we shall be able to appeal to other people openly in public places." After Ömer had become a Muslim, many other people did the same thing. And in that way Islam began to spread out rapidly.

Ebu Cehl was unable to do anything to change this course of events. He said to himself, "I shall have to go to the Fortress of Wealth."[108] Christian people from all over the world used to come to visit with the commander of that fortress, a man named Habib.[109] He was a very wise

108 Whether historical or imaginary, this fortress has no identity beyond its name.

109 Equally undocumented is the character Habib. There was a Habib who was a distinguished contemporary of Mohammed—he was only seventeen years old when the Prophet died—but he

scholar of the Christian community. He had read all of the Bible carefully, and he was a very learned man.

Ebu Cehl and half the people of Mecca went to Habib's fortress. Gentlemen, the events in stories roll swiftly off the tongues of narrators, but it took days and nights before these people reached that fortress. When Habib's men reported to him that Ebu Cehl and half the population of Mecca were arriving at the fortress, the commander ordered that they be properly welcomed. From his reading in the Bible, Ebul Cehl knew that Mohammed would be the last of the prophets.[110] Gentlemen, there were four divine books revealed to mankind from heaven. Three of them were revealed to Jews and Christians,[111] but the fourth, the Koran, was for us. The richness of the Koran was worth that of the other three books combined. Habib knew about and read all of these books.

Ebu Cehl and his people were welcomed at the Fortress of Wealth. There they prepared beds for Ebu Cehl and his men, for Ebu Cehl was a powerful and a very influential man. After dinner Ebu Cehl said to his host, "I have come here to consult with you about a very important problem."

When Habib heard this statement, he gathered all of his advisors there, and he then said to Ebu Cehl, "Tell us your problem. We shall listen as a group, and as a group we shall try to find a solution for it."

Ebu Cehl then began to explain to them the situation that concerned him. He began by saying, "His name is Mohammed." (Look, look, gentlemen, and listen! If Allah favors you, He causes even your enemies to speak well of you. After a while you will realize why I am saying this.) Ebu Cehl continued his comments. "He has a very appealing personality. He never tells lies but only the truth. He does nothing evil or unjust."

(Gentlemen, the most important principle in the Muslim religion is truth. If a man's word does not express the truth, the man's heart does not contain justice. Our mother told us, "Your words and your heart should reflect the truth always.")

---

fitted the description of Behçet Mahir's Habib in only one respect: he was—actually *was to become*—a powerful general. However, he was neither a Christian nor a friend of Christians. Quite the contrary, much of his military reputation was earned by his devastating attacks against Christian Armenians and Christian Byzantines. So effective were his incursions against the Byzantine Empire that he was honored with the title *Habib of Byzantium* (Fück 1971: 12).

110 This is a cherished folk belief in Turkey. There is not, however, any passage in the Bible which foretells the coming of a final prophet, Mohammed.

111 Although the entire Koran is said to have been revealed by the Deity, only parts of the Bible were derived from revelation. The three "revealed" Hebrew scriptures referred to by Behçet Mahir and other narrators are said to be the Old Testament (*Tevrat*), the Psalms of David (*Zebur*), and the New Testament (*İncil*). See the comments of another narrator on this subject in ATON tale No. 493. Although numerous fragments of the Old Testament appear in the Koran, uneducated Turks have only a vague comprehension of the contents of that work. Here the Psalms of David are set apart from the Old Testament. Sometimes the Pentateuch is given independent status as The Book of Moses.

Habib was taking notes all the while that Ebu Cehl was speaking. Ebul Cehl added, "He is also a very handsome being."

(Gentlemen, if you are a believer, you will also be handsome. Men of great faith speak so pleasantly that their listeners think, "I do not want to eat or drink but simply to listen to these words." Believers are able to chat in such an engaging way that conversation with them is always pleasant.)

Habib asked, "How tall is he?" Then, after Ebu Cehl had described Mohammed's height and appearance, Habib asked, "Does he have compassion?"

Ebu Cehl answered, "There is no more compassionate man in the world than he. He is so compassionate that if someone asked him to cut himself, he would do so out of compassion for that person."

Habib opened his Bible and examined certain parts of it. Everything that Ebu Cehl had said about Mohammed conformed exactly with accounts that were in the Bible.

[At this point an unidentified listener addressed a question to the narrator. He was, however, so far from the microphone that his query is not audible on the tape. It may in part be inferred from the narrator's answer.]

Behçet Mahir: I shall try to answer your question. Allah himself once wished to test Mohammed's compassion. He called the angels Michael and Israfel[112] to Him. Then He said, "Michael, I want you to become a pigeon. Then fly to Mohammed's window and place yourself under his arm.[113] Israfel, you are to become a hunter who will go there and demand your prey from Mohammed."

The pigeon flew to Mohammed's window and began speaking to the Prophet. He said, "O Mohammed, light of my life, please protect me!"

After a short while the hunter arrived and said, "O light of my life, give me back my prey."

Mohammed answered, "Please relinquish your prey this time and give it to me."

---

112 Israfel (or Israfil) is a Muslim archangel so huge that his head can enter heaven while his feet stand on the seventh level below the earth. He serves as an announcer, relaying the decrees of Allah to the appropriate other angels while remaining in constant readiness to blow his trumpet to announce the arrival of Judgment Day. In the latter capacity he assumes a responsibility assigned to Gabriel in Judeo-Christian angelology. His entire body is covered with mouths and tongues, which symbolize his communicative activities. He it was who tutored Mohammed for three years to prepare him to receive the message of the Koran from Allah, a message borne to the Prophet by the archangel Gabriel. Israfel was thrice daily overcome with grief and tears at the prospect of human beings in hell. It may have been his compassion which led the Deity to select him for participation in this episode.

113 This is a figurative expression for being protected or supported by someone with superior wealth or power.

But the hunter replied, "O Mohammed, this is my family's livelihood. I cannot give up my family's daily food."

Mohammed said, "Get a sheep for your family's food. This pigeon requested my protection."

The hunter said, "No, I cannot do that. But if you will give me a piece of your own flesh, I shall accept that in exchange for this pigeon."

Mohammed said, "Very well! I shall give you some flesh from my own body in exchange for this pigeon." Saying that, he picked up a knife and was just about to cut himself when he was stopped by Israfel.

Israfel said, "O light of my life, don't cut yourself! Don't! Allah simply wished to test your compassion, and He sent us to do that testing."

(Gentlemen, I am seventy years old and I have been telling this story for fifty years. Today is today; this hour is this hour. The past does not return. Once it has gone, it is gone forever.)

Ebu Cehl told Habib and his men about the Blessed Mohammed. When Ebu Cehl had finished his comments, Habib said, "You have answered my questions. You reported that he would not tell lies, and that is a great credit to him. Then you indicated that he was a just and compassionate man."

"Yes," said Ebu Cehl, "and all of my words were accurate. You asked me about Mohammed, and I told you the truth about him."

"All right," said Habib. "Now collect your men to return to Mecca, and I shall go along with you. I should like to see this man with my own eyes. I shall also collect my soldiers, and we shall all go to Mecca together. I shall test Mohammed to see if you are really telling the truth about him."

"All right, but be aware of what is going on in Mecca," said Ebu Cehl. "Half of the people of Mecca are believers in his religion. The other half are my people, who have chosen to block what he is doing."

Mohammed Performs Miracles

They all went to Mecca, where Habib invited all of the people to witness his testing of Mohammed. They came from all directions to see this spectacle. Habib had an infant daughter who lacked eyesight and had withered arms and legs. She looked like a pile of lifeless flesh. Everyone knew that Habib had a daughter, but only Allah, Habib, and his wife knew how abnormal she was. Inasmuch as Habib felt embarrassed about her condition, he had never said a word about it to anyone. To himself he said, "I shall take my daughter to Mohammed. If he is really a holy man, he will be able to change her condition so that she will become a normal human being." Ebu Cehl had told Habib how very powerful Mohammed was.

When the large group went to Mecca, Habib took his wife and daughter along too. Habib had read in the Bible that soon the last prophet would arrive. He said to himself, "I shall ask him some questions and determine whether or not he is the last prophet."

Those people of Mecca who believed in Mohammed were of the Haşimi clan, and the other half of the people of Mecca were of the Hurişi clan. Tents were pitched, and Habib's wife and daughter were placed inside one of those tents. Habib allowed no one else to enter that tent but himself, for he did not wish anyone else to know about the condition of his daughter.

After dinner had been eaten, the Blessed Mohammed was called. He went to Habib's tent, where Ebu Cehl was sitting alongside the commander of the Fortress of Wealth. As soon as Habib saw Mohammed, he immediately arose and welcomed him. He had the Prophet sit down beside him, but this politeness of Habib to Mohammed infuriated Ebu Cehl. He could not understand it.

After they had talked in a light manner for some time, Habib said to Mohammed, "I have heard that you founded a new religion and that you are spreading it in every direction. I have also been told that you have cursed our churches and our idols, saying that our idols could not be gods."

Mohammed answered, "Yes, there is only one god, Allah, Who created our universe. He gives life, and He also takes life away. Your idols, like fire and like the ocean, were all created by Allah."

Habib replied, "Very well, then. I respect your religion. It is your religion and your god."

Mohammed disagreed with this. He said, "No, He is not only my god but also yours, for He created you too. Your idols cannot create any living thing, nor can they perform miracles. Allah created you from nothing. Your way of thinking is the wrong way. The right way follows Allah's directions."

Habib answered, "It may be so, but to prove it, you are requested to do something for me, and I want everyone here to observe you doing it. If you are really telling the truth, and if your god is as powerful as you say he is, then you should be able, with his help, to do almost anything. I want you to bring both the moon and the sun down from the sky. Then you are to split the moon into two moons. One of them is to go to the south and the other to the north. After that you will reunite them into one moon again. And while you are doing this, the whole world will be observing you."

"All right," answered Mohammed. "If Allah is with me, He will not allow any obstacle to hinder me from doing that."

During the previous night Gabriel had visited Mohammed, who was rather sad at the time. Gabriel said, "Mohammed, do not be sad! O brother, Allah sent His greetings to you. He said, 'Tell my beloved Mohammed not to be sad and not to worry. He may request from Me anything that he wishes.'"

Mohammed was greatly cheered by these words of Gabriel, and he remembered those words when he was asked by Habib to perform a great miracle. He climbed the nearby Kureyiz mountain.[114] Not only the people of Mecca but also the people of the whole world would witness what he would do, for they would see the same sun and the same moon. He called out to those near him, "Do not be frightened!" He then looked upward and said, "O Sultan of the sky and earth, I want the sun and moon." It was noontime by then, but suddenly it grew dark everywhere. The sky was no longer visible. The sun had gone from the sky to the chest of Mohammed, where it remained for some time. Not just Habib but also everyone else observed that miracle. Later the sun returned to its place in the sky. That night he called to the moon, saying, "Come, come!" Again it grew dark everywhere. The moon, now split into halves, went to Mohammed, one piece to his left arm and the other to his right. Then, when he said, "Return to your regular place," the two halves reunited and went back to the sky. All of the people observed these miracles.

After Habib had witnessed these events, he turned to Ebu Cehl and said, "Boo[115] to you, Ebu Cehl! How could you fail to see his power? Why didn't you believe in him? These miracles are written about in the Bible. If the sun and moon were both under his spell, how could you have any doubt about his being a prophet?" Then turning toward the mountain, he called, "Do not come to me, Mohammed! I shall come to you!" Going then to Kureyiz Mountain, he prostrated himself before Mohammed and said, "O Mohammed, may anyone who looks at you with evil intentions have his eyes blinded! Even your enemy Ebu Cehl praised you greatly. O Blessed Mohammed, I have just one more request to make of you."

"What is it, Habib?"

"Come with me to my tent, and I shall explain my wish to you there. If I explain my request here, everyone will hear it." Habib led him to the tent where his daughter was sleeping. With her were her mother and Habib's brother, who had one blind eye. Habib said to those in the tent, "Come and accept the religion of Mohammed and kiss his hand." Then, turning to the Prophet again, he said, "O Mohammed, let me pull back this blanket. I have a daughter here who lacks eyesight and has shrunken arms and legs. Only I, my family, and Allah know about this. Can you cure her?"

"I shall ask Allah about this," answered Mohammed. "If He wills it, we can do it. All strength comes from Him." Placing his right hand on the girl's forehead, he said, "*Bismillahirrahmanirrahim.*"[116]

---

[114] Apparently in one of the outskirts of Mecca where the Hurişi clan lived.

[115] The most common Turkish word for *boo* is *yuha*. The narrator here uses *tuu*.

[116] *Bismillahirrahmanirrahim*, the opening expression of the Koran, means "In the name of Allah the Compassionate, the Merciful." By extension it is thought to be the appropriate remark to be made at the beginning of any undertaking in order to insure its success. Besides the pious sentiment it voices, the expression calls attention to the fact that the speaker is

The eyes of the girl were suddenly opened. Then her arms and legs were restored. Although she was only a three-or-five-month-old[117] baby, she started speaking and said, "O Mohammed, you are the last of the prophets."

When Habib saw this, he took Mohammed's hand and said, "Forgive me! I did not believe that you could do that. May the eyes that don't believe the miracles you perform be blinded."

Then Habib's brother spoke up, saying, "Mohammed, one of my eyes was blinded in an accident. Please place your blessed right hand on my eyes too."

After he had placed his right hand on the man's eyes, Mohammed said, "*Bismillah.*" Immediately the blind eye of Habib's brother began once again to see.

Nobody from the outside saw what happened in the tent of Habib's family. It was all kept secret. But people observed that the blind eye of Habib's brother had been healed. They saw the results of what had happened.

But even after this evidence of Mohammed's favor in the sight of Allah, Ebu Cehl went on saying that the man was no more than a magician. His eyes were blind in a different way. He could see clearly the divinely inspired power of Mohammed, but he did not believe what he saw. His family home in Mecca has now become a latrine. Yes, it became a latrine.

Habib and his army returned to their own country. Soon after that the number of Muslims increased rapidly and steadily. Habib permitted his people to become Muslims, and the Muslim world expanded more and more. The voice of Islam was heard from north to south.

Hamzai Accepts His Fated Role as Giant Slayer

Now we shall give the news about Hamzai Sahip Kıran. Time passed rapidly, and the first seven years of the truce had been completed, but Hamzai Sahip Kıran had granted Nuşirvan an additional three years. He had offered a ten-year armistice to Nuşirvan. Now let us turn to the Mirror of Fate[118] and find out what we can see in it.

Gentlemen, the people who lived in this world before our time often had greater difficulties than those we experience. One day a man entered the

---

auspiciously starting a venture with the name of the Deity. For everyday occasions the term is often shortened to *Bismillah.*

117 The Turkish expression *three or five* is rarely meant literally. It does not indicate any specific number but can mean *a couple*, *a few*, or *a small number*.

118 Few objects have had more folklore generated about them than has the mirror. Middle Eastern literatures and mysticism are filled with mirrors, real and figurative. For an analysis of the concept of the world as a mirror of God's will, see Chapter 3 of *Mystique et poésie* . . . (Vitray-Meyerovich 1972). For a discussion of the mirror in Middle Eastern religious art, consult Chapter 6 of *The Feather of Simurgh* . . . (Bürgel 1988).

central mosque[119] and said, "O light of my life, when most of the giants were killed, why were three of those infidel, demonic creatures spared?"

When Solomon, the son of David, was on his throne, he said to the three infidel giants, "I could have had you smashed to pieces except for the fact that Allah had already assigned the power of controlling your fates to three Arabs." The fate of the first one, the Red Giant, had been assigned to Hamzai Sahip Kıran. The fate of the second, the Kasır[120] Giant, had been put in the control of İmam Ali.[121] And the fate of the third, the Black Giant, had been given over to Çirman Shah.[122]

But later, in the time of the Prophet, people began complaining about the abuses they were suffering at the hands of the Red Giant. They said to the Prophet Mohammed, "This giant cuts off our sources of water. He has taken many people from among us, people whom he either eats or enslaves. Help us, O Mohammed! Help us!"

As Prophet Mohammed was gazing at the faces of the men around him, Hamzai Sahip Kıran jumped to his feet. He said to the Prophet, "My master, order me to do so, and I shall go and kill him."

The Prophet answered, "Hamzai, Allah made you stand up, and Allah made you say what you said. I cannot, therefore, tell you to sit down, nor can I tell you to go. Orders come from Allah. You are older than I, and you are my uncle. You have received your orders from Allah, not from me."

When Hamzai Sahip Kıran buckled on his sword, one of those who had been seated near him asked, "How many days will you be gone, Hamzai? How long will it be before you are back here with us again?"

Hamzai answered, "I shall be back in seventeen days." But because he failed to say *İnşallah*,[123] Allah turned each one of the days he thought he

---

[119] For *mosque* the narrator here, atypically, uses *mescit*, derived from the Arabic *masjdid*. In Turkey the most commonly used word for that public structure is *cami*. *Mescit* more often refers to a small, private mosque incorporated into a palace or into the home of a wealthy person.

[120] This giant may have been named after the place where he lived. Kasır is a town in Turkey's Mardin Province, at the 48th degree east longitude and the 11th parallel north latitude. It is just five kilometers from the Syrian border.

[121] An *imam* is the leader of the Muslim prayer service. Although he was later to have the much more prestigious title of *caliph*, Ali in his younger years is often referred to in Turkish folktales as *imam*.

[122] Kirman is a province of Iran, and Kirmanşah is its capital. A leader named Kirman Shah is the protagonist of a long heroic romance. Behçet Mahir's version of that romance is ATON tale No. 1699. Although he did not usually do so, Behçet Mahir here used the sound *Ç* (English *ch*) for the sound *K*. This pronunciation is not uncommon in extreme eastern Turkey, especially among people influenced by the Azeri branch of the Turkic language. Although the narrator referred to his three giant killers as Arabs, Kirman Shah was Persian (Iranian) rather than Arabian.

[123] See Note 48.

A 1961 taping session that failed at a coffeehouse in the mountain town of Nallıhan, Ankara Province. Seconds after the picture was taken, the narrator, Ali Bahar, fled in panic. He had suddenly decided that the collector, Warren Walker, had an evil eye.

İsmail Doğan telling tales in field where wheat had just been harvested, August 1964. Doğan was the *muhtar* (headman) of the village of Çetme in Kastamonu Province.

would be away into a year! (That is the reason I request that you say *inşallah* for everything that you wish to do. You must remember Allah's name and say *inşallah* ! You must also start doing anything only after first saying *Bismillah.* If you undertake to do anything—even to eat—first say *Bismillah*, for the virtue of *Bismillah* is great. Even before you start reading or reciting from the Koran, you should say *Bismillah.*)

Hamzai traveled night and day until he finally entered the area where the fortress of the Red Giant was located. But because everything is under the dome of Allah, it does not matter how far you go. You will always remain under that dome.

(One day I went to call upon Zinci Ağa.[124] I found him outside staring at the sky. He was a very much respected man who liked me, and so I did not interrupt him but stood patiently near him for thirty minutes. When he noticed me after a while, he said, "Oh, Mahir, come here and sit down with me! *Aleykümselam!*"[125]

He ordered tea, and after we had finished drinking that tea, I asked him, "Zinci Ağa, why were you standing with your head back looking upward for so long?"

He answered, "I was looking at the dome of Allah. Did you guess why I was doing that?"

"Yes," I answered. "I stood by your side for thirty minutes and I thought that you were probably looking at the dome of the sky and comparing it with the mere man-made domes."

He said to me, "Mahir, you are very intelligent. I was indeed looking at Allah's dome and comparing it with those domes made by human beings."

We talked with each other for some time. There were three men with whom I used to talk at length in those days. We used to tell our problems and our concerns to each other. These men were Zinci Ağa, Kindar Hakkı Efendi, and a dervish named Hacı[126] Mehmet Baba,[127] who used to sell soap. When we shared our concerns, we spoke openly and never concealed

---

124 An *ağa*—*agha* in English—is a rural landholder, often affluent, sometimes very influential. It is not a hereditary title. The word *ağa* is also used in a different context. It is frequently a term of politeness or flattery added to a man's first name, as it is here.

125 *Selamünaleyküm/Aleykümselam*—a traditional exchange of greetings between Muslims not well acquainted or who have not seen each other for some time. It means *May peace be unto you/May peace be unto you also*. If *Selamünaleyküm* is not responded to, the speaker should be wary of the one so addressed. Only the response is given here. Perhaps Zinci Ağa simply assumed that the initial greeting had been made but had gone unnoticed by him.

126 The *hac* is the pilgrimage to the sacred city of Mecca, and a *hacı* is a person who has completed that pilgrimage. One who has returned from that religious journey—formerly arduous and very expensive for many Muslims—has this honorific prefixed automatically and permanently to his or her first name.

127 *Baba*, meaning *father*, is often used as a term of respect for an older man.

any of the details. All three of them passed away and are beneath the surface of the earth. I am the only survivor of our group.)

Hamzai traveled day and night to reach the Red Giant. At one point along his way he saw an old man standing by the side of the road. Gazing at this old man, Hamzai thought, "Alas, neither human being nor jinn lives in this desolate area. Why, then, should there be an old man standing here?" He dismounted and started to walk toward the old man.

But the old man said, "Stop, Hamzai! Stay where you are. I should be the one to come to you!" That old man was the Blessed Hızır.[128]

"How did he know my name?" Hamzai asked himself.

The Blessed Grandfatherly Patron Saint[129] went to Hamzai and kissed his eyes.[130] He then said, "Thanks be to Allah, I have kissed the eyes which have looked upon the Prophet Mohammed."

(Someone once asked Prophet Mohammed, "O Mohammed, is there really someone named Hızır?"

Mohammed answered, "Yes, Hızır really exists, but he is not seen by everyone. He remains invisible much of the time. He often goes to the rescue of those in deep distress.")

Hızır said to Hamzai, "When you return, tell our Prophet not to forget to serve as my intercessor on the Day of Judgment.—Oh, Hamzai, because you failed to say *inşallah*, Allah lengthened your journey from seventeen days to seventeen years. But I have prayed for you, requesting that Allah keep you from ever feeling fatigue, hunger, or thirst." Having spoken in this way, the old man suddenly vanished.

Between this evening and tomorrow evening when we meet again, all of the seventeen years of Hamzai's punishment will have passed. We shall stop telling the story for now, and we shall continue it tomorrow evening.

---

128 Once a water deity and fertility god—and still both those figures to many farmers in southern Turkey—Hızır is more widely known now as a granter of wishes, a last-minute rescuer from disaster, and a special messenger and agent of Allah. In these latter three functions he appears frequently in Turkish folktales. Not mentioned by name in the original Koran, he had a chapter of the work later named after him. He is assumed to be the person instructing Moses in Chapter 18 of the Koran, where he is referred to by Allah simply as "our servant." *Hıdrellez* (May 6) is a day honoring Hızır (Walker and Uysal 1973).

129 The narrator's words here are *Hazreti Piri Dede.*

130 A younger person may show respect for an older person by kissing his/her hands and/or feet. An older person may show affection for or approval of a child or anyone his/her junior by "kissing the eyes" of the younger person. Actually it is the eyelids, not the eyes, that are kissed.

Fourth night; narration of January 12, 1977

Before I return to our story, I wish to recite for you some additional quatrains of the late Summani Father.

A dirty dungeon is our earthly life.
In all my views of it I but see filth,
Both in our errors and our better deeds;
In everything the blots and stains prevail.

Tyrants attack Islam without rebuff.
Both left and right betray the virtuous man.
With gardeners thieves, the garden yields no fruit.
Thus honor fades, replaced by ugly blots.

Our scholars fail to give each other aid.
They fail to offer or to seek advice.
The artisan neglects to use his skills,
And every craft and trade is smudged with spots.

With every passing day our lot grows worse.
There is no remedy for all its ills.
In misery the poor endure their plight,
While rotted wisdom sullies all our thoughts.

[In the last two quatrains it is Behçet Mahir, not Summani, who continues this jeremiad.]

Behçet laments the failure of our youth,
Who curse the past but shun the present need,
Who cannot know their sterile age will bear
But empty days, the heirs of all their ways.

Declining Summani foretold our lot,
Foresaw our workers' sloth and negligence,
Guessed at the vapid sermons preached to us,
Anticipated all our blemishment.

Gentlemen, please begin to quiet down. As you can see, in all this noise I have almost forgotten what I was going to say. If someone is speaking, it is proper to listen and discover what he has to say. Whether he says good things or bad things, listen to everything he says, and then keep those thoughts that may be useful to you and leave the rest behind. Let me also say that moving new thoughts through your mind may in itself be beneficial. If water stands in the same place over a long period of time, it may eventually develop a very bad smell.

Fated Marriage of Hamzai to Mine Hatun

Yes, Hamzai Sahip Kıran had been continuing on his way. After a while he came into view of a fortress which belonged to Firdevs Shah.[131] The guards at the gate reported to Firdevs Shah, "There is a rider approaching. He and his horse are each more magnificent than the other."[132] This Firdevs Shah had dreamed of the Prophet Mohammed, and on the strength of that dream, he and all his people had become Muslims. He believed in Allah with all his heart, and he accepted Mohammed as the last prophet. Firdevs had only one child, a daughter named Mine Hatun.[133] Firdevs Shah said to some of his men, "Go and find out who that rider is."

Those men went to Hamzai Sahip Kıran and asked, "Hey, stranger, who are you? Where have you come from, and where are you going?"

Hamzai Sahip Kıran answered them with a question of his own: "Who sent you to me?"

"The shah of this fortress sent us."

"What is his name?" asked Hamzai.

The soldiers replied, "His name is Firdevs Shah."

Hamzai then said, "Go and tell him that I have come from Mecca and that I have no interest in his fortress. I am only passing through this land, and I shall continue on my journey." When they again asked him his name, he answered, "I am Hamzai Sahip Kıran."

Firdevs Shah had heard that Hamzai Sahip Kıran was going to be in that area at about that time. He said to his men, "He is the uncle of the Prophet Mohammed. Go back to him and make him very welcome here." The soldiers did as Firdevs Shah had ordered, and they welcomed Hamzai Sahip Kıran with great respect.

---

131 Not identified as an historical person.

132 This is a commonly used paradox in Turkish tales, especially for distinguishing degrees of beauty. When a group of attractive girls is described, its members are "each more beautiful than all the others."

133 *Hatun* is probably not part of the girl's name but rather a term of respect. *Hatun* seems to be an earlier form of *hanım*, meaning *lady*. It appears in Seljuk Turkish records of the 11th to 13th centuries.

When Hamzai was brought into the presence of the owner of that fortress, Firdevs Shah said to him, "I have just one child, a beloved[134] daughter. I should like to join my family to yours by having her married to you."

This stunned Hamzai Sahip Kıran, who said to himself, "I did not even mention his daughter, but here he suddenly offers to give her to me in marriage!" After a few moments, he said to Firdevs Shah, "Thank you, but please give me some time to think about this proposal."

When night came and everyone else in the fortress had gone to bed, Hamzai Sahip Kıran took his ritual ablutions and performed four *rekats*[135] of prayer service. Shortly after he had gone to bed, he had a dream in which the Prophet Mohammed spoke to him: "Hamzai, take Firdevs' daughter as a wife. It is your fate to do so, and your offspring from that marriage will bring great benefit to you." Upon hearing this, Hamzai jumped from his bed, renewed his ablutions, and performed four more *rekats* of prayer.

In the morning Firdevs Shah went to Hamzai's room and asked him, "What do you have to say about my offer?"

Hamzai answered, "I have nothing to say about it, but someone far more important than I did. In a dream last night, I received the answer to your question. If you give your daughter to me, I shall accept her, but I must tell you first that I am deeply in love with Mehli Nigâr, the daughter of Nuşirvan."

Firdevs said, "That is all right, Hamzai Sahip Kıran."

The two were married according to the custom of the day, and after sherbet had been drunk, he entered the bridal chamber with the daughter of Firdevs Shah before he did with the daughter of Nuşirvan, Mehli Nigâr.

On the following day, Hamzai Sahip Kıran said to his father-in-law, "O Firdevs Shah, I am on a mission which I still have to complete. With your permission, I should like to leave now." After securing that permission, he

---

134 The father does not actually use the Turkish equivalent of *beloved*. He expresses his affection for his daughter by describing her as "a corner of his liver" (*ciğerimin köşesi*). See Note 62.

135 Besides its verbal and spiritual elements, a Muslim prayer service includes considerable physical movement and gesture. Starting from a standing position, the worshiper bends forward, placing his hands on his thighs; he then moves to a kneeling position; and he finally presses his forehead to the floor. The movements are then reversed, and when the worshiper is again standing, he has completed one *rekat*. When the prayer service is held in a mosque, all of this movement is made under the direction of the prayer leader, the *imam*. Completion of a *rekat* takes from 2.5 to 3 minutes. The number of required *rekats* varies for different kinds of services. At a high point of Ramazan, the *teravih* service has thirty-three *rekats*. Before praying, one is required to take ritual ablutions. The worshiper must wash—just water, no soap—three times his/her hands, face, eyes, ears, nose, mouth and feet. To facilitate this process of purification, each mosque yard is equipped with several faucets which flow into marble drainage basins.

said to Mine Hatun, "My beloved wife, if we have a daughter, you may name her what you wish; but if we have a son, I want him to be named Hamzai Yunan." He then departed from the fortress of Firdevs Shah.

Mine Hatun was pregnant, and Hamzai Sahip Kıran continued on his journey. After nine months, nine days, and nine hours,[136] Mine Hatun gave birth to a child. It was a boy, and Mine Hatun named him Hamzai Yunan. While the child is growing, let us turn to the activities of Hamzai Sahip Kıran.

The Lessons of Two Gardens

After another year had passed, Hamzai reached the Garden of Solomon, son of David. There he saw a sign addressed to him which said, "O my beloved child, remember me to the last prophet. Give him my greetings, and tell the Prophet Mohammed not to withhold his intercession on my behalf on the day of the Last Judgment. O Hamzai, I was here long before you, and I had seven large stones placed here to be cast by seven different heroes. The first three stones have already been cast, and the fourth is for you to throw. After you leave here there will be three more visitors to this garden, each of whom will cast the stone left here specifically for him. These stones were assigned to different people according to their respective ages and strengths.[137] Oh, son Hamzai, do not be overly influenced by your power. I ruled this land long before you entered the world, and I can tell you that at the end of this mortal life is death. Live all your life until the very last day of it, doing good deeds. Do not leave the way of Allah.

"After you have left this garden, you will travel for three days, at which time you will enter another garden, the Garden of Allah's Wisdom. That Garden of Allah's Wisdom does not look at all like my garden. You will see many different things there. When you blink your eyes after your arrival there, you will see a sign, which you will be able to read."

Hamzai looked along the right side of the garden and saw where the seven stones had been placed. He saw that three of the stones had already been removed and that his own name was on the fourth. Picking up that fourth stone, he threw it, saying, "O my great Allah, You are mighty. You are able to do everything."

---

136 According to a folk formula, human gestation lasts for nine months, nine days, nine hours, nine minutes, and nine seconds. This appears in several ATON tales. Here only the first three units of time are cited.

137 What is the meaning of the casting of these large stones? Who are the other six stone casters? The context seems to suggest that the seven stones represented fated commitments of seven individuals. Why should these stones be in the Garden of Solomon rather than in any other place? The answer to this last question may lie in the great attraction Solomon held for Behçet Mahir. He mentions Solomon in several of his tales, and he has already referred to him earlier in this tale.

Then Hamzai Sahip Kıran remounted his horse, Askeri Devzade, and rode on steadily for three days. On the fourth day he came to a garden with a sign on the gate which read "Garden of Allah's Wisdom." Dismounting from Askeri Devzade, he said to himself, "I cannot very well enter this garden with my horse."

Before he entered the garden, however, he saw by the gate a pregnant dog whose puppies, though still in the womb, were barking at him. Hamzai thought, "O Allah, what kind of situation is this? Although the puppies are not yet even born, they are barking at me!" After entering the garden, the first thing that he observed was a set of forty pomegranates, thirty-nine of which were hollow, and the fortieth was only half full. As he passed the pomegranate tree, he said, "O Allah, what kind of wisdom of Yours is this?" Then he saw a group of people sitting around two large pieces of meat, one of which was *helâl* [permitted] for human beings and the other was *haram* [forbidden]. For some reason which he did not understand, all of the people were eating only the forbidden meat. Then he came to a fire over which were hung three cauldrons. The two cauldrons on the outer edge of the fire were full of something which was boiling. The center cauldron was empty, though the fire beneath it was burning furiously. After he had walked a little farther, he came upon a man who was struggling to lift a large bundle of wood. Because the bundle was too heavy for him, he could not lift it, but in spite of that, he kept adding piece after piece of wood to the top of the bundle. Then with the additional weight on the bundle, he again tried in vain to lift it. Passing on, Hamzai came to a bird which was reciting the Koran as it pecked a tree. Next he came to a group of people who were crying and begging something from a beautiful young lady seated upon a throne, but the young lady just looked past the people and laughed. Finally, he came upon a camel, into the open mouth of which the water of the ocean was flowing.

When Hamzai Sahip Kıran blinked his eyes, he found himself outside the garden and standing beside his horse. Then he noticed nearby a large sign upon which were written explanations of all of the things he had witnessed in the garden. This sign read, "Hamzai Sahip Kıran, you first saw a pregnant dog whose puppies were barking at you from their mother's womb. That represents the fact that the younger generation will one day no longer have any respect for its elders. It will fail to speak properly or behave courteously. The pomegranates were meant to show that eventually thirty-nine out of every forty people will be completely lacking in religious faith, and the fortieth will be only a halfway believer. [Behçet Mahir addressing the coffeehouse audience, quite outside this interpolated story, said, "May Allah keep us from ever seeing such days!" Several listeners responded, "Amen! Amen!"] The third thing that you saw was a group of people eating forbidden meat. This represents the unfaithfulness of men who leave their wives and consort with other women. In doing so, they are forsaking what is permitted and indulging in what is forbidden. The fourth thing you observed was the set of three cauldrons. The two full cauldrons stand for rich people, and the overheated empty cauldron between them stands for the poor, who will burn with hunger and suffer even as they stand between wealthy people. The fifth spectacle you beheld was that of a man trying unsuccessfully to lift a very heavy load of wood and yet adding still more wood to the load. This indicates that we shall see the time when people will not only sin from dawn to dark but will also fail to repent for their sins. The seventh scene showed a bird reciting the Koran but at the same time pecking away at a tree. This represents the preacher who will include in his sermons the virtue and high morality of the Koran but who will himself later engage in sin. He illustrates the fact that knowledge without sincere belief is not enough. The eighth scene pictured a beautiful young woman seated upon a throne and ignoring those who were begging her for help. The world seems as attractive as that beautiful young lady, but, like her, it will smile at us and lead us astray. It will give us the impression that there is no death, no eventual ending. Finally you saw a camel that was trying to drink an ocean of water. That camel was like those people who are never satisfied with what they have in this world. They always want more, more, more."

Hamzai blinked his eyes again, and both the sign and the garden disappeared. Hamzai then continued on his way. After a while he saw again the old man, Grandfather Hızır. He immediately dismounted from his horse, Askeri Devzade, and embraced the old man. Grandfather Hızır then said, "My beloved son, you are now getting quite close to your destination, but from this point forward you will have to be committed to your faith with all your heart. You must believe in and trust Allah completely. If you encounter difficulties, you must discover their solution from Allah. Allah is even closer to you than you are to yourself!" The Patron Grandfather gave him this advice and said, "I am leaving you in the care of Allah." Hızır then vanished.

Hamzai's Pursuit of the Red Giant

Gentlemen, now let us hear some information about the tyrannical giant. Solomon, son of David, had known this giant long before this time, and he had said to the giant, "I could have you killed and torn into pieces, but it is not in my fate to do so. You will die at the hands of Hamzai Sahip Kıran. The appointed hour when Hamzai will kill you has already been set."

When most of the giants had been killed, there were three allowed to continue life for a while longer. One of them would eventually be killed by the caliph Ali, one by Çirman Shah, and the third by Hamzai Sahip Kıran. This third giant took every precaution to avoid Hamzai Sahip Kıran.

Hamzai finally reached Crystal Mountain,[138] which was aglow with fire at its base but covered with snow at its peak. Hamzai rode Askeri Devzade through the fiery part in order to reach the snowy peak above. Only with Allah's assistance would he have been able to have reached the snow-covered top of the mountain. He prayed, "O my great Allah, the helper of those in trouble, now help me to pass unharmed through this fiery zone." After he had uttered those words, a strong wind arose. It at once blew out the fire below and melted the snow above. The weather became pleasantly warm.

Gentlemen, this giant secluded himself in a very deep well.[139] As Hamzai was approaching that well, he suddenly heard a voice speaking to him. It said, "Hamzai, you will not return without having killed this giant, no matter how much time it takes to do so. Because you did not say, '*İnşallah,*' Allah lengthened your seventeen-day journey to seventeen years."

Hamzai saw dense smoke rising from the mouth of the well. He tied Askeri Devzade to a stone. Then tying himself to another stone with a very long rope, he lowered himself very carefully into the well. When he reached the bottom of that well, he heard a very strange noise. Turning his head to right and left to locate the source of the sound, he saw a very beautiful girl who from her waist downward had the body of a snake. She said, "Oh, Hamzai, welcome, welcome."

Surprised, Hamzai asked, "How do you know my name? How do you know who I am?"

She answered, "Solomon, the son of David, told us about you, and then later Allah told us about you. I am the Sultana of Snakes, and my name is Şahmeran.[140] Before you arrived here, I warned all of my subjects not to harm you, and so you should not be afraid of them. In fact, every one of them will help you. O Hamzai, I should like to make a request of you. Please ask

---

[138] The context, more than the words used in the text, suggests the title used here. The actual words of the narrator are *Billuri Elzem* (Crystal Indispensable).

[139] In Turkish folktales the word *kuyu* (well) often does not refer to a source of water. It means *pit* or *deep hole*, sometimes an entrance to the underworld.

[140] The snake-woman is a familiar figure in folklore (Motif B 29.2.3) (Thompson 1955-58). One of Behçet Mahir's longer tales is devoted to Seyfülmülük, a queen of snakes. See Note 14 of the Introduction to the present volume. Here he refers to Şahmeran as a similar queen. Both of Behçet's tales are probably of Persian origin. Altan Gökalp also writes about a female Şameran, likening her to the Melusine fairy of medieval European tales and to the protagonist of "The Tale of Yamlika, Queen of the Serpents" of the 355th night of *The Thousand Nights and a Night* (Gökalp 1987).

To keep the record straight, however, it should be noted that in most Turkish tales about the snake monarch, Şahmeran is male, the King of Snakes. For a printed version (in Turkish) of this male Şahmeran see *Şahmeran Hikâyesi* (Yurdatap 1970). For ATON variants see tales numbered 921, 923, 951, and 1180. For the basic Turkish version see Type 57—*Der Schlangenkönig Şahmaran* [sic] (Eberhard and Boratav 1953).

the Prophet Mohammed not to forget to intercede for me on the Day of Judgment."

"All right. I shall tell him that," answered Hamzai.

Hamzai Sahip Kıran began to search for the giant both in the depths of that well and above ground. With sword in hand, he began pursuing the giant by following his tracks, but for some time he did not seem to get any closer to the monster. That giant had a very keen sense of smell, and he could detect Hamzai's approach at some distance by his human scent. Dreading the arrival of Hamzai, the giant had for years been building barricades and other means of defense, and he kept retreating from one of these to another as Hamzai approached. As this pursuit continued, more and more time elapsed. Hamzai had said he would return in seventeen days, but because he had failed to say, "*İnşallah,*" Allah had extended those seventeen days to seventeen years. Those seventeen years had now expired, and his son, Hamzai Yunan, had reached the age of fifteen.

Hamzai's Son, Hamzai Yunan, Defends Islam

While Hamzai Sahip Kıran's lengthy activities had been going on, Ömer Ümmiye had been visiting Mehli Nigâr every month, and every time that he did so, the princess would ask him whether Hamzai had returned. He would answer, "No, my coquettish beauty. When he does return, I shall inform you of this immediately."

But Hamzai Sahip Kıran had been gone for such a long time that many people felt that he must have died. Nuşirvan decided to take advantage of this situation. He said to his council, "We must use this opportunity well," and he gave orders to his troops to attack the Muslim forces from all directions. The Muslims resisted as hard as they could, but Nuşirvan's soldiers continued to attack them on all fronts and capture fortress after fortress. The Muslim forces were growing weaker and weaker day by day.

While this was going on, Hamzai Yunan's mother said to him, "O my son, your father went to kill a giant, but after all this time he has not returned. I believe that he will arrive here soon, but so far there have been no messages from him. As his son, you have his blood in your veins, and you have an obligation to help the Muslim troops who are steadily growing weaker under the constant attacks of Nuşirvan's army. Your duty is to help them in their fight. I reared you to be able to help the Muslim cause."

Hamzai Yunan was given a horse and a sword, but it was only his mother and Allah who knew that he was the son of Hamzai Sahip Kıran. Hamzai Yunan rode to the battlefront to join the greatly outnumbered Muslim forces. There had been many *şehit* among them. When the young man saw this, he put his hand on his side and gave forth a great shout. Then he announced, "If you know me, then you recognize me; but if you do not know me, I am called Hamzai Yunan." He then began assaulting the soldiers of

Nuşirvan who were besieging a Muslim fortress and drove them back. When night arrived, the defenders of the fortress opened the gates and welcomed the young warrior into their midst. He then said to them, "I am Hamzai Yunan, son of Hamzai Sahip Kıran."

Ömer Ümmiye immediately reported this news to Mehli Nigâr. He said, "Mehli, our forces have been rescued, and I have news for you. Hamzai Sahip Kıran is alive, and it was his fifteen-year-old son, Hamzai Yunan, who saved us."

Upon hearing this, Mehli Nigâr grew very sad. In tears she said, "Oh, I never suspected that Hamzai would marry anyone else! It now seems that whenever he sees a pretty face, he falls in love. I sacrificed my sleep, and I sacrificed my father's love for the sake of Hamzai's love. But he cared nothing for me, for he married someone else and now has a son who is fifteen years old. If he and I had been married, we would now have a son of that same age." Ömer regretted having given the news to Mehli Nigâr, but it was too late now for him to do anything about it.

Hamzai's Fated Marriage to the Sultana of Fairies

We must return now to Hamzai Sahip Kıran, who was still searching for the giant. One day he approached a very large castle. As he drew closer, the castle gate opened and several men came riding out to meet him. "What do you want?" he asked them.

They answered, "This castle belongs to the Sultana of Fairies, and she wants to have you enter her presence." It seems that Allah had caused the Sultana of Fairies to fall in love with Hamzai Sahip Kıran, but Hamzai knew nothing whatsoever about this. No one knows what Fate has prepared for him. Prophet Joseph had no idea that Züleyha had developed a passion for him, but Allah had caused her to have such a feeling. Other women in the neighborhood used to laugh about her love of Joseph, and they had reason for doing so, because the first and last word that she uttered every day was *Joseph*. One day when she was being teased excessively by the other women, she reached the conclusion that her attraction to Joseph was not just an unreasonable whim. She said to the other women, "I know that you are laughing at me because of my great love for Joseph, but I shall show you why I have that love. I am going to give each of you a cucumber and a knife, and when I shout 'Joseph,' you are to start peeling the cucumber." Each woman took a cucumber and a knife and prepared to do as Züleyha had directed. Züleyha called, "Joseph," and the young man entered the room. When the other women saw Joseph's handsome face, they all peeled their fingers instead of the cucumbers they were holding. Züleyha then said, "Do you see now? Do you understand now the reason for my love of Joseph? You saw his face just once, but I see it every day. How do you suppose that I could fail to love him?"[141]

As I told you before, love is a great and powerful feeling. It is able to conquer anything. You can understand this by observing the condition of Mehli Nigâr while all these other things were going on. She was crying, "Oh, Hamzai, Hamzai!" But at the same time she was consoling herself by thinking, "Someday Hamzai will marry me too."

Now let us gaze into the Mirror of Fortune again to see what it will show us. Only seventeen years had passed, but during that time Hamzai Sahip Kıran had suffered a great deal. He went into the presence of the Sultana of Fairies, who said to him, "Oh, Hamzai, Allah caused me to fall in love with you! I am the ruler of all the fairies."

Hamzai was astonished by what he heard. He stood in silence, quite bewildered. When he looked into the face of the Sultana of Fairies, there was something which passed from her heart to his, as if his heart had been struck by some strange, powerful arrow. What was the power? What was the arrow? I shall answer these questions with another story. We shall leave Hamzai there, and I shall tell you a story from Erzurum Province, which is my native region.

Once in the past there was a *bey*[142] who was very rich. This *bey* had a servant, a very honest young man, who had worked for him for seven years. One day the *bey*'s wife said to the *bey*, "Husband, our servant has now been working for us for seven years, and he has been a good man. Let us now show him what kind of master you are and what kind of master's wife I am. I shall look for a suitable bride for him, and then after I have found one, you can give him some money with which to start a business of his own. After that has been done, we can let him live in the building which is attached to the

---

141 The crosscultural episode that ends here draws upon Biblical, Koranic, and folkloric sources. In *Genesis* 39, Joseph is bought as a household slave by an Egyptian official named Potiphar. When handsome Joseph rejects efforts of Potiphar's wife to seduce him, she reports falsely to her husband that Joseph has made immoral advances toward her. He is jailed as a result. The Koran (Chapter 12, verses 23-29 and 33-35) echoes this quite closely but adds the moving scene (verses 30-32) in which other women testify to Joseph's attractiveness by absentmindedly using their knives to cut their own hands instead of their food when Joseph walks into their midst.

In neither the Bible nor the Koran does Joseph's temptress have a name. In post-Koranic legend she was initially called Ra'il but later almost always Zulaika or (in Turkish) Züleyha. In Arabian lore her husband is not named Potiphar but most frequently Kitfir, Kutifar, or Kittifin (Heller 1987: 1178). In the Koranic version the rebuffed woman invites mocking female friends to a dinner at which their infatuation with Joseph causes them to cut themselves. But in Turkish folktales—Mahir's, as well as others'—the guests much more graphically peel their fingers instead of the cucumbers they had been given.

142 In earlier times a *bey* was a landholder and an aristocrat roughly equivalent to a British baron. Thus the term *bey* was similar to the English *lord*. There are no longer *bey*s of that type in Turkey. The word *bey* placed after a man's first name is now a term of respect or flattery.

back of our own house." The *bey* agreed heartily with these thoughts of his wife.

One day the *bey*'s wife said to their young helper, "Son, get the carriage ready. I am going to take some of the neighborhood girls and go to Cermik[143] for a day's outing." The servant hitched the horses to the carriage and then drove the *bey*'s wife and the girls to Cermik. When they arrived at Cermik, he pitched a tent for the ladies.

As the wife of the *bey* and her guests were preparing to go to the hot mineral baths at Cermik, they took off all of their jewelry. The *bey*'s wife wrapped all of this jewelry in a large handkerchief, but instead of putting the handkerchief into a chest in the tent, as she had intended to do, she placed it in her bosom. When they were ready to go to the bath, the woman said to her servant, "Get the meal ready for our return, and you should eat something too."

She then started walking to the bath with her guests. Along the way, she stumbled and fell to the ground. Although no one noticed it, when she fell, the handkerchief full of jewelry dropped from her bosom and slid under an overhanging stone. The *bey*'s wife was not injured, and so they proceeded to the bath. After they had finished bathing, they returned to the tent, where the servant had the meal prepared for them. But when the *bey*'s wife opened the chest, she could not find within it the handkerchief of jewels which she thought she had left there. She called the servant at once and asked, "Son, have you seen a handkerchief full of jewelry which I placed in the chest before we went to the bath?"

The helper answered, "No, lady, I have seen no such handkerchief. I did not touch the chest during your absence."

She repeated the same question, and the helper gave the same answer. Because the jewelry was very valuable, she wanted some explanation of what had happened to it. She questioned him very rigorously and accused him of having stolen the jewelry. They then returned home in great haste.

The woman went to the *bey* and said, "Sit down, Husband. I have something very serious to tell you. It has snowed upon the mountain that we thought was safe. I am very sad because the male servant who has hitherto always been so honest today stole all of my and my guests' jewelry. But he denies this completely."

---

143 This place-name is actually *Çermik*. (In eastern Turkey, the sounds of the Turkish letters *c*, *ç* [English *ch*] and *k* often deviate from their pronunciation in standard Turkish. See Note 122.) Çermik is a village just west of Erzurum. It is named after the hot-spring bath there. *Çermik* and *kaplıca* are both terms used for thermal springs; the latter is the more common in most of Turkey today.

The *bey* called the helper to him and asked him the same question that his wife had asked. He got the same answer that his wife had received. This made the *bey* very angry, and so he decided to take the helper to court.

On the day of the trial the judge said to the helper, "Son, take your ritual ablutions and then take an oath in the name of Allah that you neither took nor even saw the jewelry."

But when the helper had taken his ablutions and had placed his hand upon the Koran to take his oath, he saw the sword of Allah descending from the ceiling over the head of his master because the master had accused him falsely. When he withdrew his hand from the Koran, he saw that the sword ascended again into the ceiling. The judge spoke to him again, saying, "Son, do not be afraid. Tell us the truth."

The helper thought for a moment. He looked at his master, at his master's wife, and at their children. He thought, "If I take that oath on the Koran, I believe that sword will cut off my master's head. Therefore, I shall not take that oath." To the judge he said, "I cannot take an oath upon the Koran. Tell me how many years I shall be required to work to pay for the missing jewelry."

The judge said to the *bey*, "Your servant was afraid to take an oath on the Koran. Tell me how much time he would have to work to pay for the jewelry."

"Very well," answered the *bey*. "To do that he would have to work for seven years without any pay." The servant agreed to this, and he began at once to work for another seven years.

Time passed, and at the end of a year the *bey*'s wife said to the helper, "Son, take me to Cermik again. Last year at this same time we went to Cermik, and there I had a very bad experience. This time I want to go there and enjoy myself."

The helper got everything ready, and they went to Cermik again. There he pitched the tent at exactly the same spot it had been the year before. The *bey*'s wife then said, "This time I shall give you my jewelry with my own hand so that we shall not have any confusion about it later."

The helper said, "Yes, lady. Now I am placing your jewelry in this chest. When you return from the bath, I shall give it back to you. In this way you will be able to go anywhere you wish with peace of mind."

The wife left the tent and started toward the bath. Along the way she saw her old handkerchief on the ground under the edge of a stone. Taking the handkerchief up from the ground, she opened it and found inside all of the jewelry that she thought had been stolen. She was greatly surprised and puzzled. Returning at once to the tent, she said to the servant, "Son, I have found all of the jewelry that I thought I lost last year. But, son, you knew that you had not stolen it. Why did you not take an oath to that effect?"

The helper replied, "I shall answer that question only if we appear in the same court and before the same judge."

They again returned home from Cermik in great haste. Then the master, his wife, and their helper went back to the same judge. After the recovery of the lost jewelry had been explained to the judge, the judge asked the servant, "What was the matter when you were here before, son? Why didn't you tell the truth to us a year ago here in this court?"

The servant answered, "O judge, when I was about to take the oath, with my hand upon the Koran, I saw the sword of Allah descending upon the head of my master. If I had taken the oath, my master's head would have been cut off by that sword. That is the reason that I did not take the oath." Upon hearing that, the judge arose and kissed both the eyes of the servant.

(Oh, gentlemen, you may not be able to see the sword of Allah, but it exists anyway. If you act unjustly or injure defenseless people, the sword of Allah will punish you in one way or another. You will be severely punished. There is a proverbial piece of verse that warns us about this:

Avoid the curse of those without defense.
Their curse can bring protracted suffering.
A faith in Allah shatters even thrones
And makes the rulers feel enduring pain.[144]

He who is cursed by those he has oppressed will never prosper. The curse of a sufferer damns the oppressor to failure.)

Hamzai Sahip Kıran fell in love with the appearance of the Sultana of Fairies. He therefore married this girl too.[145] Then he said to his new bride, "O my sultana, O my great beauty, I did not even know that you were here, but Allah led me to you and caused me to fall in love with you. But I have been traveling for seventeen years on a mission that has still not been completed. I must kill the Red Giant, who lives in this area."

---

144 While the whole quatrain may not be proverbial, its message could have been inspired by a well-known proverb listed in *A Dictionary of Turkish Proverbs* (Yurtbaşı 1993: 349): "Do not be cursed by the poor, for you will suffer sorely for that" ("Alma garibi ahınlı çekersin günahını").

145 In his treatment of Hamzai's meeting with and marriage to the sultana, Behçet Mahir has ignored all of the conventions—the magic, the mystery, the enchantment—of human/fairy relationships in Turkish folklore. The numerous protagonists who establish contact with fairies usually do so only after overcoming formidable obstacles. Otherworldly creatures, fairies live outside mortal time and space in a dimension inaccessible to human beings except through the assistance of some other supernatural agency. That Mahir knew well all of the traditional agonies involved in bridging the gulf between the two worlds is demonstrated in his "The Ordeal of Lâtif Shah . . . " (Walker and Uysal 1992: 5-71). There is nothing whatsoever fairylike about Hamzai's second wife, and she brings to their marriage none of the special powers with which other fairy spouses aid their husbands. Perhaps Mahir's omission of all the fairy trappings was one of the ways in which he and his storytelling predecessors truncated what he himself subsequently admits would otherwise have been an impossibly long tale.

The sultana's subjects had been complaining for some time about the abuses they had suffered from that giant. Hamzai Sahip Kıran finally caught up with him while that monster was sleeping. He drew his sword quietly and approached the giant. Then Hamzai gave a shout so loud that it must have been heard in all four corners of the world. That shout was both a battle cry and an expression of Hamzai's great fatigue. After seventeen years of pursuit, he was so tired that his mother's milk ran out of his nose.[146]. If I were to tell you about all of the difficulties he had encountered during those seventeen years, this story could not be completed in less than a year. Because of its extreme length, storytellers who preceded me presented this tale in one word instead of three.[147] But to the wise one word is sufficient.[148]

When the giant was awakened by Hamzai's great shout, he said, "Ah-h-h, Hamzai, you have come!"

"Yes, infidel, I have come. Get up and fight. It is your right to attack first. Come on!" (When you challenge an enemy to fight, it is his right to attack first. When he has used his turn without success and all his hopes are gone, then you should invite him to accept the Muslim religion. If he accepts your invitation, he will become your brother. If he refuses, then you may kill him.) The giant made his first move against Hamzai Sahip Kıran, but it was wasted. Then Hamzai made his first move, which split the giant's shield in half. There were words of prayer written on Hamzai's sword.

Three Ancient Physicians

There were three great medical doctors in history. The first was the Blessed Lokman.[149] The second was Plato,[150] and the third was Çüllü.[151]

---

146 Another figurative expression used by Turks to indicate extreme fatigue is this: "He was so weak that all his lice fell to the ground around his feet."

147 Condensing either an oral or a written text is sometimes described in this way.

148 Because he took himself and his stories very seriously, Behçet Mahir rarely indulged in this kind of wordplay.

149 Although Lokman is commented upon frequently in Turkish folktales as a legendary physician, this imaginary Arab was not until very recently acknowledged by the *Encyclopaedia of Islam* as having had any medical role. He was credited with having been (1) a pre-Islamic sage. In Chapter 31 of the Koran he was praised as (2) a maker of pious proverbs. In late medieval Arabian literature he was cited as (3) a writer of fables, which were compared with those of Aesop. In a brief addendum to the Lokman (Lukman) entry in a later edition of the encyclopaedia (Heller 1986: 813) he was finally recognized as being perceived in Turkey almost exclusively as a famous physician. That reference work cites as its sources for this belated information Eberhard and Boratav (1953: 346) and Walker and Uysal (1966: 33). For ATON tales devoted entirely to Lokman as an exceptionally skilled doctor, see those numbered 654, 922, 1018, and 1639.

150 In Turkish he is called *Eflatûn*.

151 Unidentified.

The Blessed Lokman found his answers to medical problems in herbs. He found a cure even for death in herbs. Herbs could speak and tell of their usefulness, and they could speak so well that they even chanted the ninety-nine names of Allah. Lokman's real name was *Camasep*;[152] the word *lokman* means *doctor.*[153]

When he found the cure for death, Lokman said, "From now on no one will have to be buried in the earth." Wishing to test this cure, Lokman cut to pieces an apprentice named Joseph and then poured his medicine over the parts. After a short while the sections of the apprentice's body were reunited, and he stood up. Lokman then said to Joseph, "Now it is your turn to cut me to pieces and then pour the medicine on the parts of my body. I found the cure for death, but all of us will still have to be questioned about our deeds on Judgment Day."

(Gentlemen, we must all give thought to the day of the Last Judgment. Don't deceive yourself by thinking that the last word has been spoken about any of your actions on earth. You might think, "I cheated this or that person. I committed many injustices against him. He took me to court, but I won the case. He could not do anything to me." Don't tell yourself that you have won any case in this world. What will you do on Judgment Day? How will you answer Allah's questions about that case? Don't try to justify a murder that you may have committed by saying to yourself, "Oh, I killed that person only in order to take my revenge against him." You may have gotten your revenge in this world, but have you considered how the matter may be decided in the next world? Gentlemen, we must all face the Day of Judgment. We will be questioned and we will be judged on the basis of our deeds in this mortal world. People may appeal to Adam for help, or to Jesus or other prophets. But they will all respond, "Go to the very last prophet [Mohammed], for it is only he who can save you." I always say that we do not have anything greater than the Koran. The answers to all of our problems are written in the Koran.)

Yes, gentlemen, Apprentice Joseph cut Lokman into pieces, as he had been directed to do. But at that very moment Allah called Gabriel to him and said, "Lokman has discovered a cure for death. Go and knock against the apprentice's arm so that he will spill that medicine on the ground."

Only three parts of Lokman's body were touched by any of the medicine. Those three parts came to life and cried out, "Joseph, pour the

152 The narrator has here confused two traditions. Camasep is a character in tales about Şahmeran, King of Snakes, commented on above.

153 The word *lokman* does not mean *doctor*. If it did, the ancient physician would not so frequently be called Lokman Hekim (Doctor Lokman). What may have confused the narrator is the fact that *Lokman* is occasionally used as a generic term. A gravely ill person may be told, "Only a Lokman can cure you."

In the hilltop village of Yukarı Kise, 1970. During a week, several reels of tape were filled by this triumvirate of narrators—(from left to right) Mehmet Beder, Yakup Kara, and Hacı Gönen. Most of the taping was done inside the home of Hacı Gönen, but for this session we were comfortably seated on Turkish rugs in the backyard.

medicine on the other parts! Pour it!" But Joseph was helpless. There was nothing that he could do to save Lokman.[154]

After Lokman's time there was his student Plato.[155] Plato found his answers to medical problems in the Koran.[156] He read the Koran very carefully. One day while he was walking along with the Koran under his arm, he was met by Gabriel on a bridge. Gabriel asked Plato, "Where are you going?"

Plato answered, "I am going to a certain mountain to get the herb which can prevent death. I read about it in the Koran."

Gabriel said, "Very well! If you are such a learned man, you can probably tell me where Gabriel is at this very moment."

Plato answered, "Let me look in my book." He opened the Koran, read from it for a minute, and then said, "He is neither in the sky nor on the ground. He is on the water."

As they stood there on the bridge, Gabriel said, "Look again, and more carefully this time."

"All right," said Plato, and when he looked into the Koran again, he understood. He said, "You are Gabriel."[157]

Gabriel fluttered his great wings, and in doing so, he knocked the book out of Plato's hands, and it fell into the water below. Only three pages remained in the hands of Plato, but from those three pages was derived all medical knowledge. All of the other pages fell into the river which watered a barley field along its bank. That is why it is now said that barley can cure many illnesses.[158]

---

[154] We have found no evidence in any other folktale or in any scholarly study that the life of the legendary Lokman ended in this way.

[155] The works of many classical authors circulated in the ancient Middle East. Several Greek authors were especially popular. Although they did not have the impact of Aristotle, Plato and the neo-Platonists (notably Plotinus) influenced Arabian and Persian philosophy (Fakhry 1970: 32-44). There is no indication that Behçet Mahir was acquainted with other than apocryphal accounts of Plato.

[156] Plato died 958 years before the first verses of the Koran were revealed to Mohammed in 610.

[157] There is very little information in the Koran that might be considered to be of a medical nature. Accepting for the moment the anachronism of Plato's having a copy of the Koran, one is led to infer that he is using it to engage in a widely practiced form of divination. The diviner opens at random a prestigious book: the Bible, a volume of Homer, of Virgil, of Hafez (the fourteenth-century Persian poet). The line on the page which the diviner then blindly touches supposedly contains one or more clues that will lead him/her to the information sought. During the Middle Ages in Europe much reliance was placed upon the *Sortes Virgilianae* (Virgilian Lots). See as sources Cary 1949: 293; Harvey 1967: 769.

[158] This story is usually told about Lokman rather than about Plato, and the book involved is not the Koran but the doctor's notebook. When Gabriel knocks that notebook into the river, it sets in motion a chain reaction of what Sir James Frazer called "contagious magic." The medical formulae in the notebook contact the water, which in turn contacts the barley—thus

After Plato came Doctor Çüllü, who could detect the presence of death or the absence of death by smell. One day while he was going somewhere, he saw a crowd of people before a certain house. He asked, "What has happened?"

One of the people of the crowd said, "There was a young pregnant woman here who has died. She died very suddenly just halfway through her period of pregnancy."

Doctor Çüllü sniffed the body of that woman, and the smell told him that she was not really dead. He asked, "Where are the relatives of this woman? I want to inform them that she is not actually dead." When the relatives appeared, he told them of the woman's condition and asked them for a long, narrow piece of glass. He said, "This woman is not dead. I think that the fetus in her womb may have grasped tightly a large blood vessel and shut off the flow of her blood. That is the reason that she seems to most people to be dead." He measured and calculated very carefully, and then he inserted the strip of glass into the woman's womb. As soon as he did this, the woman regained consciousness immediately. She did so because the strip of glass had struck the hand of the fetus and forced it away from the vital vein. Doctor Çüllü then said to the people standing there, "When the baby is born, you will see that it has a hole in its right hand." Then he left.

Time passed. In fact, a year and two days [sic] passed, and finally the woman gave birth to a baby girl. It was seen at once that the baby had a large hole in its right hand. But, gentlemen, no matter how many wonderful things they might do, doctors were not permitted to have a cure for death.

The Giant Killer Returns to Religious War

The world of Islam had been reduced to desperate conditions during the seventeen years Hamzai Sahip Kıran had been pursuing the giant. Hamzai Yunan had been wounded several times, and as a result, he had been greatly weakened. And the whole Muslim force was growing weaker day by day.

But we have forgotten to finish the fight between Hamzai and the giant, and so we must return to that. Hamzai Sahip Kıran said, "Ho, giant! You have used your turn to attack, and now you have nothing to hope for and no way to protect yourself. It is my turn now, but let me ask you something first. Do you recognize the true way of Allah? Do you accept the Muslim religion and believe in the Prophet Mohammed? If so, then I shall forgive you." But when in response the giant began to curse all Muslims, Hamzai Sahip Kıran drew his sword and cut the giant into two pieces. He struck the giant such a terribly hard blow that his sword also cut the giant's throne in

transferring the curative potency to that grain. In 1981 a different narrator (Ali Çiftçi of Yozgat Province) recounted a variant of this tale in "Legendary Lokman and Barley Soup." This is ATON No. 922.

half. After wiping the giant's blood from his sword, Hamzai replaced it in its scabbard. Then he prayed, "O my great Allah, it was You who gave me the strength to kill this giant, and You gave me the courage to face him. I am not as large as even one foot of this giant, but with Your help, I killed him."

After the giant had been killed, the Sultana of Fairies ordered her fairy forces to take Hamzai to his own country. Before he left, however, she said to him, "Hamzai, we have just been married, but now you are leaving. Do not forget me, Hamzai."

"No, my fairy, I shall not forget you." The fairies then returned him to his own country in twenty-four hours.

(Gentlemen, Allah created human beings, and nothing has been created superior to human beings so far. The human being is the best part of Creation in this world.)

Back in his own country, Hamzai saw at once that everyone there was engaged in warfare. This fighting had raised such a large cloud of dust that it hung over the entire country. Hamzai Sahip Kıran rode to the battlefield and there he raised one of his loud shouts. Immediately the fighting stopped, and everyone gazed upon Hamzai sitting on his horse with great dignity. Hamzai Yunan saw his father for the first time, and Hamzai Sahip Kıran saw the boy but did not recognize his son right away. The father dismounted, and the son did the same. Then Hamzai Yunan ran to his father and threw himself at his feet.

Confused, Hamzai Sahip Kıran asked, "Son, who are you? What should I call you? To what family do you belong?"

Hamzai Yunan kissed his father's hands and said, "You are my father, and you named me. I am Hamzai Yunan."

Hamzai Sahip Kıran was delighted to find his son there, but he asked him, "Son, you haven't revealed your identity to anyone—have you?" He was worried that Mehli Nigâr might have heard about this son and might have been saddened by the news. Hamzai did not know that Ömer Ümmiye had already informed Mehli Nigâr of the presence of Hamzai Yunan.

All of the Muslim forces were greatly encouraged by the news that Hamzai Sahip Kıran had returned alive. They began celebrating that happy event, but Hamzai's return had a very different effect on the idol worshipers. It made them uncomfortable, even afraid. They said among themselves, "We thought that Hamzai Sahip Kıran was beneath the ground by this time, but he is not!" (Of course, in due time Hamzai would go beneath the ground like everyone else.)

When Hamzai Sahip Kıran saw what the situation was, he said to himself, "The Muslim world is struggling through very difficult times. It is my duty to fight until we win this war." Drawing his sword, he passed through the length of the battlefield. When the Muslim soldiers saw Hamzai's courage, their own courage returned, and they renewed their fighting. Yes, without a shepherd, the flock can scatter easily and quickly.

Many of the idol worshipers said, "Stop, Hamzai! We are willing to pay you tribute to end this war."

But Nuşirvan rejected that solution. He said, "No, I shall never pay tribute to Hamzai Sahip Kıran. We shall carry on the war in the future." He was the richest and most powerful ruler in that part of the world, but some of the lesser rulers agreed to pay tribute to Hamzai Sahip Kıran in order to make him stop attacking their troops.

Hamzai said to Ömer Ümmiye, "Go and take this good news to Mehli Nigâr and let her know that I have returned alive."

Ömer replied, "I gave this news to Mehli Nigâr some time ago. She was very happy to hear of your return, but she is also disappointed about you."

"Why, Ömer?"

Ömer said, "I told her about your son, Hamzai Yunan."

"Why did you do that, Ömer?"

"Oh, Hamzai, after I had told her about him, I regretted what I had done, but by then it was too late to prevent her sadness."

Hamzai Sahip Kıran's forces made many attacks against Barber Castle,[159] but he was unable to capture it. Ali also attempted to take that castle, but he too failed. There was a very heavy hailstorm during one of their attacks on Barber Castle, and while that storm raged, one of the strongest Muslim wrestlers was made a prisoner of war. But Prophet Mohammed received a message from Allah which said, "Mohammed, do not worry. Ali will eventually conquer Barber Castle."

(You may tell a lie in order to save the helpless from injustice. If you tell a lie for that reason, it is not a sin. Prophet Mohammed was once asked if his people lied. He answered, "No, Muslims do not lie." But still you may lie if you have to do so in order to save Muslims from tyranny.

First you must save your own life and then the lives of your loved ones. Unless you preserve your own life, you cannot preserve the lives of others. If you are dead, you can do nothing for others. I am reminded now of one of my poems, which I shall recite for you.

A cloud of smoky grief surrounds my head.
Encircling sorrow aches without a cure.
There is no cure unless a Lokman comes.
A bloody sadness stains my very heart.

This love of mine has driven me insane.
When I'm awake, I'm like the dizzy moth

159 Unidentified.

That flutters round and round the flame of love.
A bloody sadness stains my very heart.

Behçet Mahir now grieves for lovers' grief,
For those who suffer all the pangs I know.
You live within the throb of my own pain.
A bloody sadness stains my very heart.

You need your life to find the loved one's life. Without your life you cannot offer prayers to Allah.)

Gentlemen, the smaller rulers paid tribute to Hamzai Sahip Kıran, but Nuşirvan refused to accept that solution. He was not only the strongest ruler in that part of the world, but with the passage of time he had also become one of the most just. He felt, therefore, that he could defeat a thousand Hamzai Sahip Kırans and that there was no one who could defeat him. As a matter of fact, Hamzai Sahip Kıran never defeated Nuşirvan. Why? Because Nuşirvan had grown to become a very just ruler, and his justice saved him from suffering defeat.

One of Nuşirvan's wrestlers fell in love with a girl named Miyase, but her father said to the wrestler, "You must bring me my daughter's weight in gold and silver before I shall give her to you." The wrestler went to Nuşirvan's room in tears. The ruler asked this man what was bothering him. When the wrestler explained his difficulty, Nuşirvan ordered his attendants to give the wrestler enough gold and silver to pay the bride-price for Miyase. Oh-h-h, if someone is as just a man as Nuşirvan was, there is no way he can be defeated.

Hamzai Sahip Kıran knew that inasmuch as Nuşirvan had fed him throughout his childhood, his sword would never be able to kill that ruler. Hamzai therefore wrote a second letter to Nuşirvan and had Ömer Ümmiye deliver it. When the ruler saw Ömer approaching, he grasped his crown and held it tightly, for he knew that Ömer could steal it and put it into his pouch without being detected.

Nuşirvan read the second letter from Hamzai Sahip Kıran. It said, "O Nuşirvan, this is my second letter to you. You supported me during my childhood. I ate your bread. As a result of that, I felt that I should go and visit you, but I shall not visit you a second time. Because of our quarrel over Mehli Nigâr, many people have been killed, and if we continue fighting, all of the rest may die too. Let us end this war. Give your daughter to me. I can get her by means of my sword, but since I ate your bread, I should prefer to get her with your permission."

At a meeting of his council Nuşirvan asked his grand vizier for his opinion about how to settle this matter. The grand vizier said, "Oh, my padishah, Allah will eventually ask questions about the great number of people who have been killed here. We have had enough fighting. Your daughter, Mehli Nigâr, wants Hamzai Sahip Kıran as much as he wants her. They want each other, and they have now been wanting each other for a very long time. If you are a just man, a just padishah, you will not cause your daughter to cry any longer. Allow them to be married. Allow these two young lovers to attain their wish."

But others in the ruler's council said to the grand vizier, "You sit down!" Then turning to Nuşirvan, they said, "O Nuşirvan, if you give your blessing to this marriage, people will think that you are a very weak padishah and that you are afraid of Hamzai Sahip Kıran. Secondly, Hamzai Sahip Kıran is a very poor person. How could you view Hamzai as a suitable husband for your only daughter, Mehli Nigâr? You are a very rich and powerful padishah. Don't listen to what your grand vizier says. If there were a hundred Hamzais, they still could not defeat us."

As a result of these latter comments, Nuşirvan did not accept the request of Hamzai Sahip Kıran's letter. He said to Ömer Ümmiye, "Ömer, write down my answer. Say, 'I do not have any daughter for Hamzai Sahip Kıran,' and then deliver this message to him."

After Ömer Ümmiye had received this answer from Nuşirvan, he went at midnight to the palace of Mehli Nigâr. He said to her, "Mehli Nigâr, some members of your father's council influenced him against giving you in marriage to Hamzai. The war will now begin again, and many more people will die."

When she heard this report, Mehli Nigâr became even sadder than she had been before. Speaking in tears, she said to Ömer, "Give my greetings to Hamzai Sahip Kıran. Hasn't he grown tired of using the sword? He could have me without the use of his sword."

Ömer then left and delivered Nuşirvan's letter to Hamzai Sahip Kıran. After reading it, Hamzai ordered his army to prepare to continue the fighting. Every soldier mounted his horse or camel and began riding toward Nuşirvan's country. While this was going on, Nuşirvan had prepared his own army for renewed fighting.

Hamzai Sahip Kıran knew that Nuşirvan's army was strong, but he sent Ömer Ümmiye to determine exactly how strong it was. He said, "Ömer, go and observe closely Nuşirvan's army in order to discover how powerful it really is."

Ömer Ümmiye entered enemy territory to get the information that Hamzai had requested. He arrived at midnight near the place where Nuşirvan's army was stationed in readiness for an attack by Hamzai's forces. There was no moon that night, and everywhere it was totally dark. While Nuşirvan's troops were sleeping, Ömer began throwing large stones upon them and shouting, "Hamzai Sahip Kıran's army has arrived! Hamzai Sahip Kıran's army has arrived! Start fighting them!" The enemy troops were thrown into utter confusion. They began fighting wildly in the dark, but no one knew whom he was striking. This battle continued until dawn, when they discovered that they had been fighting each other. None of Hamzai's troops were there, and they realized that all night long they had been killing their own men. Yes, the cleverness of Ömer Ümmiye had caused the enemy forces to spend the night destroying themselves.

Ömer Ümmiye then returned to Hamzai Sahip Kıran and reported on the strength of the enemy. "But they are fighting among themselves and killing each other. We, on the other hand, are ready to attack."

The Muslim forces now moved to the battlefield. As he had done earlier, Hamzai Sahip Kıran rode out in front of them into the open space between the two armies. There he shouted with all his might, "Ho-o-o! I am called Hamzai Sahip Kıran!" and then he rode his horse forward at a gallop against the enemy. The battle raged until the end of the day, and all of the streams in the area ran with blood instead of water.

That night Nuşirvan gathered his men and said to them, "The heavenly light of the Fire God is no longer helping us." (As you know, they were fire worshipers, and they had been expecting to receive help from the Fire God.) Now the Muslim forces were advancing, and they were conquering Nuşirvan's fortresses one after another. What had been Nuşirvan's fortresses were steadily becoming Muslim fortresses. Nuşirvan said, "What are we to do? We are now losing this war very badly. We are losing a fortress every day to the Muslims. What should we do? Should we not end the war by surrendering?"

But his men replied, "No, no, Nuşirvan! We cannot do that! You are far stronger than Hamzai Sahip Kıran, and you are too just a person to be defeated by him. We shall win this war eventually."

During that discussion Ömer Ümmiye was present all the time, but no one there could recognize him because he had disguised himself as one of Nuşirvan's soldiers. He thought, "If I cannot somehow stop Nuşirvan's commander Mehdi, he will surely persuade the padishah to continue fighting against Hamzai Sahip Kıran." Therefore, after the meeting, he began following Mehdi. If Ömer had wished to kill Mehdi, or even Nuşirvan himself, he would have been capable of doing so, but he was under very strict orders from Hamzai Sahip Kıran not to commit such a crime. Ömer now posed as one of the personal guards of Mehdi, and when midnight arrived, he went to Mehdi's tent. After he saw that Mehdi was sleeping, Ömer took from his magic pouch a strong herb and held it under Mehdi's nose. Within a few minutes Mehdi became completely unconscious. Ömer then put this military commander on his back and carried him to a very isolated place in a nearby forest. There he stripped off all of Mehdi's clothes, and after tying him securely to a tree, he inserted into Mehdi's anus a candle and lighted that candle. Ömer then left him there.

When morning arrived, it was discovered that Mehdi was missing. Everyone began searching for him, but for some time nobody could find him. Then some horsemen were sent to search in places farther and farther from the city. After several days they finally heard the voice of Mehdi. By then his voice was very hoarse from his having called for help day and night. In most ways Mehdi was not seriously injured, but he had a severe burn all around his anus. They returned him to his tent, but he was too ill to sit up. They asked him, "Who did this to you?"

He answered, "It must have been Ömer Ümmiye."

When Mehdi's experience was reported to Nuşirvan, that ruler laughed. By then Ömer Ümmiye had changed his appearance again, this time disguising himself as one of Nuşirvan's regular soldiers. In the twinkling of an eye, he stole Nuşirvan's precious crown. When the palace people realized this, they shouted, "Stop that man! Catch that thief!" But their efforts went for nothing. The crown was gone, and there was no way to recover it.

Mehli Nigâr Joins Hamzai

Now let us find out what Mehli Nigâr was doing at that time. She had been giving very serious thought to her situation. She said to herself, "What am I going to do? The fighting between my father and Hamzai will not end soon. They may continue to fight forever." Then she decided to call Ömer Ümmiye.

When Ömer arrived at her palace, she said to him, "Oh, Ömer, I have thought and thought about my problem, and I have finally reached a decision about it. I have said to you repeatedly, 'Take me to Hamzai,' but you refused to do that. Listen now to what I have decided to do. I shall mount a horse, unsheathe my sword, and ride against my father's army. I shall attack them from one side, and you will attack them from the other. In this way I shall be united with Hamzai by the strength of my sword. When I proceed in this way, Hamzai will have no responsibility for my going to him."

Ömer Ümmiye answered, "O beauty, I cannot say anything without first consulting Hamzai. I must ask him about this."

Mehli Nigâr replied, "All right, Ömer. Go and tell Hamzai about my plan. Then return and tell me his final words on this matter."

Ömer Ümmiye left Mehli Nigâr's palace and went directly to Hamzai Sahip Kıran. He reported to Hamzai, word for word, what Mehli Nigâr had said. After listening to this carefully, Hamzai said, "Ömer, these words spoke the same thoughts that have been crossing my mind. But I said nothing of these thoughts to Mehli Nigâr, for I did not wish to force her into a difficult position. However, inasmuch as her thoughts are the same as mine, ask her if she can make her attack tomorrow evening. I shall attack from another side, and you will do so from a third side. In that way we may be able to end this fighting."

Returning to Mehli Nigâr's palace, Ömer repeated Hamzai's words to the girl. He said, "O Mehli Nigâr, I have good news for you! I told Hamzai about your thoughts, and he said that they were the same as his thoughts.

He wants you to think about it all again very carefully, however, before you carry out your plan."

Mehli answered, "Ömer, I have been dying forty times every day. I have thought this over very carefully already. It would be far better to die just once instead of dying forty times each passing day. I have made up my mind about this."

Gentlemen, on the following evening Mehli Nigâr selected a good horse for herself. Then mounting her horse and unsheathing her sword, she passed through her father's army. Ömer Ümmiye attacked from a second side, and at the same time Hamzai Sahip Kıran advanced from yet another side. This battle lasted for three days and three nights, and during that time Mehli Nigâr was wounded. Hamzai said to Ömer, "Mehli Nigâr has received several wounds. Take her to my tent and tend to her needs." Following this order, Ömer took Mehli Nigâr to Hamzai's tent and wrapped her wounds.

Soon after the battle had begun, messengers arrived at Nuşirvan's palace. They announced, "O Nuşirvan, your daughter has left us and has gone over to the side of Hamzai Sahip Kıran."

Nuşirvan asked, "Who came and got her and took her there?"

"Nobody," they said. "She went over to Hamzai by herself, and it was as a result of her own will that she did so." When Nuşirvan heard this he was stunned. He suddenly realized at that moment that he had lost not only his daughter but also the war.

Now let us see what is happening on Hamzai's side of the battlefield. Hamzai gathered all of his wrestlers and said to them, "I did not have any personal enmity against Nuşirvan. My only concern was to get Mehli Nigâr. Since she is now here with me, I can no longer continue the war against her father's forces. It would not be proper for me to do so. I got what I want." Gathering all of his troops, he turned back toward his own country.

Love's Labor Lost to Pride

On their way home they stopped in a deserted area to rest. While they were there, Hamzai noticed a white deer standing at the top of a small hill. He said to his wrestler friends, "I shall shoot at that deer, but my arrow will strike only its ear. When it passes through its ear, the deer will think that a fly is on its ear, and it will scratch its ear. My arrow will not harm the deer in any other way." Placing an arrow in his bow, Hamzai aimed very carefully. The arrow passed through the deer's ear, and—as Hamzai had predicted—the deer, supposing it was a fly, scratched its ear with a hind foot. Hamzai then turned to Mehli Nigâr and asked, "Did you see that, O Mehli?"

Mehli answered, "Yes, my shah, I saw that, but it must have been the result of a great amount of practice."

When Hamzai heard this remark, he became furious. He shouted, "*Vay*! *Vay*![160] You do not recognize my excellent marksmanship! I do not want to see you anymore!" Then turning to Ömer Ümmiye, he said, "Ömer, call the black executioner to me." And when the black executioner arrived, Hamzai gave him this command: "Take this woman to some isolated place, kill her, and bring her bloody shirt back to me."

Mehli Nigâr began to cry. All of the wrestlers begged Hamzai to change his mind, but he remained steadfast in his decision; he did not alter his position at all.

The black executioner placed Mehli Nigâr on his horse behind him and started to search for a lonely place. As they were riding along, Mehli said to the black executioner, "If you kill me and take my bloody shirt back to Hamzai, he will sooner or later kill you. He made his decision in great haste, and it will not be long before he regrets that decision. He will then hold you responsible for my death, and he may even try to kill you, because you will have been the one who actually took my life. Instead of killing me, catch an animal, kill it, and dip my shirt in its blood. Then take the shirt to Hamzai as evidence that you have killed me. If you do that, you will not regret it, for I shall someday have occasion to repay you."

The executioner thought for only a moment before he realized how reasonable were Mehli Nigâr's remarks. He took her to his home and hid her there. After Mehli Nigâr had taken off her shirt and given it to him, the black executioner killed an animal and soaked up its blood with her shirt. Taking that blood-soaked shirt, he returned with it to Hamzai Sahip Kıran.

"What did you do, black executioner?" asked Hamzai.

"Oh, Hamzai Sahip Kıran, as you ordered me to do, I killed Mehli Nigâr and brought you this shirt soaked with her blood."

When Hamzai saw Mehli Nigâr's bloodstained shirt, he was shocked, and he then realized how rash his sudden decision had been. He said to the black executioner, "I do not want to see you ever again. Remove yourself permanently from my presence."

When the black executioner heard what Hamzai said, he thought, "I did the right thing. I listened to the wise words of Mehli Nigâr and decided not to kill her."

The cow of the black executioner had a calf on the day that Mehli Nigâr arrived there. Mehli Nigâr carried the calf in her arms to her room. To do this, she had to take it up the flight of forty steps that led upstairs to the living quarters of the executioner's house.[161] She petted the calf for a while

---

[160] An interjection expressing either surprise or regret.

[161] In many parts of the world, including much of the Middle East, barns to house livestock are not separate buildings. They are the first or ground-level stories of the farmhouses. Because of the low latitudes in which many Middle Eastern homes are located, they often do not have

and then carried it back down the forty steps to its mother. She repeated this twice every day. Every morning and every evening she carried the calf to her room, petted it, and then returned it to its mother. Of course, the calf grew and grew, getting heavier and heavier. And, of course, as she continued carrying it up and down the forty steps of the stairway, Mehli Nigâr grew stronger and stronger.

As the days passed, Hamzai Sahip Kıran grew sadder and sadder. He was living with his son, Hamzai Yunan, but his eyes were not seeing anything at all, for he grieved continuously about the death of Mehli Nigâr. He hardly knew whether he was dead or alive. He did nothing but breathe in and out, not caring about anything that was going on around him. He was frantic with sorrow and regret for his decision to have Mehli Nigâr killed. He kept her bloody shirt, and every time he looked at it, he cried. He thought over and over, "O Allah, how could I have decided to have Mehli Nigâr killed when she was the person for whom I cared most? How could I do that? If I ever see that black executioner again, I shall kill him. I shall strangle him with my own hands. How could he kill my Mehli Nigâr? He has no compassion in his heart!" But the black executioner was so afraid of Hamzai that he did not leave his house even for a single moment.

The calf reached the age of one year, and Mehli Nigâr was still carrying it in her arms up and down the forty steps twice a day.

But, gentlemen, this is as far as we can carry our story this evening. We shall continue tomorrow evening by discovering what Mehli Nigâr will do to improve her situation.

[*Editorial note*: Earlier in this tale the narrator inserted a passage on three legendary physicians: Lokman, Plato, and Çüllü Hekim. The passage seemed unrelated to the story of Hamzai Sahip Kıran, but we included it because there was no break in the recording and because it was Behçet Mahir's spontaneous offering, not something solicited. At this point, however, Ahmet Uysal queried the narrator about the three ancient physicians referred to earlier. There followed then a very lengthy question-and-answer dialogue on the three physicians, plus an offshoot anecdote which had nothing to do with the Hamzai story. We have omitted that extraneous material from this text.]

regular heating systems. The residents are kept warm on chilly days by heat from the massed animal bodies beneath their living quarters.

Fifth night; narration of January 13, 1977

Mehli Nigâr had been living at the home of the black executioner. The calf was now a year old, and every day since its birth she had been carrying it up and down the forty stairs twice a day. Whenever the calf saw her, it stood perfectly still and waited quietly for her to carry it up the flight of forty steps.

Hamzai Sahip Kıran remained very angry at the black executioner, and he made a vow that he would take vengeance against that man. Hamzai said to himself, "What a heartless man he is! How could he separate me from a beauty like Mehli Nigâr? How could he kill her? How could he obey an order of mine given in a moment of weakness? How could he be so heartless?"

In the meantime, the black executioner knew that Hamzai Sahip Kıran would eventually find him and avenge himself. He had no way of knowing, however, at what time that revenge would occur.

One day while Hamzai and his wrestlers were hunting, their course led them past the house of the black executioner. The hunters were very impressed by a house so high that a stairway of forty steps was required to reach from the ground to the living quarters. They asked one of the local people who lived in that house, and they were told, "That mansion belongs to the black executioner."

Hamzai Sahip Kıran said to his wrestlers, "Bring the black executioner into my presence."

When the wrestlers brought him before Hamzai, the black executioner said, "Yes, my shah? What is your wish?"

Hamzai Sahip Kıran answered, "I should like to see the inside of your great house."

The black executioner replied, "Of course, my shah! Come right in." Then he went to Mehli's room and said, "O beauty, Hamzai is here, and he is looking for an excuse to take his revenge against me. I have kept you in my home, and I have kept your secret in my heart. Now it is time to keep your promise to help me. Save me from the rage of Hamzai Sahip Kıran!"

"Do not worry, black executioner. I shall save you. I have experienced nothing but kindness from you. You spared my life and you have kept me in your home. I shall in turn help you now."

(This is something that we should all know. Do a good deed and throw it into the ocean. Even if the fish do not recognize it, Allah will.[162])

---

[162] See Note 86.

While Mehli Nigâr began to make coffee for the guests,[163] Hamzai Sahip Kıran and the black executioner engaged in conversation. Hamzai was still looking for a convincing reason to take vengeance against the black executioner. He said to him, "Tell me, black executioner, how do you manage to climb all those steps several times a day? It made me very tired to climb them just once. What is your secret? Tell me."

The black executioner answered, "O my shah, you complain about climbing those stairs just once, but I have a daughter who climbs and descends those steps twice a day every day with a year-old calf in her arms."

Astonished, Hamzai said, "If this is the case, then tell your daughter that I should like to see her."

The black executioner went immediately to Mehli Nigâr and said to her, "Oh, my beauty, it is time now! He is looking for an excuse to kill me. Help me now!"

Mehli Nigâr went immediately to the barn below. Picking up the year-old calf, she carried it up the flight of stairs in a single breath. Hamzai Sahip Kıran was bewildered when he saw Mehli Nigâr before his eyes. He could not at first believe what he saw. He closed his eyes and then opened them again, and he still saw Mehli Nigâr standing before him. Yes, she was Mehli Nigâr, the daughter of Nuşirvan. The three hundred and sixty-six veins of Hamzai began to vibrate, and he said, "Oh, Mehli, I thought that you were dead, and my heart missed you badly. Now I have discovered that you are alive!"

Crying, Mehli Nigâr grasped Hamzai's hand, but she then said, "Stop, my shah! Stop!" As soon as she spoke, Hamzai fainted. Mehli rubbed some rose water on his face, and he soon recovered consciousness.

After a brief pause, Mehli Nigâr said, "Oh, my shah, do you remember that some time ago many of us were resting on the way from my father's country to your country? We saw a deer on a nearby hill, and you said, 'Observe my marksmanship, Mehli. I shall shoot an arrow through the ear of the deer, and the deer, thinking it is only a fly, will scratch its ear with its foot.' You did shoot the deer through its ear, and it did scratch its ear as if a fly were there. I then said, 'Hamzai, you were able to do that because you have had a great amount of practice shooting arrows for a long time.' You became furious, and you turned me over to this executioner. This black executioner has taken care of me as if I were his daughter. During the first day that I spent in his house, his cow gave birth to a calf, and from that time until now I have twice daily carried that calf up the forty steps to my room and back down again. Now you cannot do that, but I can because I have been

163 This is almost certainly an anachronism. Most authorities on the subject agree that coffee drinking began in Arabia sometime during the thirteenth century, roughly 600 years after the time of the action of this tale.

practicing. Such difficult things can be accomplished only by practice and hard work." Then picking up the calf and placing it before Hamzai Sahip Kıran, Mehli said, "I can carry this calf up and down the forty steps while taking just one breath in each direction. You can try to do the same thing, but it may not be possible for you to do it right away. After practicing, you would be able to do it. Everything must be accomplished through practice. You were a great marksman because of your lengthy practice."

Hamzai Sahip Kıran realized that Mehli was describing reality and that she had been right all along. Turning to the black executioner, he said, "Executioner, I forgive you for not carrying out my order. You did a good deed in disobeying that order. I am very pleased with you." He then kissed the eyes of the black executioner and added, "If you had actually killed Mehli Nigâr, I should not have left this house without having killed you."

This is the way that Hamzai Sahip Kıran found Nuşirvan's daughter, Mehli Nigâr. This was the way in which his happiness was restored. Then Mehli and Hamzai joined the wrestlers for the return trip. Before they left, however, Hamzai said to the black executioner, "You have now become one of my eyes. No one can look at you with evil intentions from this moment onward, for if anyone does, he will find me to be his enemy." He gave several presents to the black executioner, and then they returned to their homes.

Muslim Elite Corps Poisoned

But while this was going on, something very different was happening elsewhere. There is a proverb which says, "Although a friend may sleep, an enemy never does so." The treacherous advisors of Nuşirvan were again sowing discord and trying to plant suspicion in the mind of that ruler. They said to him, "You were unable to prevent Hamzai from getting your daughter, but Mehli Nigâr deserved a far better husband than that. She was worthy of a greater man."

"All right! All right!" answered Nuşirvan. "But what can we do about that now?"

One of his advisors said, "Oh, there is an easy way to handle the matter. We should pretend to be friendly to Hamzai Sahip Kıran and invite him here for a big feast. Then it will be a simple matter to put poison in his food. After that, your daughter, Mehli Nigâr, will remain here with you."

Nuşirvan answered, "That is a very clever plan."

(We should all learn something from this. May Allah keep us from having friends of this kind! Their tongues seem friendly, but their hearts are hostile. Such treachery has caused the suffering and deaths of a great many brave men. No one but Allah knows for certain what is in the hearts of others.

Everyone knows that our father Adam was created from mud [Koran 15: 28] by Allah. It was at a time when Satan was chief of all the angels.

When he heard that Allah had created Adam from mud, Satan entered that body before it was given life and tried to examine all of its parts. The human body has three hundred and sixty-six parts, and each part has its own function. But Allah hid one part of Adam from Satan's eyes, and that was Adam's heart. Later Satan said to the other angels, "I entered the body of Adam and examined all of its parts except one; that one part somehow remains hidden." Allah hid the heart of Adam, and since that time all of Adam's heirs have had hidden hearts. That is the reason that no one but Allah understands the heart of any human being. If Satan had been permitted to see the heart of Adam, then everyone would be able to look into the hearts of others, but as it is, no one can penetrate the mystery of another's heart.)

Following the suggestion of his evil advisor, Nuşirvan invited Hamzai Sahip Kıran to his palace for a feast. Nuşirvan wrote a letter which said, "O Hamzai, we have been at war for a long time, and many people have been killed on both sides. Inasmuch as my daughter chose, by her own will, to move over to your side, I cannot any longer hold anything against you. Therefore, let us become friends. Come here and be properly married to my daughter."

Hamzai Sahip Kıran received this letter from Nuşirvan. After reading it, he concluded that Nuşirvan was no longer angry at him and that Nuşirvan now wanted peace. He therefore called together all of his wrestlers and Ömer Ümmiye and ordered that preparations be made for the journey to Nuşirvan's country. At the same time other preparations were being made at the palace of Nuşirvan for the reception of Hamzai Sahip Kıran.

After a journey of a few days, Hamzai Sahip Kıran and his people reached Nuşirvan's city. There they were welcomed warmly by Nuşirvan's attendants and then shown into the presence of the ruler. When everything was ready for the feast, Nuşirvan asked all those present to be seated. Food was placed upon the tables; music was played; and servants were bringing the drinks. The eating and drinking then began.

But at that point Ömer Ümmiye asked Hamzai Sahip Kıran for permission to leave the room. As soon as he was outside that room, he disguised himself as one of Nuşirvan's servants. Mingling with the other servants, he listened to their conversation and discovered the deadly plot against the life of Hamzai Sahip Kıran. He learned of the plan to poison Hamzai and all of his wrestlers. But it was now too late for Ömer to foil this plot, for everyone was already eating and drinking. Hamzai and all his followers began to shake and quiver, and their bodies began to swell. One by one they began to die. At first quite bewildered and unable to act, Ömer Ümmiye then decided that he must get Hamzai out of the palace. Returning to the dining room, he grabbed Hamzai, put him on his own back, and rushed out of the building.

Ömer Ümmiye ran steadily with Hamzai on his back until he reached Mecca. He then took the extremely ill Hamzai to the house of Mehli Nigâr, who burst into tears when she realized the gravity of Hamzai's condition. She was so shocked that she was unable to look at him a second time. The strong poison was lethal, and Hamzai was dying.

Ömer Ümmiye knew what kind of poison had been given to Hamzai Sahip Kıran, and he consulted all of the doctors about medicine that could overcome the effect of that poison. Most of the doctors said, "There is no antidote for that poison. Furthermore, people should not enter the room where Hamzai is lying, or they too may be killed by the fumes given off by his body."

But one doctor declared, "There is a medicinal plant which could save Hamzai, but it grows in a very distant place. It would take six months to go there and return, and you do not have that much time before Hamzai dies." When Ömer Ümmiye heard this, he immediately began racing to the location of that plant, and his speed was so great that he completed the six-month journey in forty-eight hours. While Ömer was gone, they kept Hamzai in a large room and they allowed no one to see him. Mehli Nigâr was so distraught that she never stopped sobbing. But Ömer Ümmiye sped like the wind and brought back the medicinal plant.

Let us now return to the palace of Nuşirvan. All of the wrestlers who had gone there with Hamzai Sahip Kıran were now dead. All of Hamzai's strongest and bravest men had been killed by poison. Not a one of them survived. Nuşirvan's men knew that Hamzai had been rescued by Ömer Ümmiye, but they also knew that he must be very close to death. Consequently, Nuşirvan ordered his army to attack Hamzai Sahip Kıran's country.

Let us now look again into the Mirror of Fortune. Ömer Ümmiye went to get the medicinal herb and returned with it within the space of forty-eight hours. He was given the herb by a physician in the distant land to which he traveled when, in tears, he said that it was to be used to save the life of Hamzai Sahip Kıran. The physician knew everything about the Bible, and he had known that Hamzai Sahip Kıran would be born and that he would engage in battle against Nuşirvan.[164] He asked Ömer, "Is your name Ömer?"

"Yes, my name is Ömer."

"Very well, then," said the physician. "I would not give this medicine to anyone else, but I shall give it to you."

Ömer Ümmiye secured the medicine and returned to Hamzai within forty-eight hours from the time he had departed. He rubbed the medicine all over Hamzai's body, and then he forced him to swallow some of it. By this time Nuşirvan's army was attacking Hamzai's Muslim country, and so to

---

164 Here again the Turkish folk imagination recreates the Bible for its own purposes. It is of course impossible to determine whether this invention is Mahir's or that of some preceding narrator.

protect Hamzai, Ömer took him to the fortified city of Aleppo.[165] At that time Aleppo was surrounded by very high walls. It was not long, however, before spies of Nuşirvan discovered the whereabouts of Hamzai. Nuşirvan then ordered his troops to attack Aleppo and to conquer the citadel at its center. Nuşirvan's troops were so numerous that they were able to attack the fortified city from all four directions at the same time.

Mehli Nigâr was crying as she climbed up to the tower of the citadel. She saw Nuşirvan's soldiers attacking the city, but she also observed that the Muslim forces were prepared to defend the fortress.

Hamzai Sahip Kıran was kept in a secret room, the location of which was known only to Ömer Ümmiye and Mehli Nigâr. Ömer continued to give the herb medicine to Hamzai. The open sores on Hamzai's head and face were beginning to heal, and he was starting to recover. The poison had begun to leave his liver. There is a proverb which says, "The inside of your body must first begin to heal before the outside can recover."

The forces of Nuşirvan had completely surrounded the fortress, and they stood all around it fourteen ranks deep. It was impossible to enter or leave the fortress. The Muslim troops tried to protect the city by shooting thousands of arrows at the invaders and hurling rocks down upon them from the fortress walls. Ömer Ümmiye ran back and forth helping Muslim soldiers who were growing tired, and he himself was casting very large stones upon Nuşirvan's men. Hamzai's forces fought courageously, but they were growing weak from hunger. The food supply of the defenders kept dwindling and dwindling, and after forty days of the siege, there was nothing left for them to eat. After most of the Muslims had eaten nothing for several days, their situation became truly desperate.

As this was going on, the condition of Hamzai Sahip Kıran was improving. He was recovering slightly more every day. Ömer Ümmiye visited him every night after the day's fighting had ended, and he kept giving Hamzai the herb medicine he had gone so far to get. Mehli Nigâr was fighting against her father's troops by throwing stones down upon them. These soldiers recognized her and shouted up to her, "Come out and surrender! Your father will forgive you. He will not kill you."

But Mehli Nigâr shouted back, "I shall never surrender, even if I am cut into small pieces. I cannot be separated from Hamzai. If Hamzai should die, I would die at the same time. I have vowed to fight at Hamzai's side until I am dead." In response to these remarks the enemy troops shot arrows at her. During the forty days of fighting, Mehli Nigâr had been wounded by arrows in at least seven different places, and as a result, she was growing weaker and weaker.

---

[165] An extremely ancient city in what is now Syria, Aleppo was for many centuries an important caravan terminal and commercial center, especially during the Ottoman era.

Despite the fact that the resistance of the fortress was steadily being reduced, the health of Hamzai Sahip Kıran was improving. Finally there came a day when he called, "Hey, Ömer, get my horse ready. I am now well enough to fight again."

Ömer went at once among the defenders and gave them the good news: "Muslim soldiers! Hamzai Sahip Kıran is well again, and he will soon join the battle!"

Nuşirvan's troops also heard this news, but they did not believe it. They said among themselves, "Oh-h-h, Ömer Ümmiye is again trying to deceive us, but this time we shall not be fooled."

After his horse had been prepared by Ömer Ümmiye, Hamzai Sahip Kıran mounted and was ready to fight again. The fortress gate was opened, and he rode out swiftly against the large enemy force. Placing his hands on his hips, he shouted out in his powerful voice, "Oh, you infidels, they call me Hamzai Sahip Kıran!" Then he began to slash to left and to right with his sword against his enemies. When Nuşirvan's men saw once again Hamzai's great fighting skill, they were filled with fear, and many fled without even looking back. They thought only of saving their lives.

Hamzai Sahip Kıran had known from the beginning that he would never attempt to kill Nuşirvan, because he had for years eaten the bread of that ruler. At times he had also wondered if he was justified in killing even the soldiers of Nuşirvan who were attacking him. Should he not try to wound them instead of killing them? But now that they had killed his best wrestlers with poison and had almost killed him in the same way, Hamzai lost all respect for Nuşirvan and all pity for Nuşirvan's men. He closed his heart against Nuşirvan and fought with more deadly fury than he had in earlier battles. His onslaught against the enemy was so fierce that the fighting lasted only until noon. At that time Nuşirvan's troops abandoned the battlefield and fled, leaving all of their supplies behind them. The Muslim soldiers prayed to Allah to thank Him for saving them. Then they prayed again to give thanks that they were no longer hungry.

Nuşirvan's troops had run in every direction because they were terrified by Hamzai Sahip Kıran's sword. The Muslims captured many of them but did not kill them. They took all of their captives' supplies and then set them free. It is a sin for Muslims to kill prisoners of war. Hamzai had given to his troops this order: "Set them free, for we are Muslims. We should neither kill nor harm prisoners of war." A week after the time that Hamzai had entered the battle there were none of Nuşirvan's troops left in Aleppo.

Hamzai Sahip Kıran's health improved and improved, and he felt as if he had been born a second time. He kissed Ömer Ümmiye on both cheeks and said to him, "Oh, Ömer, you saved my life! If you had not been there then, I should not be here now. I would be dead." They then left the fortress of Aleppo and moved to Medina. There Hamzai Sahip Kıran declared a forty-day period of mourning for the forty wrestlers who had been poisoned by

Nuşirvan's men. During that time everyone wore black clothing, and all of the flags were flown at a lower level.

Hamzai Sahip Kıran Killed in Holy War

Now let us see what the Prophet Mohammed was doing at this time. He was greatly pleased that the forces of Islam were gaining strength every day. They had been compelled to flee from Mecca to Medina, but now Mohammed announced that they would soon recapture Mecca.

While the Muslim troops were preparing for their campaign against Mecca, our Prophet had a dream. On the following morning he told those around him about that dream. He said, "I had a dream last night. I saw a ram being sacrificed even as I was holding it in my hands. I cried aloud, and the sound of my own crying awakened me. The meaning of my dream is that one of my beloved followers will die in one of the battles leading to the capture of the city of Mecca. Who will that be? Which one of my followers will be that man? Whoever it is that dies in that effort will go directly to heaven, and he will remain there forever with me."[166]

Upon hearing this, Hamzai Sahip Kıran stood up immediately and said, "O light of my life, I pray that I may be that ram. I pray that I may be the one to die for you and then go to heaven and remain there with you throughout all eternity." When our Prophet heard these words, he gazed sadly into the face of Hamzai Sahip Kıran.

Soon after that the forces of Islam began their attack against the city of Mecca. At the head of the Muslim army were Hamzai and his remaining wrestlers. Among the Meccans killed early in the battle[167] was Mu'awiya. When Mu'awiya's mother, Hind, heard of his death at the hands of Hamzai Sahip Kıran, she vowed to take vengeance against Hamzai.

Whenever Hamzai Sahip Kıran was fighting, he never looked behind him; he always looked forward at the battle ahead of him. Hind knew this, and so she watched and waited for an opportunity to sneak up behind Hamzai and kill him. No one paid any attention to this woman during the fierce battle,

---

166 Any Muslim who dies in a religious war (*jihad* in English, *cihad* in Turkish) automatically becomes a martyr (*şehit*) and goes immediately to heaven, bypassing both examination on Judgment Day and any purgatorial delay. Not a matter of folk whimsy, this idea is fundamental in Islamic belief. It has also been shown to be an important military factor, producing warriors endowed with fearlessness—indeed quite reckless abandon—in the face of danger. The war against Nuşirvan had a religious dimension in that it struck unmistakable infidels, but that was incidental to the actual cause of the conflict. The campaign to recapture the holy city of Mecca was clearly a religious war.

167 This was the Battle of Uhud (625), which occurred at a considerable distance from Mecca. It was fought against Meccan forces and was intended to be an initial step toward the conquest of Mecca, but it was actually a disaster for the Muslim troops. The present tale makes it sound as if the Muslim forces were at the very gates of Mecca.

and so she was able to come upon Hamzai from behind and fulfill her vow. In this way Hamzai Sahip Kıran was killed in a battle to retake Mecca.[168]

Everyone who heard the news of Hamzai's death was struck by grief. Yes, all who knew him grieved, even though the Muslim forces had taken Mecca and all of the members of the opposing Hurişi clan were converted to Islam.[169]

When our Prophet heard the news of Hamzai's death in the battle for Mecca, three tears fell from his eyes. At that very moment the angel Gabriel appeared before him and asked, "O Mohammed, why are you crying? You knew in advance that he would die during a battle to regain Mecca. You received the message in a dream, and you understood the meaning of that dream. You also know that he is in heaven at this very moment."

Prophet Mohammed said, "Thanks be to you, O Allah!" He rejoiced that Allah had indeed accepted Hamzai into heaven immediately.

Hamzai Sahip Kıran's funeral was then prepared. During the funeral ceremony thousands of Muslims followed Hamzai's body to the place where it was buried.

Gentlemen, Hamzai Sahip Kıran's life was ended there, and the story of Hamzai Sahip Kıran's life has ended here. May Allah grant you all of your wishes.

---

168 According to historical records, this was not quite the way in which Hamzai was killed. Although Hind was indeed implicated in the death of Hamzai (and allegedly chewed either the heart or liver that was later taken from his mutilated corpse), she did not kill him. That act was committed by an Abyssinian slave named Wahshi, who pierced Hamzai's chest with a javelin (Meredith-Owens 1971: 152).

169 This was not the great day of victory here suggested.

Bibliography

Aarne, Antti, and Stith Thompson. 1961. *The Types of the Folktale: A Classification and Bibliography*. Folklore Fellows Communications, no. 184. Helsinki: Suomalainen Tiedeakatemia.

Akkad, Moustapha. 1977. *The Message*. Cairo: Akkad.

And, Metin. 1975. *Karagöz: Turkish Shadow Theatre*. Ankara: Dost Yayınları.

Arnold, Thomas W. 1965. *The Caliphate*. London: Routledge and Kegan Paul.

Attar, Farid al-Din. 1976. *The Alahi-Nama* [Legend], *or Book of God*, trans. John A. Boyle. Manchester: Manchester University Press.

Başgöz, Ilhan. 1952. "Turkish Folk Stories about the Lives of Minstrels." *Journal of American Folklore* 65: 331-39.

Başgöz, Ilhan, and Andreas Tietze. 1973. *Bilmece: A Corpus of Turkish Riddles*. Berkeley: University of California Press.

Boratav, Pertev Naili. 1951. "Notes sur 'Azrail' dans le Folklore turc." *Oriens* 4: 58-79.

Bürgel, Christopher. 1988. *The Feather of Simurgh: The "Licit Magic" of Medieval Islam*. New York: New York University Press.

Burton, Richard, ed. and trans. 1934. *The Thousand Nights and a Night*, 1. New York: Heritage.

Caroe, Olaf. 1958. *The Pathans 559 B.C.—A.D. 1957*. London: Oxford University Press.

Cary, M., et al. 1949. *The Oxford Classical Dictionary*. London: Oxford University Press.

Chadwick, Nora, and Victor Zhirmunsky. 1969. *Oral Epics of Central Asia*. Cambridge: Cambridge University Press.

Denny, Frederick, et al. 1981. *Islamic Ritual Practices*. New York: American Council of Learned Societies.

Eberhard, Wolfram. 1955. *Minstrel Tales from Southeastern Turkey*. Berkeley: University of California Press.

Eberhard, Wolfram, and Pertev Naili Boratav. 1953. *Typen Türkischer Volksmärchen*. Wiesbaden: Steiner.

Fakhry, Majid. 1970. *A History of Islamic Philosophy*. New York: Columbia University Press.

Ferdowsi. 1967. *The Epic of the Kings: Shah-Nama, the National Epic of Persia*, trans. Reuben Levy. Chicago: University of Chicago Press.

Foley, John Miles. 1988. *The Theory of Oral Composition: History and Methodology*. Bloomington: Indiana University Press.

Frye, R.N., ed. 1975. *The Cambridge History of Iran*, 4. Cambridge: Cambridge University Press.

Fück, J.W. "Habib b. Maslam." *Encyclopaedia of Islam*, New Edition, 3. Leiden: Brill.

Gökalp, Altan. 1987. "The Melusine Fairy and Şahmeran in Asia Minor," in Akuta, Sabri M., ed. *Turkish Culture: Continuity and Change*. Bloomington: Indiana University Press.

Gülensoy, Tuncer. 1979. "Erzurum Ağzı İle 'Hatem Ta'i Masalı.'" *Türkoloji Dergisi* 8: 403-58.

Harvey, Sir Paul. 1967. *The Oxford Companion to English Literature*. London: Oxford University Press.

Heller, Bernard. 1987 [orig. 1938]. "Yusuf b. Yakub." *First Encyclopaedia of Islam*, 8. Leiden: Brill.

——. 1986. "Lukman." *Encyclopaedia of Islam*, New Edition, 5. Leiden: Brill.

Hitti, Philip. 1945. *The Arabs: A Short History*. Princeton: Princeton University Press.

Khoneli, Mose. 1958. *Amir Darejian—A Cycle of Medieval Georgian Tales Traditionally Ascribed to Mose Khoneli*, trans. R.G. Stevenson. Oxford: Oxford University Press.

Leach, Maria. 1950. *Standard Dictionary of Folklore, Mythology, and Legend*, 2 vols. New York: Funk and Wagnalls.

Lord, Albert B. 1960. *The Singer of Tales*. Cambridge: Harvard University Press.

Mahir, Behçet. 1973. *Köroğlu Destanı*, ed. Mehmet Kaplan, Mehmet Akalın, and Muhan Bali. Erzurum: Atatürk University Press.

May, Herbert G., and Bruce M. Metzger, eds. 1962. *The Oxford Annotated Bible*, Revised Standard Version. New York: Oxford University Press.

Meredith-Owens, G.M. 1971. "Hamza b. 'Abd al-Muttalib." *Encyclopaedia of Islam*, New Edition, 3. Leiden: Brill.

Nutku, Özdemir. 1977. *Meddalık ve Meddah Hikâyeleri* [Meddah Art and Meddah Stories]. Ankara: İş Bankası Kültür Yayınları.

Önder, Mehmet. 1967-68. "Kubâd-Ârad Sarayı Harpi ve Simurg'ları." *Türk Etnografya Dergisi* 10: 5-16.

Ong, Walter. 1982. *Orality and Literature: The Technologizing of the Word*. London: Methuen.

Pickthall, Mohammed M., ed. and trans. 1930. *The Meaning of the Glorious Koran*. London: Allen and Unwin.

Rentz, G. 1965. "Hashimids." *Encyclopaedia of Islam*, New Edition, 3. Leiden: Brill.

Sterling, Paul. 1956. *Turkish Village*. London: Weidenfeld.

al-Tabari. 1988. *The History of al-Tabari*, 6, ed. H. Montgomery Watt and M.V. McDonald. Albany: State University of New York Press.

Thompson, Stith. 1955-58. *Motif-Index of Folk-Literature*, 6 vols. Bloomington: Indiana University Press.

Uysal, Ahmet E. 1983a. "The Making of a Turkish Folk Narrator: Behçet Mahir of Erzurum." *International Folklore Review* 3: 29-33.

——. 1983b. "Turkish Treasure Lore: Traditions and Practices." *International Folklore Review* 3: 135-42.

Virolleaud, C. 1958-59. "Le roman de l'Émir Hamza, oncle de Mahomet." *Ethnographie* 51: 3-10.

Vitray-Meyerovich, Eva de. 1972. *Mystique et poésie en Islam: Djalâl-ud Dîn Rumî et l'ordre des derviches tourneurs*. Paris: Brouwer.

Walker, Barbara K. 1990. *The Art of the Turkish Tale*, 1. Lubbock: Texas Tech University Press.

Walker, Warren S. 1987. "Structural Complexity in the Turkish Folktale." *Proceedings of the Third International Congress on Turkish Folklore*, 2: 403-12.

Walker, Warren S., and Ahmet E. Uysal. 1966. *Tales Alive in Turkey*. Cambridge: Harvard University Press; rpt. 1990. Lubbock: Texas Tech University Press.

——. 1973. "An Ancient God in Modern Turkey: The Cult of Hızır." *Journal of American Folklore* 86: 286-89.

——. 1981. "Solomon and the Vulture." *Parabola: Myth and the Quest for Meaning* 4, ii: 52-54.

——. 1992. *More Tales Alive in Turkey*. Lubbock: Texas Tech University Press.

Watt, W. Montgomery. 1967. *Companion to the Qur'an*. London: Allen and Unwin.

Wensinck, A.J. 1985. "Kibla." *Encyclopaedia of Islam*, New Edition, 5. Leiden: Brill.

Yarshater, Ehsan, ed. 1983. *Cambridge History of Iran*, 3. Cambridge: Cambridge University Press.

Yurdatap, Selâmi Münir. 1970. *Şahmeran Hikâyesi*. Istanbul: Aziz Bozkurt.

Yurtbaşı, Metin. 1993. *A Dictionary of Turkish Proverbs*. Ankara: Turkish Daily News.

Index of Tale Types

I

These type numbers are from Antti Aarne and Stith Thompson. 1961. *The Types of the Folktale: A Classification and Bibliography.* Folklore Fellows Communications, no. 184. Helsinki: Suomalainen Tiedeakatemia.

Type No.		Page Nos.
155	*The Ungrateful Serpent Returned to Captivity.*	50-51
670	*The Animal Languages.*	8-12
934A	*Predestined Death.*	30

II

These type numbers are from Wolfram Eberhard and Pertev Naili Boratav.1953. *Typen Türkischer Volksmärchen.* Wiesbaden: Steiner.

Type No.		Page Nos.
48	*Die Schlange und der Mann.*	50-51
56	*Die Vogelsprache.*	8-12
57	*Der Schlangenkönig Şahmaran.*	89-90

Index of Motifs

Motif numbers come from Stith Thompson. 1955-58. *Motif-Index of Folk-Literature*, 6 vols. Bloomington: Indiana University Press.

Motif No.		Page Nos.
	A. Mythological Motifs	
A52.1.1	Angel of death created by God.	18
A52.3	Material of which angels are created (fire, water, snow).	3
A63.5.1	Satan jealous of Adam.	3
A157.5	God's sword.	96, 97
A1002	Doomsday.	37, 65, 83, 88, 92, 99
A1210	Creation of man by creator.	3
A1241	Man made from clay (earth).	3, 115-116
	B. Animals	
B11.11	Fight with dragon.	7-8
B29.2.3	Snake body—woman's head.	91-92
B31.1	Roc (giant bird).	6
B36	Milk-producing bird.	8
B122.3	Bird can recite sacred writings.	89-90
B215.1	Bird language.	5, 7, 8, 11
B215.2	Dog language.	9, 10
B216	Knowledge of animal languages.	9
B217	Animal language learned.	9
B242	King of birds.	6
B244.1	King [queen] of serpents (snakes).	91-92
B312.1	Helpful animals a gift.	15, 16
B319.1	Helpful animal sent by God.	15, 16
B365.0.1	Bird grateful for rescue of its young.	8
B435.1	Helpful fox.	51
B469.5	Helpful cock.	10
B735	Bird gives milk.	8

C. Tabu

C220	Tabu: eating certain things.	70-71, 89
C425	Tabu: revealing knowledge of animal language.	8, 9
C770	Tabu: overweening pride.	80, 110

D. Magic

D811	Magic object received from God.	16, 17
D1025.8	Magic sheepskin.	16
D1040.1	Drink supplied by magic.	58
D1193	Magic bag (sack).	16, 17, 44, 58
D1311.14	Divination from chance reading of sacred (magic) book.	74, 101
D1323.1	Magic clairvoyant mirror.	19, 94, 117
D1325.1	Magic book wherein is written family's destiny.	30
D1344.4	Charm (written) renders invulnerable.	96
D1361	Magic object renders invisible.	26
D1451.2	Inexhaustible sack furnishes treasure.	16, 17
D1470.1.27	Magic wishing-bag.	16, 17-18, 42, 44, 58
D1472	Food and drink from magic object.	17-18, 42, 44, 58
D1472.1.22	Magic bag supplies food.	42
D1500.1.4	Magic healing plant.	117, 118
D1500.1.19	Magic healing salve.	99-100
D1610.3	Speaking plant.	99
D1645.10	Man's body emits light.	22, 63, 67, 72
D1651.12	Box [pouch] can be opened only by right person.	26
D1654.3.1.1	Indelible writing: the scraped-off word found written as before.	30
D1655	Invisible object.	26
D1712	Soothsayer (diviner, oracle, etc.).	12, 14
D1766.7.1	Magic results produced in name of deity.	68, 78, 79
D1810.0.10	Magic knowledge of Solomon.	88, 90
D1810.8.2	Information received through dream.	120
D1812.0.1.2	Foreknowledge of means of death.	80, 90
D1812.3	Means of learning future.	30
D1812.3.3	Future revealed in dream.	120, 121
D1812.3.3.9	Future husband (wife) revealed in dream.	84
D1850	Immortality.	99
D1855	Time of death postponed.	18, 19

D1936	Magic fleetness of foot.	43, 45
D2087	Theft by magic.	24, 25
D2087.5	Gold stolen by magic.	24, 25
D2157.3	Withered and dead tree suddenly blossoms at saint's command.	69
D2188	Magic disappearance.	26

E. The Dead

E100	Resuscitation by medicines.	99, 100
E101	Resuscitation by salve (oil).	100
E751	Souls at Judgment Day.	37, 52, 99

F. Marvels

F92.7	Underworld snake kingdom.	91
F162.1.2	Contrasting qualities found in otherworldly garden.	89-90
F171	Extraordinary sights in other world.	89-90
F171.0.1	Enigmatic happenings in otherworld, which are later explained.	89-90
F171.6.1	Man in otherworld loaded down with wood. Then more and more put on him.	89, 90
F252.2	Fairy queen.	93, 94, 97, 98
F302.3	Fairy woos mortal man.	94
F517	Person unusual as to his legs.	18
F531.6.12.6	Giant slain by man.	102-103
F574	Luminous person.	22, 63, 67, 72
F575.1	Remarkably beautiful woman.	23
F610.0.1	Remarkably strong woman.	111, 114
F610.9	God's spirit aids strong man.	103
F617	Mighty wrestler.	14
F628.1.3.1	Man kills dragon with own hands.	7-8
F628.2.3	Strong man kills giant.	102-103
F660	Remarkable skill.	7
F661	Skillful marksman.	109
F681	Marvelous runner.	18
F751	Glass mountain.	91
F813.8	Extraordinary pomegranates.	89
F818	Extraordinary garden.	89-90
F952	Blindness miraculously cured.	68, 79
F959.6	Marvelous cure for poison.	117, 118

F997	Sword pierces rock.	38
F1034.4	Person's armpit as hiding place.	75
F1041.21.1	Illness from excessive grief.	111
F1041.3	Person goes blind from overweeping.	68

G. Ogres

G303.4.1.2.7	Devil is blind.	36
G303.4.8.6	Devil is swift of foot.	36
G303.7.9	Devil flies like bird.	36
G303.9.4	Devil as tempter.	36

H. Tests

H509.4.2	Riddles proposed as tests of poetic ability.	46
H530	Riddles.	46-48
H617	Symbolic interpretations of dreams.	120
H1333.2	Quest for extraordinary plant.	117-118
H1333.2.3	Quest for extraordinary herb.	117-118
H1558.6	Test of friendship: the imagined refusal.	15, 16
H1561.2	Single combat to prove valor.	52-55
H1573.5	Steadfastness of love for God tested.	35-38
H1573.7.1	Test of repentance: culprit exposed to situation identical to that in which he sinned.	114-115

J. The Wise and the Foolish

J151.4	Always say, "If it pleases God."	82-83
J157	Wisdom (knowledge) from dream.	120, 121
J643	Care against future tyranny.	12, 14
J645	Avoiding power of future enemy.	12, 14
J701	Provision for the future.	12, 14
J1172.3	Ungrateful animal returned to captivity.	51

K. Deceptions

K512	Compassionate executioner. A servant charged with killing heroine arranges the escape of the latter.	110
K512.0.2	"Prince will soon want me back." Executioner persuaded to let hero (heroine) go.	110
K512.1	Compassionate executioner: bloody coat.	110
K1826	Disguise as churchman (cleric).	52
K1853	Substitute sacrifice.	16, 38

K2100	False accusation.	95, 97
K2111	Potiphar's wife.	93-94
K2298	Treacherous counselor.	40, 41, 115
K2357	Disguise to enter enemy's camp (castle).	42, 43
K2357.0.1	Disguise to spy on enemy.	52, 58, 116
K2357.1	Disguise as musician to enter enemy camp.	63
K2357.7	Disguise in killed [drugged] enemy's clothes.	42
K2369.7	Shammed discussing of peace while getting reinforcements.	61-63, 64-65
K2369.11	Hero causes confusion in enemy camp in dead of night: army men fall upon one another.	106-107
K2369.12.1	Enemy leaders invited to banquet and poisoned.	115-116

M. Ordaining the Future

M161.2	Vow to revenge or die.	120-121
M302	Means of learning the future.	12, 87, 94
M302.7	Prophecy through dreams.	120, 121
M302.8	Prophecy from book.	30
M311	Prophecy: future greatness of unborn child.	12, 88
M311.0.2	Prophecy: hero's birth at certain time, place.	12, 13
M311.6	Prophecy: unborn child will be prophet.	67
M341	Death prophesied.	30, 90, 120
M341.1	Prophecy: death at (before, within) certain time.	30, 90
M341.3	Prophecy: death in particular place.	30
M361	Fated hero. Only certain hero will succeed in exploit.	87, 90
M363	Coming of religious leader prophesied.	67, 75
M369.3	Prophecy that certain person will fight particular battle.	120-121
M370	Vain attempt to escape fulfillment of prophecy.	30, 90
M370.1	Prophecy of death fulfilled.	30, 121
M391.1	Fulfillment of prophecy successfully avoided.	12-13, 14
M394	Hero's coming prophesied.	12-13, 86

N. Chance and Fate

N111.3	Fortune's wheel.	4
N121	Fate decided before birth.	24, 30
N385.1	Misfortune from forgetting to say, "If God wills."	80, 82, 83, 91, 92
N456	Enigmatic smile (laugh) reveals secret knowledge.	9-10, 11
N511	Treasure in ground.	17, 18, 66

N511.1	Treasure buried by men.	17, 18, 66
N621	Lucky shot with arrow—foot and ear of deer. Deer is scratching ear.	109
N731	Unexpected meeting of father and son.	103

P. Society

P14.15.1	Court counselor.	40, 41
P361	Faithful servant.	94-97
P623	Fasting as means of distraint.	71

Q. Rewards and Punishments

Q20	Piety rewarded.	38
Q20.2	Fulfillment of precepts rewarded.	38
Q22	Reward for faith.	37-38
Q40	Kindness rewarded.	51-52
Q261	Treachery punished.	51
Q556	Curse as punishment.	3-4

R. Captives and Fugitives

R122	Miraculous rescue.	38
R131	Exposed or abandoned child rescued.	6

S. Unnatural Cruelty

S140	Cruel abandonment and exposure.	107-108
S255	Deity saves person about to be sacrificed.	38
S263.2.3	Man willing to sacrifice child to God.	35-38
S301	Children abandoned.	5-6
S325.0.1	Monstrous child exposed.	5-6

T. Sex

T11	Falling in love with person never seen.	93-94
T15	Love at first sight.	22-23
T22	Predestined lovers.	86, 93-94
T22.2	Predestined wife.	86, 93-94, 97
T22.3	Predestined husband.	86, 93-94, 97
T24	Symptoms of love.	93-94

T26.1	Finger cut because of absorption in the charms of beloved.	93-94
T50.2.1	King unwilling to marry his daughter to man not her equal.	42, 106, 115, 116
T52	Bride purchase.	11, 105
T52.3	Bride purchased for her weight in gold.	105
T55	Girl as wooer.	93, 94
T88.1	Love kept up even after one of the parties is married.	94
T95.0.1	Princess falls in love with father's enemy.	22
T96	Lovers reunited after many adventures.	115
T97	Father opposed to daughter's marriage.	42-115
T102	Hero returns and marries first love.	109
T104.1	Rejected suitor wages war.	46
T145	Polygamous marriages.	97, 109
T252.2	Cock shows browbeaten husband how to rule his wife.	10
T253.1	Nagging wife drives husband to prepare for suicide.	9-10
T298	Reconciliation of separated couple.	115
T575.1	Child [pup] speaks in mother's womb.	89
T584.3	Caesarean childbirth a custom.	5

V. Religion

V1.6.3	Worship of fire.	55, 57, 107
V1.11	Worship of idols.	67
V10	Religious sacrifice.	35, 36, 37, 38
V223.1	Saint gives advice.	83
V231.1	Angel in shape of bird.	75-76
V330	Conversion from one religion to another.	54, 79, 86, 121
V340	Miracle manifested to non-believers.	69, 78, 79
V350	Conflict between religions.	92, 103-104, 118-119
V463	Religious martyrdom.	120-121

W. Traits of Character

W154	Ingratitude.	50, 51-52
W154.2.1	Rescued animal threatens rescuer.	50-51

Z. Miscellaneous Groups of Motifs

Z65	Proverbs.	3, 23, 26, 31, 33, 52, 74, 97, 113, 115, 118
Z254	Destined hero.	12
Z292	Death of hero.	121

For Product Safety Concerns and Information please contact our EU
representative GPSR@taylorandfrancis.com
Taylor & Francis Verlag GmbH, Kaufingerstraße 24, 80331 München, Germany

www.ingramcontent.com/pod-product-compliance
Lightning Source LLC
Chambersburg PA
CBHW081357090726
47908CB00011B/2704

* 9 7 8 1 1 3 8 9 8 6 2 4 4 *